THE ART OF PLEASURE

With stories by
Monica Burns
Charlotte Featherstone

Erotic Historical Romance

New Concepts　　　　　　　　　　　　　Georgia

Be sure to check out our website for the very best in fiction at fantastic prices!

When you visit our webpage, you can:

* Read excerpts of currently available books
* View cover art of upcoming books and current releases
* Find out more about the talented artists who capture the magic of the writer's imagination on the covers
* Order books from our backlist
* Find out the latest NCP and author news--including any upcoming book signings by your favorite NCP author
* Read author bios and reviews of our books
* Get NCP submission guidelines
* And so much more!

We offer a 20% discount on all new Trade Paperback releases ordered from our website!

We also have contests and sales regularly, so be sure to visit our webpage to find the best deals in ebooks and paperbacks! To find out about our new releases as soon as they are available, please be sure to sign up for our newsletter (http://www.newconceptspublishing.com/newsletter.htm) or join our reader group (http://groups.yahoo.com/group/new_concepts_pub/join) !

The newsletter is available by double opt in only and our customer information is *never* shared!

Visit our webpage at:
www.newconceptspublishing.com

The Art of Pleasure is an original publication of NCP. This work has never before appeared in book form. This work is a novel. Any similarity to actual persons or events is purely coincidental.

New Concepts Publishing
5202 Humphreys Rd.
Lake Park, GA 31636

ISBN 1-58608-710-X
Rogue in Disguise © copyright 2005 Monica Burns
Tutoring Lady Jane © copyright 2005, Charlotte Featherstone
Cover art by Eliza Black, © copyright 2005

All rights reserved, which includes the right to reproduce this book or portions thereof in any form whatsoever except as provided by the U.S. Copyright Law.

If you purchased this book without a cover you should be aware this book is stolen property.

NCP books are available at special quantity discounts for bulk purchases for sales promotions, premiums, fund raising, or educational use. For details, write, email, or phone New Concepts Publishing, 5202Humphreys Rd., Lake Park, GA 31636, ncp@newconceptspublishing.com, Ph. 229-257-0367, Fax 229-219-1097.

First NCP Paperback Printing: 2005

TABLE OF CONTENTS

Rogue in Disguise — Page 5

Tutoring Lady Jane — Page 97

ROGUE IN DISGUISE

By

Monica Burns

For Greg, Marie and Olivia.
Without your patience, love and
willingness to listen to my screams of joy and frustration
I would not have reached this point in my life.
I love you all very much.

And a huge thank you to Charlotte Featherstone,
a wonderful human being, terrific writer and treasured friend.
Without her encouragement to stretch myself
and her invaluable critiques, I would have failed to grow as a
writer.

Chapter 1

London, 1875

Ophelia's heart sank as she stared at the handsome man across the room. Her gaze skimmed over him seeking evidence of the monster within. She snapped open her peach-colored fan and fluttered it in front of her as she studied him with care. Although she was too far away to determine the color of his eyes, she could easily make out the sensual curve of his firm mouth.

With a cynical tilt of her lips, she shook her head slightly. How on earth could this man be the heartless libertine her father had described? The man's golden locks glinted in the candlelight as he nodded his head at something the man next to him said. There was almost an angelic look to him. Without shifting her gaze, she leaned to one side.

"Patience, are you certain this is the man father lost to? He doesn't look anything like the rake and scoundrel Father described." The dubious note in her voice prompted Ophelia's sister to bristle just as crisply as the bustle beneath her skirt.

"Of course, I'm certain. Everyone knows who the Earl of Rotherham is."

Ophelia arched an eyebrow at her younger sister. "And when were you introduced to the earl?"

"Well ... I've not been." Patience tilted her head haughtily at the affront. "But it's him, I tell you. He stole Sheffield Park from Papa, and if we don't do something we'll have nowhere to go."

"Naturally, Father is completely blameless in this entire debacle," Ophelia bit out as she sent her sister a scathing look. "After all, he was in his cups when he wagered our home and proceeded to lose everything at a game of cards."

"Ophelia Sheffield! The man took advantage of Papa. You know he's far too polite to refuse a drink, and the man kept plying him with wine."

"Oh, of course. Father would never turn down a drink."

Ophelia returned her attention to the earl as he sipped champagne from the flute he held. Firm lips pressed against the crystal as he drank. His long fingers encircled the fragile neck of the glass, evoking the sensual image of a strong hand trailing down the side of her throat. Excitement swirled in her stomach at the sight of his tongue flicking out to erase a droplet of wine from his mouth.

The man's reputation with the fairer sex was legendary, and his prowess as a lover equally touted. A dangerous quality resounded in his sleek, muscular movements. She was entranced and alarmed all in the same instant. Although there was a reckless air in his mannerisms, she still found it difficult to believe this was the same man who'd callously ordered her father to vacate Sheffield Park in five days. How could such a gorgeous specimen of man be such a heartless rake? Surely, the earl would let them stay on as tenants. Her father had to be wrong. Perhaps he'd misunderstood the earl's instructions. It would not be the first time her wayward father had been mistaken.

A grimace of irritation tugged at her mouth. Although for him to make a mistake in their favor would be a rare thing indeed. In fact, in the two years since the quiet debut of his two daughters, Sir Thomas Sheffield had never erred in a positive way. He had merely reinforced Ophelia's jaded view of noblemen. They saw fit only to indulge in reckless games of chance and debauched pleasures. With an imperceptible shake of her head, she watched the golden-haired man across the room. What a pity the man looked the part of Lancelot, but did not play the role.

"So are you going to approach him or shall I?" Patience's name had never been a reflection of her temperament. Ophelia frowned.

They rarely moved in the same exalted circles as Rotherham, but tonight was an exception. Patience had been convinced they would be able to appeal to the earl's benevolent side if they could just capture his ear. Now, watching the earl from a distance, Ophelia knew how fruitless it was to think they would have a moment alone with the earl. No. The only thing she could hope for was the ultimate act of desperation.

Fanning herself, she shifted her gaze from the earl to the dance floor. Vibrantly colored dresses sparkled under the chandeliers as dancers swirled around the dance floor. "We shall do neither. I have a plan, but it will require your cooperation."

"What do you want me to do?"

"I shall visit the earl tonight, and plead our case with him. I need you to make sure I have a way back into the house."

"Ophelia Sheffield! You'll be ruined."

A smile pulled at her lips as she dragged her eyes away from the earl. Closing her fan, Ophelia lightly tapped her sister's arm. "If I went during the day to see the man, my ruin would be assured, but in the dark, I'll not be recognized."

"You're mad."

"I am not about to let Sheffield be torn from us, simply because Father hasn't shown any restraint when it comes to drinking and betting," she snapped.

The icy words effectively ended Patience's protests. Would her plan work? She prayed it would. A twinge of sorrow nipped at her heart. Mama would be devastated if she had lived to see Father lose their home. They'd all been so happy there until her death. No, Sheffield Park was far too dear just to give it up without a fight. But would the earl be willing to exchange her home for what she would offer him? Ophelia bit her lip as she turned to study the man once more. There was no other alternative.

* * * *

The Honorable Charles Lynton entered Rotherham House with a weary sigh. If not for his promise to Robert, he would forgo the remainder of invitations for the next two weeks. The younger by one year, he'd served as his brother's counsel since the death of their father more than five years ago. On a whim, Robert had left earlier in the day for the continent, leaving Charles to fulfill the social obligations his brother had accepted before his sudden absence.

He heaved another sigh. One would think Robert would outgrow the need for switching identities. As children, it had been great fun to fool the servants and even their father, but the game had grown wearisome. The only real way one could tell the brothers apart was by their different colored eyes. Fortunately, with the exception of their friends, the Marlborough Set was too superficial to notice such a small difference.

What he really longed for was a quiet visit to the family estate north of London. Robert rarely visited Roth Manor, and no doubt, the holdings were in need of some oversight. Peeling off his gloves, Charles dropped them into his hat. The butler took the accessories from him with a pointed bow.

"Sir, a young woman presented herself for an appointment with his lordship a short time ago."

Charles glanced at the hall clock. It was after two in the morning. Had his brother arranged for some amusement and not bothered to tell him? "Did she say what she wanted?"

"No, sir. Although I was a bit surprised, sir."

"Surprised?"

"Yes, sir. The woman is not one of his lordship's usual appointments. She appeared to be a genteel woman, sir. Nevertheless, I showed her to the usual suite of rooms."

With a low growl of irritation, Charles raked a hand through his hair. It had been a long night, and the last thing he wanted to deal with was someone after his brother's title. He loosened the black tie at his neck. "Thank you, Bateson. I'll tend to the young lady. If I have need of you, I'll ring."

"Very good, sir."

Charles stifled a yawn as he climbed the stairs. Once again, he was his brother's savior. Tired and irritable, he strode down the hall toward the opulent den Robert used for his ladyloves. He would rid himself of the tart and turn in for a well-earned night of rest. Throwing open the door, he strode into the room prepared for anything. At least he thought he was prepared.

A branch of candles illuminated a mere portion of the room, while the fire in the hearth threw into relief the bewitching creature reclining on the chaise lounge. Lushly rounded hips accompanied long silk-covered legs, stretching the length of the couch. White drawers of the sheerest material revealed a small thatch of hair at the apex of voluptuous thighs beckoning him to explore beyond those curly dark locks. Contrasted against the virginal lingerie were black garters holding her stockings in place. A black, French-designed corset clung with aching seduction to her luxuriant figure. Full breasts crested the top of the enticing stays, and he found himself longing to run his tongue over the top of the plump mounds. To caress the shadowy valley that existed between each succulent breast would be heaven. Dark brown hair framed the soft peach complexion of her animated face. She was not a beauty by the Set's standards. Rather it was the expressive and inviting look on her lovely face that excited him.

His body hardened automatically in response to the tempting picture she made. It had been a long time since he'd alleviated his sexual needs, and his cock reminded him of it. Silence stretched between them before a smile curved her lips.

"Good evening." The sultry quiet of her voice trailed across his skin like a feather. Where the devil had this enchantress come from? Thank God, Robert wasn't here. The man would not have hesitated to bed the woman, without considering the consequences. No doubt, the minx had already arranged for a family member to charge in at any moment to rescue her. Folding his arms over his chest, he swallowed the desire threatening to take control of him.

"You look extremely comfortable."

Surprise furrowed her brow, and she sent him a puzzled look. With a small wave of an elegant hand, her fingers caressed the fabric of the couch. He found himself wishing he were the couch. With a mental shake of his head, he quelled the urges rising inside him as he saw her lovely pink lips turn down in a fit of pique.

"Looks are often deceiving, my lord. In truth, this couch is very uncomfortable."

Charles couldn't restrain his humor. He laughed outright for the first time in months. "If you find the couch ill-suited, would the bed be more to your liking?"

An indecipherable flash of emotion flitted across her animated features before it vanished. She smiled with genuine amusement. "Your reputation in that area is considerable, my lord; however, I'm also aware that word of mouth does much to feed one's reputation."

There was a mischievous bite to her words, and his lips curled in a smile. What a disappointment she would experience when her family burst in to find her en dishabille with the earl of Rotherham's brother. A far cry from the fat purse they were no doubt angling for. She wasn't the first social climber who'd attempted to secure the countess of Rotherham title.

"So you know of my reputation. And what precisely do you know?"

Contemplation danced across her expressive face, and he found himself thinking her features were quite exquisite. What a delight it would be to teach this lovely creature a thing or two.

"Well, I know that you bore easily, and enjoy a challenge. I thought perhaps a novice might intrigue you for a period of time."

"A novice?" He narrowed his eyes with suspicion and his muscles bunched with tension. If the woman was a virgin, his brother would have been doomed by now.

"Someone virtually untrained in the art of pleasure. I think you will find me an apt pupil." The sultry look she sent him eased his doubt. No virgin could be this enticing without displaying some sense of trepidation.

"I see, and in exchange for this delightful proposition, what is expected of me."

"Very little--in fact, I'm certain you'd never even miss it."

"It?" He unfolded his arms and clasped his hand behind his back. Frowning at her, he waited for her to issue her ultimatum. Even despite his irritation, his groin told him it cared little about the how or why of their conversation. All it wanted was to assuage the tension making him rock hard.

"Yes, you won a small estate at cards the other night, and I'm here to offer myself in exchange for its return."

"And if I refuse?"

"Then I shall leave."

His amusement returned and he moved toward the couch. Before she could swing her legs off, he seated himself beside her and rested his hand on a warm leg. "Ah, but what if I refuse to let you leave? It would be so easy to take my pleasure without any commitment on my part."

"Yes, but from your reputation, I understand you believe in a mutual sharing of passion. You would find me unresponsive, which would make any victory of yours quite hollow."

"Are you so certain I'm unable to make you respond to my touch?" His fingers slid up to the delectable expanse of skin exposed between the corset and her stocking. Smiling he watched her tremble at the light caress.

"So your reputed gentlemanly behavior in the boudoir is simply a mask." The gold flecks in her warm brown gaze flashed fiery contempt at him.

"Don't we all wear masks? After all, most gentlemen are really rogues in disguise."

"More's the pity for the women they marry."

The stinging response alerted him to the change in her mood. Narrowing his eyes, he studied the regal look on her face with curiosity. The cynical tilt of her lips intrigued him.

"You say that with great cynicism for one so young."

"I am twenty-two."

"Ah, a mature age, indeed." The humor in his voice made her stiffen with umbrage.

"Do not mock me, my lord. I've offered myself in exchange for the return of my home, but if you intend to take what you want without fair compensation, make quick about it."

"But you asked me to introduce you to the art of pleasure, and that is something which requires time."

His fingers itched to explore the length of her sweetly curved body. With a feather light stroke, he gently squeezed the plump curve of her thigh then proceeded to trace small circles atop her leg. Leaning toward her, he grinned as she retreated and pressed deeper into the back of the couch. The soft mounds pushing up against her corset rose and fell at a rapid pace. Charles lowered his mouth and lightly caressed the creamy skin of one plump breast.

"What is the name of this small estate you think I could do without?" he murmured against her skin.

"Sheffield Park," she breathed.

"And if I return this prize to you, what guarantee do I have you will honor your debt to me?"

With a violent shove she pushed him off her. The suddenness of the move surprised him, and he found himself sprawled on the floor. In a flash, she had scrambled to her knees. Hands on her hips, she scowled down at him with the fury of an untamed filly. "Unlike you, my lord, I am not a rogue in disguise, and when I give my word to someone, I honor it."

He rarely savored playing the role of his brother, but tonight he was thoroughly enjoying himself. Leaning back onto his elbows, he smiled, enjoying the sultry picture of indignation she made. God, but he would enjoy instructing her in the art of lovemaking. In fact, he might even go so far as to set her up as his mistress.

"Very well, my sweet. I shall prepare the transfer of deed back to you with the understanding that you will return here each night for as long as I deem fit."

Triumph sparkled in her eyes before they grew somber. Her sensual mouth formed a moue of dismay as she sank back on her heels. "But I thought ... I mean ... surely we could set a time limit."

"Hmmm," he arched his brow. Robert would be back in a month, more than enough time for him to introduce her to the pleasures he envisioned. "A month then."

Another enigmatic expression flitted across her lively features, but she gave him a resolute nod. "One month."

"Well, now that we've settled our arrangement, perhaps we should begin our instruction tonight."

"I think not," she said archly, her spine going rigid. "I will have the deed first."

"Don't you trust me?"

"Trust is never warranted for a rogue in disguise, my lord."

"Hmm, perhaps you're right to be cautious where I'm concerned." He laughed at her expression of annoyance. Climbing to his feet, he extended his hand to her. "Come, I'll help you dress. Then I'll secure a carriage to take you home."

"Thank you." She gave him haughty nod. It reminded him of the Queen's regal bearing, although her apparel cried out a different persona entirely.

"There is one more thing, though. I prefer to know the name of any lady I intend to bed." Pink color crested over her cheeks, and consternation made her bite her lip. For a novice she displayed an innocence that he found entrancing. Whatever lovers she'd had in the past, they'd failed to remove that elusive air about her. The one thing he was certain of, a virgin would not be as daring as this lovely creature.

"My name is Ophelia."

"Ophelia, a lovely name, although a tragic one."

"Shakespeare's character did not have the strength to withstand her madness, whereas I am far stronger than I look."

"Of that I have no doubt." The memory of how he landed on the floor made his response rueful.

"And you, my lord. Am I to address you as Rotherham?"

"Actually, I prefer Charles."

With another nod, she slid off the couch and reached for the dress she'd laid over the back of a nearby chair. She pulled the dress over her head and reached behind her to fasten the buttons. Watching her struggle to do up the fasteners, he strode toward her. Before she could evade him, he grasped her by the shoulders and turned her so her back faced him. Nimble fingers latched the cloth hooks over the small buttons.

"How the devil did you manage to get these undone without assistance?"

"With great difficulty."

"Do I detect a trace of humor in that remark?" His task completed, he turned her around. The vivid blue of the gown suited her.

"Yes." The corners of her mouth lifted in a mischievous smile.

"I think we shall suit each other quite well, my sweet Ophelia."

"For a month only, my lord."

"A month only," he repeated, but a voice in his head told him it would be much longer than that before he would part with her."

Chapter 2

Reclined against the plush cushions of the earl's unmarked carriage, Ophelia barely noticed the luxurious interior. Eyes closed, her head against the plump padding, she contemplated the evening's events. Tonight had not gone as she'd expected. She had been determined to dislike the earl, but he had been far more charming than expected. If anything, the man's charms were potent enough to put any woman's heart at risk. It was understandable how women flocked to the man, eager for his kisses. And if his reputation in the bedroom was to be believed, then she'd opened a door into a veritable heaven and hell.

The carriage rolled to a halt with a small jerk. The door opened almost immediately, and she accepted the hand of an older footman who helped her descend from the carriage. She uttered her gratitude in a whisper before scurrying toward the back of the townhouse her father had rented for the season. Her hand grasped the cool, brass doorknob, grateful her irresponsible sire had paid the rental in full. At least they would have a roof over their heads until her bargain with the earl was completed.

Patience had seen to it the rear door of the house was unlocked, and Ophelia sighed with relief. Reaching the sanctuary of her bedroom, she stopped to stand in front of her full-length mirror. As she unbuttoned her gown, she quivered at the memory of the earl's fingers against her back as he'd helped her dress. Locked in her recollections, she let the dress fall to her feet unnoticed.

The color of his eyes had surprised her. For some reason she had expected them to be blue. Instead, his gaze was as darkly mysterious as the deep jade brooch she owned. One moment they sparked with fiery temptation, the next they danced with mischief. The manner in which his blonde hair dropped across his brow only enhanced the rakish expression in his eyes.

She tipped her head to one side, studying her reflection in the mirror. One hand trailed her fingers across her breast as she recalled the searing heat his kiss had radiated over her skin. The memory made her suck in a quick breath. Even now, her heart raced at the remembrance. What was it going to feel like when those heavenly lips touched her mouth or other parts of her body? The wicked thought teased her, and hot color burned her cheeks.

When he'd caressed her thigh, it had lit a fire in her belly that was new and unexpected. No man had ever made her skin tingle in such a wicked way. Then there was the ache inside her that cried out for fulfillment. It was an ache she'd never experienced before, and she had mixed emotions about discovering exactly what would quell the sensation.

The click of her bedroom door opening made her heart plunge into her stomach then back up into her throat. Whirling around, the constricted muscles in her chest relaxed and she exhaled a sigh of relief as Patience scurried into the room. She reached for her robe and wrapped it around her, knotting the belt around her waist. Patience bit her lip, hope and fear playing across her face.

"Well? What did he say?"

"He said yes." Ophelia forced a smile to her lips to hide the apprehension she felt about her bargain with the earl. A flash of panic snagged her heart. How in the world was she going to explain her visits to Rotherham House every night for the next month?

"Oh, Ophelia! You did it." Patience launched herself forward and embraced Ophelia in an elated hug. "I didn't think you'd be able to convince him, but you did. Oh, won't Papa be surprised! The poor dear has been so despondent."

Patience's excitement made Ophelia flinch. The idea of explaining to her father how she had managed to reacquire their home was far from appealing. In fact, the idea filled her with dread. She knew her father well enough to know he would encourage her to trick the earl into marriage. It was the last thing she wanted. The idea of marrying a rake of the earl's reputation appalled her. Frantic to avoid such a confrontation until her bargain was complete she shook her head.

"No. No, you can't tell Father yet."

"Well, why ever not? You said Rotherham agreed to return Sheffield Park. I don't understand what the problem is."

Hesitating, Ophelia turned away from her sister. "That's true, he did agree to return Sheffield to us."

"Then what's the matter?" The suspicion in Patience voice forced Ophelia to press her fingers against her temple. What was she going to say?

"He's demanded a form of compensation for returning Sheffield to us."

"Compensation! Dear heaven, has he ... oh Ophelia, you didn't."

"No, of course not," she exclaimed, aware that it was the truth only until tomorrow night. "No, it's something altogether different."

"Well, what then. What could he possibly want from you?"

Panic constricted her chest at the question. She resorted to the first thing that came into her head. "Tonight when I met with the earl, he was in foul mood. He complained of a headache, and I offered to soothe him. You know how Father says I have the best hands for alleviating a migraine."

Patience nodded her head, the suspicion in her face ebbing somewhat. Relieved that her explanation was sounding reasonable, she allowed herself a soft sigh. "Well, I managed to make the earl's pain disappear so quickly that he refused to release Sheffield unless I visit him every night for a month and relieve his migraines. He's also ordered me to teach his valet my technique."

Lies. She had never told so many before in her entire life. Patience, however, seemed to find her explanation not only reasonable, but romantic as well.

"Oh Ophelia, it's wonderful. Why the earl might even fall in love with you."

She raised her eyebrows at her sister's statement. It was highly doubtful the earl would want anything more to do with her once their month's bargain was complete. No, Patience's imagination was as impractical as their hope that Father would give up gambling. However, Sheffield Park would be theirs again, and she would have to find a way to keep her father from wagering it away in the future. If she was giving up all hope for a respectable marriage, she was not about to give Father another opportunity to lose it again.

* * * *

"Have you ever seen such a crowd?" Patience waved her fan in front of her flushed face. "The only spare room is on the dance floor, which is crowded enough."

Ophelia smiled at her sister's complaint. Studying the dancers on the floor, a strange sensation rippled against the back of her neck. Her skin tingled as if a feather were brushing across her skin. With a quick jerk of her hand, she touched the back of her neck.

Her fingers found nothing unexpected. With a slight turn, she looked over her shoulder and saw him. He was leaning against a white column, the sleek line of his body enhanced by the black tails he wore. Every bit the indolent rake, jade eyes sparkled with laughter as his gaze danced over her. Startled, she stood mesmerized by the riveting look. The moment he moved toward her, she panicked. *Oh dear lord, the man is going to speak to me in public.* Ophelia reached behind her, her hand searching for Patience's arm, but found only warm air. Frantic, she stood frozen, unable to flee. As she waited for him to stop in front of her, astonishment whipped through her as he continued past her with a slight nod of his head.

Gathering her wits, she stared after him as he moved through the crowded room until he disappeared from view. Flummoxed by his behavior, she tightened her grip on the fan she held. He'd ignored her. With a sharp snap of her wrist, she flicked open the accessory to beat the air in front of her with ferocity. Why did she care that he'd ignored her? After all, his attentions in public were the last thing she wanted--especially given the fact he was no doubt as much a wastrel as her own father. She had little use for such noblemen.

Nevertheless, a small seed of pique teased her vanity. Ophelia inhaled a deep breath, releasing it slowly as she eased the fierce motion of her fan. If anything, the man's discretion had saved her from curious looks and whispers. Her reputation was still intact, at least for the moment.

"Some refreshment, miss?"

She glanced at the servant holding a tray of champagne flutes and shook her head. "No, thank you."

"I can recommend the glass closest you as one with an intriguing flavor, miss."

The unusual reply struck her as odd, and she looked down at the tray to see a small sliver of parchment tucked under the glass. A tremor ran through her as she reached for the drink, while discreetly pulling the note into the palm of her hand. Without another word, the servant continued on his way.

There was no need to unfold the small piece of paper. Only one person would be bold enough to send her a note in such a way. Sipping her drink, the vellum tickled the palm of her skin in a manner similar to the way the earl had touched her the night before. Eager to read the note, she made her way to the ladies room. Once inside, she pretended to fuss with her hair until the room was empty.

Her fingers trembled as she unfolded the missive. Staring down at the bold script, her heart leapt at the words.

Meet me outside on the patio. C.

She bit her lip as she reread the words. Expectation skidded through her and made her breathing erratic. What did he want? And why was she so eager to find out? The voice of reason tried to restrain her, but there was something about the note that pulled at her, insisting she do as the earl asked.

Without further contemplation, she hurried out into the hall and back toward the ballroom. In the hallway outside the crowded room, she noticed a lovely pair of French doors leading out onto the patio. She did not hesitate, but quietly slid out into the sultry summer night. A small breeze stirred the air, cooling her warm skin. The brick lined walkway overlooked a garden lit by a full moon. Tree branches threw their large shadows over the ground in the manner of a lover's embrace.

No longer in the brightly lit safety of the house, she hesitated. Meeting the earl like this was madness. She was already taking far too many risks as it was by offering to become the man's lover. There was no need to risk public humiliation as well before she escaped to Sheffield Park in a month's time. About to retreat back the way she had come, her neck tingled with the sensation she'd experienced earlier. She started to turn, but strong hands stopped her. The hard strength of his chest pressed into her back, his fingers caressing her bare shoulders with a lover's touch. Heart pounding, she realized her breathing was once more as erratic as her pulse.

"Good evening, temptress." The husky sound of his voice caressed her as if he had pressed his lips to her skin.

"I ... I'm not a temptress."

"Aren't you?" His hands were now resting against her waist. The warmth of his palms seeped through her clothing to burn her skin. "Your body says otherwise."

"I don't know what you mean."

"Then let me show you."

His breath whispered against her bare shoulder with the heat of a small fire as his lips grazed the side of her neck. The touch pulled a gasp of surprised delight from her. A second later, his fingers lightly trailed across her throat.

"You tempt me, Ophelia," he whispered the words, as he feathered kisses across her shoulders. "I'm impatient to know the color of your nipples. Are they a flush pink or a dusky rose?"

She gasped, "My lord--"

"Tell me their color, Ophelia." The deep command scraped across her skin, puckering it with small bumps. She swallowed the knot in her throat.

"I think you would ... would call them dusky rose." Sweet Lord. She couldn't believe she was talking this way with a man. Especially this man, one of London's most notorious rakes. She trembled as his finger ran along the edge of her bodice in a leisurely fashion.

"I intend to suck on those dusky rose nipples, Ophelia."

"Oh."

Her breasts swelled in her bodice. They were heavy and the tips were hard. The stiff peaks pushed achingly against her bodice. Her breathing increased, while she struggled with the wanton sensations stirring in her belly. The thought of his mouth on her was the most wicked notion she'd ever had, but she wanted it. She wanted him to suck on her. A tremor ran through her at the image.

"I see the idea of my sucking on you excites you."

"I ... ye--no."

"Don't waver, Ophelia."

"I ... yes," she breathed with a reluctant sigh.

With a quick movement, he turned her to face him. She met his startling green-eyed gaze, her heart slamming into her breast. Holding her close to him, he traced the line of her bodice again. As he did so, her body longed for him to push aside her clothing and touch her. To reach her nipples and suckle her. Oh God, she was insane for acting like this. If someone were to come out onto the patio, she'd be ruined.

"Dear heaven, I've never ... I don't...."

"Don't think--feel."

His mouth singed the top of her breasts as a spicy fragrance filled her nostrils. It tickled her senses in a way that urged her to forget every moral lesson she'd ever learned. The aroma of his scent stirred her, but she was unprepared for the way his tongue suddenly slid into the valley of her breasts. Fire exploded inside her and her body cried its frustrations at the trappings she wore.

A quiet moan broke past her lips as she shuddered with an emotion she didn't recognize. It heated her, encouraging her to give herself up to the pleasure that slid through her as his mouth danced lightly across her skin. Firm lips nipped playfully at her skin, pulling another soft moan from her.

Sweet heaven, she wanted-- no, she could never label this as want, this was a craving. A sharp need. She hungered for the touch of his mouth against her aching breasts and any other part of her body he might wish to explore. Beyond thinking, she did as he'd ordered. She felt.

The warmth of him seeped through her clothing until she was consumed with the essence of him. It filled her, heating her body until a shudder ripped through her. Lost in an eddy of passion, her head fell back so her throat was openly exposed to his caresses. She gasped as the rough tip of his tongue grazed her sensitive skin just above her bodice. His touch left behind a wet heat that stirred and roiled an answering fire inside her.

Flames licked their way through her veins until she burned not only on the outside but the inside as well. Clinging to the solid strength of him, she eagerly met his kiss as his tongue danced its way into her mouth. He teased, excited her with his sinful caress. Dear Lord, had she lost her mind? This was beyond ruinous behavior. Need ripped through her making her reject the idea of propriety. She didn't want to be proper. She wanted to be wicked.

An instant later, he broke the kiss and turned her away from him, cradling her against his hard chest. The leisurely caress of his hands withdrew until he was barely touching her shoulders. In a primal display, his teeth scraped across her skin in a seductive manner.

"Until midnight, temptress."

He pulled away from her. Shattered by the force of the arousal still holding her in its grip, her body trembled at the loss of his warmth. The quiet click of the French doors announced his departure from the terrace. She flinched at the sound, her heart sighing with disappointment. Her breasts pressed heavily against her stays, tingling and achy, while the place between her thighs was damp.

She shivered at how her body cried out for him with such vehemence. She remembered her worries about his ability to wreak havoc with her heart. It was a road she'd vowed not to travel. A sharp sting of fear pierced her heart. She was already treading the path to destruction.

Chapter 3

Charles found himself growing impatient as the hall clock chimed the midnight hour. At the ball this evening, he'd had a difficult time controlling his urge to do more than just arouse Ophelia. Something about the woman made him want to lose control. He wanted to claim her and sink himself into her over and over again. The erotic image of her lush body beneath him, gave him an instant erection.

Glancing about the room, he smiled with satisfaction. The soft glow of candlelight was neither too bright nor too dark. A pleasing scent of lemon and ginger lightly drifted through the air without overpowering his nose. The starkness of his white shirt reflected in the mirror, he smiled back at his image. Also visible in the looking glass was the opulent setting behind him. It looked like a sultan's den with dozens of brightly colored pillows strewn about the floor, the ceiling overhead draped with billowy curtains of equally luxuriant color. Yes, the atmosphere was perfect. It would suit his purpose for Ophelia's next lesson in the fine art of pleasure. A quiet knock on the door interrupted his thoughts.

"Enter."

A voluptuous goddess encased in navy silk, Ophelia glided into the room, her features flushed. The front of her gown rode snugly against her lush curves, while her bustle and short train billowed softly out behind her. She reminded him of the beautiful figureheads on a sleek sailing ship. The one difference was her eyes. Her eyes were alive and filled with spirit. There was hesitation there too.

It told him the possibility of achieving his ultimate goal tonight would probably not occur. No matter how much he wanted to embed himself in her warmth, it would have to wait until he had laid the foundation for all the things he wanted to do to her. More than anything, he wanted her to crave the elemental experience that would occur between them. It was necessary to tease and tantalize her into an erotic state so she gave herself willingly and passionately over to the act of lovemaking.

"Good evening." The husky quality of her voice hardened his cock even more. God, what would he do when she spoke like that during their lovemaking? It would drive him over the edge. He steadied himself against the onslaught of desire lashing him with each inhalation of air. He needed to deal with business first.

"I have the deed to your property. I took the liberty of placing it in your name so your father would not be able to wager it again."

"Thank you."

Delighted surprise flitted over her animated features. The knowledge that he enjoyed making her happy sent a jolt of fear through him. His inner conscience warned him of the consequences of becoming emotionally involved with her. Although he'd seen no indication of her intent to deceive or ensnare, he knew what skillful actresses women were. How many times had he saved his brother from just such a woman? No, he would enjoy Ophelia's luscious charms, and his heart would remain intact.

With a sweep of his hand, he showed her to a small table where he'd laid out the deed for Sheffield Park. She read over the document quickly, then folded it and placed it in her reticule. Turning to face him, she smiled, but a glimmer of resignation darkened her lovely eyes. He studied her carefully for a moment, trying to understand her quickly disguised reluctance. As if sensing his hesitation, she tipped her head to one side.

"So it begins. Your student awaits your instruction, my lord." Although her tone was light, an unrecognizable emotion threaded her sultry voice. Unable to determine what was transpiring in her head, he grasped her hand and lifted it to his lips.

"I think you would be more comfortable in the garment I have selected for you."

"Garment?" The catch in her voice made him slide the back of his hand across her cheek.

"Come."

Her brown eyes studied him with suspicion for a long moment before she nodded. He tucked her arm in his and pulled her toward a wardrobe. Opening the door, he pulled out a luxuriant deep rose cloth. The silk material rustled softly across his fingertips as he held it up for her close inspection. She reached out to run her slender fingers over the cloth, her animated features glowing with pleasure.

"It's exquisite. I've never seen anything like it before."

"I doubt seriously you will unless you travel to India. It's called a sari and is the traditional dress worn by the women there."

"Is there nothing to wear underneath it?"

The question made him smile, and he pulled a shirt and a petticoat from the wardrobe. "The sari goes over these two garments. The top is a choli and the petticoat is a lehanga. Change behind the screen, and then I'll teach you how to wear the sari."

He nodded toward a dressing screen situated close to the wardrobe. Anticipation lightened her face, and she accepted the clothing from him, her eyes lingering on the rose-colored silk as she disappeared behind the screen.

"Have you been to India?" The lyrical sound of her voice filled the room. The image of her sliding out of her austere dress to reveal her voluptuous curves made him swallow a desire threatening to spin out of control. Silently, he vowed that tomorrow night he would have the pleasure of watching her remove her clothes.

"Yes. It's quite beautiful. The women there are some of the loveliest in the world."

"Even more so than English women?" The fit of pique in her voice made him laugh.

"I can think of one Englishwoman who would hold her own among the most sensual of all hothouse flowers." Silence greeted his response, and he smiled to himself. "Do you require any help?"

"No ... ah ... I'm fine, thank you."

"I don't mind at all, if you require my assistance."

"I'm fine. Thank you."

A moment later, she emerged from behind the screen. The sight of her made him suck in a quick breath. The white choli emphasized her ample breasts, the material snug against her skin. The outline of her nipples pushing through the material lit his fingers with a burning need to feel them harden beneath his hand. Her creamy midriff made him swallow hard. Damnation, but the temptress had the milkiest stomach he'd ever seen on a woman. He wanted to explore it with his tongue, that and other areas of her body. The urge to devour her tightened his groin, and his cock painfully stood at attention, ready for action. God, but he needed to bed her. He wasn't certain he'd even be able to last the night at this rate.

"Is something wrong?" She arched her eyebrow, and he shook his head.

"Not at all. I was simply admiring you."

"Oh."

"Do you object?"

"No."

The firmly worded response held a faint trace of uneasiness. He bit back a smile. Taking the sari in hand, he walked toward her. Keeping his voice low, he began to dress her, explaining each step as he wrapped her in the luxurious cloth. When he'd finished, he pulled her toward a full-length mirror. Standing behind her, he watched her face as she stared at her reflection. Delight danced in her brown eyes as golden flecks of light sparkled and made her gaze brilliant.

"A seduction waiting to happen."

"Yours or mine, my lord." Her hazel eyes had darkened to a deep brown as she met his gaze in the mirror. There was a vulnerable look in her expression for a brief instant before it vanished.

"Ahh, I believe that would be your seduction, Ophelia. After all, I'm the master, you're the student."

His hands reached for the pins that held her hair in place. Like brown silk, her hair tumbled over his hands to hang down her back. The luxuriant feel of her hair slid over his skin like the soft material of the sari she wore. Free of its tight confines, her brown hair streamed down in a lush curtain of curls that clung to his fingers like downy feathers. His eyes met hers in the mirror, and he smiled at her sensual reflection.

A fiery color flooded her cheeks, and he squeezed her shoulders before pulling her toward the section of floor strewn with pillows. Sitting down, he gestured for her to sit next to him.

Puzzlement furrowed her brow. "I don't understand."

"The art of sexual pleasure is more than simply an act. It's a state of mind, a gratification in a manner of all things."

She sank down into the nest of silk pillows, her tongue flicking out to lick her bottom lip. The action drove him to lean forward. With his thumb, he rubbed her bottom lip for a moment. Feeling the tremor running through her, he lowered his mouth to hers and lightly brushed his lips across hers. Again, she shuddered, but she did not draw back and her hand reached up to stroke his cheek. The tentative caress sent a bolt of lightning through him.

Restraining the desire flooding through his limbs with such exquisite pain, he drew back.

Her luscious lips formed a small circle of disappointment. He shook his head. "Come, lay your head against my thigh, and we can discuss the virtues of poetry."

"Poetry? I fear I've never much cared for that form of literature."

"I'm certain you've been reading the wrong types of poetry."

Irritation flashed in her eyes but she remained silent. In an effort to prod her into obeying his command, he sent her a wolfish grin. "Of course, if you have no wish to discuss poetry, we could progress to our next lesson if you like."

Without any further protests, she turned and reclined against his leg. The warmth of her sank deep into his leg muscles, and he reached out to play with the riotous curls that wound their way across her breast. His fingers barely scraped over her nipples, but he saw the small peaks stiffen immediately. The rapid rise and fall of her chest matched the ragged breaths blowing over his hand.

"Are you familiar with the medieval text, Carmina Burana?"

"I'm afraid my tastes run more to gardening texts."

"Ah, a novice indeed." She stiffened against his leg. Leaning over her, he stared into her eyes.

"I find parts of the text quite erotic. Many focus on the pursuit of sexual pleasures. Let me think, ah, yes ... summer returns, now withdraw the rigors of winter. Ah! Now melts and disappears--ice, snow and the rest, winter flees, and now. Spring sucks at summer's breast. A wretched soul is he who does not live or lust under summer's rule. Ah! They glory and rejoice in honeyed sweetness who strive to make use of Cupid's prize, at Venus' command let us glory and rejoice in being Paris' equals. Ah!"

He reached out to trail his finger over her hand, running his forefinger across her knuckles and up her bare arm. "Do you understand the meaning of those words?"

"No, but somehow I feel certain you are about to tell me."

"You are correct." He smiled at her amusement. "The entire poem is about the act of copulation. It describes how a man and woman come together to experience the pleasures of the body."

"I ... oh..." Her breathy response shot a bolt of satisfaction through him. Surprise mingled with anticipation on her face. She might be a novice, but it was evident she would be a quick and eager student. With a languid gesture, he trailed his finger back down her arm.

"For instance, the first line, Summer returns, now withdraw the rigors of winter. That describes how passion heats a man's cock as it burgeons forth with heated desire."

She sucked in a quick breath but didn't speak. It shocked her to hear him speak in such raw terms, but it made her spine tingle and sent spirals of excitement circling across her skin. Lord, but the man's voice was dangerously hypnotic.

"Of course, the next line is equally arousing," he murmured. "Now melts and disappears, ice, snow and the rest, winter flees, and now, spring sucks at summer's breast. In other words, a man's ballocks grow warm as his hard, erect cock enjoys the hot clenches of a woman's sex."

"Good lord," she breathed.

Never in her wildest imaginings had she ever thought a man could arouse a woman with just a few simple words or the sound of his voice. His provocative words didn't just warm the air around her, they caressed her. Invisible hands, they stroked her skin with quiet seduction sending a shudder of longing through her as her heart pounded against her chest.

The sudden warmth of his hand cupping hers made her breath hitch. Gently, he guided her hand toward her breast, forcing her thumb over a stiff peak in a sensuous caress. Swallowing hard, she struggled to keep from trembling. Sweet heaven, it was the most sensually wicked touch she'd ever experienced. Again he used her own thumb to stroke her nipple.

Her body shifted slightly beneath her own fingers as he showed her how to stroke the nipple through the material of her choli. A soft moan whispered past her lips. She couldn't help it. It was erotic the way he was touching her without really doing so. The deep notes of his voice washed over her again.

"A wretched soul is he who does not live or lust under summer's rule. In other words, the soul who doesn't enjoy the heated pleasures and delights of a cock buried in a furry muff is a wretched being indeed."

She swallowed hard at the description he gave. Reading was a favorite pastime, and she knew the basics of what occurred between a man and woman. But this was beyond even some of the more risqué books she'd read. His voice alone was enough to tempt her, but his words--they swished across her skin in a lazy movement of heat.

He'd barely touched her and yet she was warm and craving his lips on hers, on her nipples. Oh God, how she wanted him to take her into his mouth. She watched his firm lips move, knowing that at some point in the future she would get her wish.

"This particular line of the poem is my favorite. They glory and rejoice in honeyed sweetness who strive to make use of Cupid's prize."

"Honeyed sweetness?"

"It's Cupid's best concoction." He sent her a wolfish grin and he continued to keep her fingers busy with her nipples. "Men and women rejoice in orgasms when the man buries his hard length deep in a woman's dark muff and her honey sweet mixture coats his hot cock. Tell me, Ophelia. If I pushed my tongue through that furry muff of yours, would you be dripping with honey?"

The image heated her blood, and a sudden gush of heat settled in the apex of her thighs. A tender ache made her muscles taut with a craving for him. His touch. She sucked in a quick breath at the thought. Yes, she wanted his touch down there, caressing her. Her gaze locked with his, and she froze as he slid his fingers under the waistband of her lehanga.

Oh, yes.

She jumped as he ran his fingers down her stomach to the crest of her mound. God, he wanted to dip into the honeyed depths of her. For he was certain she was wet and slick. Her breasts heaved against his arm, and he slowly retreated. A sigh eased past her lips, and he knew she was disappointed.

"Not yet, I think. I need to provide you with an explanation of the poem's last line. At Venus' command, let us glory and rejoice in being Paris' equals. What do you think that means?"

"I ... I don't know."

"The Goddess of love herself commands all men and women to rejoice in the pleasures of lovemaking as Paris did with his beautiful Helen of Troy. And that's precisely what we're going to do, Ophelia."

He pressed his mouth against hers in a feathery touch then raised his head. The disappointment in her doe-eyed gaze drew a smile to his lips. Without another word, he reclined back against the pillows. She rose on one elbow and turned toward him with a quick jerk of her head. Her frustration obvious, he grinned at her.

"Such disappointment."

"If you expect me to beg, I shall not."

"Ah, now that would be quite enjoyable, my concubine begging to be pleasured."

"Concubine," she hissed. "I am not your concubine."

"Then come here and prove to me that you are not a slave, but an independent woman, here of her own volition."

He chuckled at the flash of gold anger lighting her beautiful brown eyes. His challenge had infuriated her. Rigid with tension she narrowed her gaze on him, her long fingers digging into the pillow beneath her hand. The blatant indignation arching her eyebrows pulled another quiet laugh from him.

The laughter mobilized her to sit up and crawl forward. She was a beautiful lioness stalking her prey. "And how am I to prove my independence?"

Her voice had deepened to a sultry tone that vibrated through him. Hovering over him, she swept her hair over her shoulder and as she did so, the sari became dislodged from her shoulder. It fell over him, and he drank in the lavender scent of her already buried in the material.

"You do not answer, my lord. How do I prove my independence to you?"

"Kiss me."

She lowered her head and pressed her lips against his in a gentle kiss. When she drew back, there was a satisfied smile on her face. Laughing, he shook his head. "No. You must entice me. Lure me into your net. A kiss such as that will only tell a man he can expect little passion from you."

Annoyance flashed in her eyes. "Why is it the student must teach the master?"

"You are not teaching me, Ophelia, you're learning the art of pleasing me. Use your imagination. Arouse me with your hands, your lips and anything else you can think of."

Surprise replaced the irritation in her animated features, and then a smile as old as Eve curved her lips. Lowering her head once more, she brushed her lips over his brow, then down his cheek. When she sought his mouth, a thread of delight tightened a vise around his chest until his breathing became ragged. Despite her inexperience, she nipped at his lip with her teeth. The unexpected bite made him take control of the kiss.

He inhaled the floral scent of her with a deep breath before he crushed her mouth against his. With his tongue, he parted her lips to probe the inner recesses of her mouth. Warm and succulent, champagne danced off her tongue onto his. He savored the delicious taste and heat of her. Capturing her bare waist, he couldn't resist sliding his hands up to cup the fullness of her breasts. She jumped and drew back. Reaching out, he laid his palm against her bare midriff. The heat of her skin burned his hand with a desire he'd never experienced before. It roared through him with the force of a gale wind, singing a song as powerful as Circe's.

The silence remained unbroken as she stared down at him, indecision and curiosity mingled together on her full features. Curiosity won out, and she placed her hands on his chest, her fingers slowly undoing the buttons of his shirt. Thoroughly enjoying himself, he folded his arms behind his head and watched as she caressed him tentatively. With each stroke, she grew bolder. The pad of her thumb slid over his nipple before tracing a line down his breastbone to the waist of his trousers.

The fiery trail made his cock jump with excitement, and he saw her eyes widen with fascination. Swallowing hard, he reached out and undid his trousers. Free of its restraint, his cock sprang out to press against his stomach like a hard pillar. He saw her mouth move with surprise, and the image of her sucking on him made him stifle a groan. That would have to come later. He wanted to take his time with her, savoring her reactions as he initiated her with each new act.

"Touch me." He saw her eyes darken with a mixture of hesitation and anticipation. Reaching out, he caught her wrist and guided her hand to encircle him. The coolness of her slender fingers made his cock jump with delight. God, he needed release. "Please me, my beauty. Squeeze me just a bit tighter."

She learned quickly he thought as he groaned from the delight surging through his body. "That's it--now slide your hand up and down. Ah, yes."

Her hand pulled another grunt of pleasure from him. As she continued to stroke him, he settled his fingers over her nipple gently rubbing it to a stiff peak through the satin material of her top. A soft gasp parted her lips, and she slowed her pace on his cock.

"No, don't stop." She resumed the fast tempo and he jerked from the pleasure she was giving him. "God, yes! Faster. That's it."

His groin was on fire, the friction creating a delightful sting of heat. The sacs beneath his cock drew up tight and he knew he was close. The sweet fragrance of her drifted under his nose, and he recognized the scent of her passion. It sent him over the edge and he shot his seed out with a loud cry. For the next few seconds, his cock continued to spasm with his release. The torturous need alleviated, he closed his eyes with a satisfied sigh.

"Are you all right?" Curiosity filled her voice.

"Quite. It's been some time since I've had such a delightful hand encircling me. You did exceedingly well."

"I never realized a man could find pleasure in such an act." The puzzlement in her voice forced his eyes open. He grinned.

"There are many ways for a man to find pleasurable release just as there are numerous ways for a woman as well."

"Show me."

He couldn't suppress his grin at the haughty demand. "Your eagerness pleases me."

A blush tinged her cheeks with pink as he tugged her down on top of him. He teased his lips across hers nibbling at the plump skin. She tasted of sweet French wine. Eager to settle his hand and possibly his lips against the apex of her thighs, his hands urged her to lie next to him.

Rolling over, onto his side, he gently tugged the pleated sari out from underneath her until only her lehanga and choli remained. Untying the drawstring at her waist, he caressed her stomach before sliding his hand under the filmy silk cloth and downward. She jumped and he halted his progress.

With feathery kisses, he teased her lips apart. The taste of him was warm and fruity as he swept his tongue into her mouth. Delight rippled through her and a delicate tension tightened her skin the moment his hand brushed across the apex of her thighs.

Instinct made her open herself up to his touch as his fingers dipped into her wiry curls and stroked her in the most intimate of ways.

The wicked caress tugged a low moan from her at the wild sensations flooding her limbs. Nothing she'd read had ever prepared her for such unbelievable pleasure. His mouth slid off her lips to drift to the side of her neck. He nipped gently at her skin. The touch, combined with the hot caress of his fingers, forced her to arch her back.

She moaned once more. Oh God, she'd never felt so wicked in her entire life. It was glorious. Heat spiraled in her belly as his fingers found the sensitive spot in her slick folds. Intense pleasure skimmed over her as he focused his attention on that center of delight. It was impossible not to writhe beneath the increased pressure and stroking of his fingers. Dear Lord, she'd had no idea a man's touch could produce such exquisite rapture.

With each stroke of his finger the rest of her body tightened with delicious anticipation--for what she didn't know. Her breasts were full and heavy, while her nipples were rigid and aching with need. Oh God, she wanted him to suck on her. Suck on her like he'd described earlier this evening. The heat of his hot breath stirred the air over one breast. If possible, it tightened her nipple even harder. She whimpered.

He granted her unspoken wish as his teeth grazed her hard peak through the choli. The brief touch made her inhale a sharp breath of anticipation. Then his mouth clamped gently down on her and he suckled her through the thin material as he increased the strokes to her now pulsating center. She shuddered at the blinding pleasure encircling her.

Caught up in a torrent of undulating emotions, a hot pressure spread its way through her body. With each intimate stroke of his finger or flick of his tongue, he guided her toward a fevered pitch. A moment later she reached the pinnacle. Bucking against his hand, she uttered a sharp cry of pleasure while tiny frissons of delight rippled through her body.

In the back of her mind a small voice warned her she was in trouble. She ignored it. She didn't care. All that mattered was this soft, luminous glow covering her body as it sank into a languid state of relaxation.

Releasing her breast from his mouth, he slowly eased the caresses of his finger. Every moment or two she would jump against his hand as the spasms inside her slowly ebbed. Her eyes fluttered open and he smiled at the dreamy expression she wore. Withdrawing his hand, he retied the drawstring of her petticoat.

"Now you know how delightful your hand felt on me. I have no need to ask if you enjoyed yourself." He smiled at her satiated expression.

"I never realized how ... exhilarating it could be ... so incredible."

Her words startled him. God in heaven. Had he misjudged her reticence for true innocence? He had no wish to initiate a virgin in the arts of pleasure. They too often found themselves enamored with their first lover, not to mention the danger of being set upon by outraged family members. Frowning he studied her with narrowed eyes.

"I was under the impression that you were not completely innocent."

A shadow entered her gaze as she turned her head away. "It is only that I have not experienced such pleasure before. It has always ... I've never...."

"I understand," he murmured. With a firm grip of her chin, he turned her head back so he could drown in the liquid warmth of her gaze. "Your past experiences will soon fade from memory, Ophelia. I promise you that."

Relief sailed through him. Her ingenuous behavior was only the result of a poor lover. He smiled. In a month's time, she would no longer be an innocent in the ways of seduction. She would be a sultry siren that no man would be able to resist. This last thought struck an arrow through his heart. No, within that time, he would bind her to him so she would not want another man. He needed to find a small, cozy love nest. Not about to share her with anyone, he tucked a reminder away in his head to seek out suitable accommodations tomorrow.

Chapter 4

Ophelia sighed as her sister pulled her along one of the many gravel paths in Hyde Park. "Oh, do come on, Ophelia. I promised Mr. Nickens I would be at the Grand Oak at eleven sharp. And we're already five minutes late."

"If Mr. Nickens is sincere in his interest, he's certain to wait until you arrive."

"Do you think so?"

Smiling, Ophelia shook her head. "Yes, now please stop pulling on my arm. Otherwise you'll have me covered in bruises."

"Well, if you hadn't stayed so late at the earl's last night, you would have been earlier to rise."

"I must do as he asked." She shrugged at her sister's reproof. "After all, we do have Sheffield Park again."

Remorse darkened Patience's pretty features. "Oh, dear, I'm sorry, Ophelia. I'm a muttonhead. Of course you must do as the earl asks."

Her sister uttered a soft cry of excitement as she released Ophelia's arm. "There he is, and you were right, Ophelia. He did wait."

Although her sister looked as if she wanted to fly toward the gentleman waiting in the shade, she was relieved that Patience maintained a moderate pace as they approached the massive oak tree. As they drew near, the gentleman tipped his hat and smiled a welcome.

"Good morning, ladies. I'm delighted you agreed to join me for a walk."

"It's a lovely day for a walk, isn't it?"

"Indeed." Nickens offered his arm to Patience, and the three of them strolled along the path. Wishing to give the couple the opportunity to talk freely without someone eavesdropping, she dropped back to a respectable distance and breathed in the fresh air. The heat of the day was just beginning to rise, but it promised to be a comfortable day.

Glancing over toward Rotten Row, she saw the popular equestrian track was quite crowded. About to turn her head away, she caught sight of a golden-haired rider breaking away from the course and cantering in her direction. As he drew near, she sucked in her breath quickly.

The memory of the night before flooded her senses, making the spot between her legs warm and sticky. Her breasts ached as she remembered the way he had taken her in his mouth while his fingers drove her to a heated explosion of desire. Need spiraled up from her feminine core, spreading its fiery stream of lava through her limbs.

The steed he rode was a massive white stallion, which snorted angrily as he reined in the animal. He did not speak to her, but trotted up to where Patience and her companion had halted. Drawing near, Ophelia heard him greet her sister's escort.

"Good morning, Nickens."

"My lord, it's been some time since our paths crossed last."

"Indeed, the fault is mine." The earl dismounted and bowed toward Patience. "Would you do me the honor of introducing me, Nickens?"

"But of course, my lord." The young man gestured toward Patience first. "This is Miss Patience Sheffield."

Ophelia watched in dismayed alarm as the earl politely kissed her sister's hand. In a daze, she heard her own name uttered in the way of an introduction. Thank God, Patience had the sensibility not to mention the earl's benevolence in returning their home to them. Before she realized what was happening, he encased her hand in his large one. The sight of his hand reminded her how those long fingers felt against her most intimate of spots.

A tremor shook through her as his mouth brushed over her hand, and he lifted his head to smile at her. The wicked glint of amusement in his gaze made her tighten her lips. The rogue knew what she was thinking. Fire crested her cheeks and she offered him a small curtsy.

"Were the three of you planning on walking far?"

"It was my intention to escort the ladies to the Achilles Statute where my carriage awaits us."

"Then perhaps I might join you for a short distance. It would seem that Miss Sheffield is without company, and I am free at the moment."

"What a capital idea," Nickens exclaimed, followed by Patience's delighted agreement.

When she remained silent in the face of such enthusiasm, the earl turned back to her. A mischievous light danced in his jade eyes.

"That is, if the lady does not object to my somewhat scandalous reputation, which I can assure you is undeserved." He caught her hand again and lifted it to his lips. Discreetly, he traced a circle in the palm of her hand. It tickled her skin through the glove she wore.

"I rarely find that any reputation is undeserved, my lord," she hissed beneath her breath before she pulled her hand away and turning her head toward the other couple. "If his Lordship is able to withstand the rigors of our walk, he is welcome to join us."

"Excellent," Nickens said with a satisfied smile and offered his arm to Patience. "Shall we continue on our way, Miss Sheffield?"

The couple moved forward, leaving Ophelia and the earl to follow. Without speaking, she kept her distance behind the other couple, her body all too aware of the man who had fallen into step beside her. The muffled snorts of his horse made her glance at the brute of an animal with curiosity.

"Do you ride often, my lord?"

"Hmm, sometimes, but the most pleasurable ride is yet to come. In fact, I believe one night very soon will find me nestled in the saddle of a delightful creature."

The flagrant reference to their upcoming rendezvous made her splutter with indignation. Flashing him a look of fury, she increased her pace. He easily kept up with her.

"I see you enjoy brisk walks as much as I do. It tells me you will not weary of the ride to come."

"Will you stop?" she snapped.

"Stop? Now why would I wish to do that?" He grinned down at her. "I enjoy seeing those brown eyes of yours throw daggers at me, while your breasts heave with such delicious abandon."

He reached for her hand. As he lifted it to his mouth, the tip of his thumb caressed her nipple in a move that would appear perfectly innocent when viewed from a distance. The action made her inhale sharply as her breasts grew heavy with desire. Again, she remembered how his touch had elicited a wild, raging need in her. The memory reminded her of the freedom she'd experienced in his arms. She wet her dry lips at the image of lying in his arms, and he growled softly against her fingers.

"That is a move you do far too often and without any idea of the effect it has on men."

His words filled her with a strange sense of power. It was if he had freed her from all inhibitions. It emboldened her to tease him. She wanted to make him to ache for a release the same way she did.

"Do you mean this?" She tilted her head closer to his and deliberately wet her upper lip with the tip of her tongue, pulling it back across her teeth in what she knew was a daring invitation. Her eyes dropped to the point where his legs met at his hips, and she laughed softly as she saw the outline of his burgeoning flesh. Two could play this game of temptation as easily as one.

Passion mixed with irritation in his eyes, telling her she would pay dearly for her impudence, but she knew it would be a pleasurable experience. Still laughing, she pulled her hand from his and continued her walk. In step beside her, he chuckled.

"You're aware it's now necessary to punish you for such audacious behavior." His voice was playful and warmed her skin with a delicious tingle.

"Audacious?" She smiled, thoroughly enjoying herself as they traded provocative barbs. "But is that not one of the lessons you have promised to teach me, my lord? The ability to tease and tempt the man I'm with?"

The dark veil of anger that fell across his brow surprised her. His hand captured hers again, squeezing it in a painful grip. "Mark my words, Ophelia. You're mine. And I'll not tolerate any other man attempting to take you from me."

"I'm yours for only a month, my lord. After that I am free to do as I wish," she said with a firmness she didn't feel. Her statement made him inhale sharply.

"Then I shall make certain I enthrall you so completely, you will want no other man." A heated gaze of possession raked over her trembling form, and she knew he wanted to pull her into his arms. Instead, he took a step away from her. "Tonight, you're to wear the sari I gave you with your hair down. Remember, I'm still the master and you the student."

With a small bow, he ducked under the neck of his horse and quickly mounted. The tension in him was evident from the way he gripped the reins. With a sharp jerk of the leather, he wheeled his horse away from her, and galloped off. Heaving a sigh of relief, she quickly crushed the disappointment trying to wrap its tendrils around her heart. She could not afford to feel anything for the man. Giving her body to him was one thing, but she would do well to guard her heart against his roguish charms.

* * * *

Ophelia knocked on the earl's door, her hands trembling as she heard his deep voice bidding her to enter. Inside the opulent room, she glanced around expecting to find him waiting for her. The atmosphere of the room seemed different somehow. There was a strange scent filling the air, and although she couldn't place the aroma, it was a pleasing one. The light jingle of bells turned her head toward a door standing open on her right.

The sight that greeted her ripped a deep breath from her. Charles entered the room in a strange garment that gave him the appearance of a corsair from the Barbary Coast. Barefoot and naked from the waist up, he looked every inch the rogue and pirate. The muscles of his chest rippled as he raised one arm to brace himself against the door frame, while the bells he held in the opposite hand rang out a sensual message as he settled his knuckles against his waist. Warm and golden, he made her knees wobble with delight and expectation as she recognized a familiar sensation stirring in her belly.

"Do you like what you see?" The wicked smile curving his lips matched the sparkling gleam of mischief in his jade eyes.

Not about to reveal how much his appearance rattled her, she tilted her head as though to contemplate his question with deep seriousness. When her gaze returned to his face, she gave a small shrug. "I do admit to a faint stirring of the senses, but then would not any sensible female given your state of undress. After all, your costume lends itself to your reputation, does it not, my lord?"

"You are impudent and quite heartless," he said with a laugh. The bells he held filled the air with the sound of a babbling brook as he moved toward her. The fluid grace of his body held her awestruck as he stopped in front of her. His free hand reached out to grasp her chin firmly.

"Now, Miss Sheffield. I want you to repeat that enticing trick you performed this morning in the park."

The unmistakable command caused her mouth to go dry, and her tongue instinctively flicked out to wet her upper lip. The moment she did so, his head descended in a swift movement as his mouth closed over hers in a heated kiss. The kiss surprised her. It wasn't the unexpectedness of his touch that startled her, rather it was the strength of her own craving for the feel of his lips on hers that astonished her. The warmth of his tongue darted past her teeth, and she struggled to remain standing beneath the wave of pleasure rolling over her.

Her fingers traced the rigid muscles curving over one nipple before she used the pad of her thumb to rub him in the same manner he had done to her. A growl of pleasure reverberated against her lips as he deepened their kiss. Eagerly, she returned the passion he displayed with each tantalizing dance of his tongue. The heat engulfing her made her want more.

When he lifted his head, she whimpered a protest. He smiled with grim satisfaction. "If that is a signal you don't want me to stop, then perhaps you'll understand how I felt in the park today. If you ever do that to me again in public, I won't be held accountable for my actions. Is that clear?"

Irritated by his threat, she pushed herself out of his arms. "I hardly call that fair, given you were the one to provoke the entire incident."

A charming grin curved his mouth, and her breath hitched at the rakish picture he presented. The desire exploding in her belly shocked her, and she took a quick step back. His gaze narrowed, and he folded his arms across his broad, muscular chest the bells he held jingling softly.

"You will find, Ophelia, that nothing is ever fair between a man and a woman. Now then, I want you to remove your slippers."

She sent him a cautious look. Seeing nothing in his expression to warrant a refusal, she did as he commanded. Despite the modest covering the sari gave her, she experienced a ripple of decadence sluicing through her. As was her habit, she wet her lips again. A deep growl rumbled in his throat, and he moved to stand in front of her.

Gently, he encircled her wrist with one of the dainty bell bracelets he held. He then adorned her opposite wrist with a similar ornament. When he knelt at her feet, his breath fanned across the tops of her feet with the gentleness of a warm fire. The action made her pull in a sharp gasp, and he looked up with a smile on his face.

"So, you are not as unaffected as you would have me believe."

"You, my lord, have earned the title of rogue most honestly. That is, if a rogue can be honest." The pained affectation on his face made her laugh.

He adorned her ankles with the delicate bell bracelets, before rising to his feet. Capturing her hand, he led her toward the center of the pillow-strewn floor. As she moved forward, the bells attached to her limbs filled the air with their soft sound. Bowls of nuts, dried fruit and other exotic foods filled a low table in the middle of the luxurious hassocks. She watched as he seated himself among the rich, red, gold and green pillows. Surrounded by such princely decadence he had the air of a sultan. The devilish smile on his face revealed the rogue once more as he extended his hand to her.

The warmth of his hand encompassed hers as she sank down onto the vibrant silk cushions beside him. With his free hand, he retrieved what looked like a large golden-brown seed from one of the bowls. The cylindrical-shaped, slightly shriveled piece of food glistened in the candlelight as he examined it. Curious, she tipped her head to one side.

"What is it?"

"A date. Have you never seen or tasted one?"

"No. Is it a nut or a fruit?"

"A fruit. It's very sweet." White teeth gleamed in the candlelight as she watched him bite into the odd-looking food. His eyes never left hers as he offered her the remaining bit. Not merely a rogue, but a wolf.

The swift rhythm of her heart pounded against her breast as she leaned forward and pulled the food from his fingers with her lips. The bold act surprised her almost as much as him, but he recovered far more quickly.

"You are a beguiling enchantress, my sweet," he murmured with a wicked grin. "But I'm afraid temptation must wait, as I arranged for a special performance for us. Tonight I wanted to show you that pleasure between a man and woman can be found in other things, besides caresses."

He raised his arms and clapped his hands together in a sharp demand. An instant later, a strange, haunting music filled the room. The instrument producing the soulful music was unlike anything she'd ever heard before, foreign and yet exciting in its exhilaration. Its effect hypnotic, she didn't resist as Charles pulled her backwards to recline against his bare chest. The poignant melody filling the room became more erotic, and cradled in his tender embrace, a lethargic sensation sank into her limbs.

Beneath her head, the raw power of his shoulder was a firm, yet flexible support. The mesmerizing music floated through the room, but now a new sound accompanied the strange instrument. The bell-like sound soon revealed itself as a woman dressed in a simple white sari edged in gold, emerged from the room adjoining the earl's bedroom with small cymbals on her fingers.

With exquisite grace, the dark-skinned dancer performed to the music with slow, elegant steps. The woman's movements and facial expressions were emotive and sensual. The husky sound of his deep voice tickled her ear.

"This dance is called the Mohiniyattam, which means dance of the celestial enchantress. Each step or movement of the body tells part of an ancient Hindu myth."

"It's beautiful."

While the woman danced before them, he tempted her with nuts and the exotic foods on the table next to him. The strange food slid from his long fingers past her lips in a sensuous fashion. It felt perfectly natural for him to feed her in this way and yet it was unlike any experience she'd ever encountered. The erotic touch of his hands against her mouth warmed her blood. It simmered and spread its languorous heat through every part of her body.

They watched in silence for some time, the music and the dancer merging into one pleasurable picture of grace, sensuality and erotic emotion. He offered her a sip of warm tea and she sighed with enjoyment. His lips nibbled at her ear for a moment, while his fingers trailed across her arm in feathery strokes.

"Are you enjoying yourself?"

"Ummm, yes. The food is delicious and the dancer is wonderful. She's so graceful and delicate looking. Tell me the story her dance describes." Her head twisted slightly on his shoulder so she could look up at him. The wicked smile she had grown accustomed to curved his mouth. His forefinger traced the outline of her lips before he gently forced her to look at the dancer again.

"As the story goes, the ocean was made of milk. This milk was so pure that gods and demons churned the ocean to extract the elixir of life and immortality. Unfortunately, the demons made away with the divine brew."

The dancer's steps became more dramatic and evocative as the story unfolded in front of their eyes. Like the music, his husky voice tempted and enticed her. Lethargy held her tightly in its grip and the dance suddenly developed into erotic and sultry movements of frenetic proportions. Once more, his voice brushed her ear with a warm breeze.

"With the elixir gone, the gods are filled with panic. Lord Vishnu wants to help the gods, so he assumes female form in the shape of Mohini. The amorous celestial damsel seeks out the demons and captivates them with her charms. Entranced by her beauty, the demons cannot help but be mesmerized by her seductive manner and sensuality. With the demons entranced, Mohini steals the nectar from them and restores it to the gods."

A sensual nip at her ear lobe pulled a soft gasp from her. Erotic and passionate, the music swelled over them as the dancer moved through the final steps of her dance. Caught up in the melody's joyous celebration, she experienced a desire to dance alongside the woman. With a final gesture of her hands, the woman came to a stop as the unusual music faded away. Seconds later, the woman hurried from the room.

Ophelia leaned forward in protest. "Oh, wait."

"Geeta is very shy. She never dances outside her husband's establishment, and I was fortunate to convince her to perform for us tonight."

"Why would she do that for you? Is she one of your conquests?" A streak of jealousy shot through her. Soft laughter stirred her hair.

"No, her husband and I became friends while I was in India. I brought them to England when I returned."

Relief made her relax against him. He reached out for a handful of nuts, offering her some as well. The silence of the room ended as the invisible musician filled the air with another sensuous melody. It called to her, enticing her to dance as the woman called Geeta had danced. Her hands moved in time to the music, and his warm breath tickled her ear.

"Dance for me, Ophelia."

"Dance," she gasped. "I ... I don't know how."

"How do you know until you try?"

"I don't think I can."

"Use your instincts, don't think. Feel, release your mind and let the music move your body." The soft murmur of encouragement made her believe she might actually be able to do as he asked.

With a tentative nod of her head, she pushed herself out of his arms. Rising to her feet, she began to mimic the intricate steps she had witnessed earlier. Aware of her horrible inadequacy at the effort, she turned with a laugh. The mirth lodged in her throat at the blazing fire glowing in his jade eyes. She froze, unable to move.

"Continue. I don't think I've ever seen anything so enchanting."

She swallowed the knot in her throat and resumed her attempts at the native folk dance. As she moved, the bells on her wrists and ankles blended with the sultry music filling the room. It moved though her, binding her to its daring, heady rhythm. Her hands seemed to belong to someone else as she reached up and loosened the sari from its snug position on her shoulder. The rose-colored silk slid across her arm, and she held it up to her face, breathing in the softly fragrant material. She allowed the sari to fall over her arm and continued to dance. The heated intensity of his gaze burned across her skin, and it emboldened her to sway her body close to his, but she pulled away in a languid move as he leaned forward.

He wanted her. She could see it in his face, and the knowledge thrilled her, encouraged her to tease him even more. Dancing away from him, she allowed the sari to trail behind her, and then lifted it up and over her head to undo the wrap. She glanced back over her shoulder and smiled. The sight of him kneeling in a predatory fashion enticed her to return to him, her steps filled with the sound of bells and the hidden musician's melody.

With a gentle wave of her hand, she allowed the end of the sari to brush his cheek. He caught it in his fingers and with a soft tug, he pulled the sari free from the waistband of her lehanga. Freed of its restraint, the sari floated down to rest at her feet, and she danced out of the remaining length of cloth.

The music grew sultrier and she closed her eyes as she swayed to the spellbinding notes. Warm hands grasped her waist, and she sighed in contentment as she continued to move to the exotic melody. Her hips brushed against his thigh and a growl rumbled out of him. His thumbs slid up along the edge of her choli, creating a wanton stirring in her belly. She wanted to have nothing between them.

Lightly, she danced away from him. Turning so she could see his face, she crossed her arms and lifted her bodice up over her head. As she discarded the choli, she stood before him wearing only the filmy lehanga, which rested low on her hips. His expression was one of stunned delight. At her soft laugh, he stepped forward and pulled her into his arms.

Covering her mouth with his, he kissed her deeply and with a passion that sent a chill of anticipation down her spine. His tongue teased its way past her lips, and she met it with a wanton abandon that caused him to groan. Against her fingertips, the hardness of his shoulder muscles bulged and rippled. The strange fragrance in the room had settled on his skin, mixing with his normal scent of spice and leather.

The music heightened to a fervent pitch before it melted into a slow rhythm and faded into nothingness. All that remained was the sound of her quick breaths as his lips singed her cheek and then bare shoulder with heat. As his hands rode up from her waist to her breasts, her heartbeat spiraled out of control. Instinct made her arch backward, thrusting her breasts into his bare chest. The sensation of her nipples against the fine hairs of his chest created an instant reaction between her legs.

She was wet and aching for release. Her hand captured one of his, and with a gentle tug she placed his hand on her thigh. With a slight shift of her body, his warm fingers pressed against the apex of her thighs. Moaning, her head fell back as he suckled one breast, while he stroked her through the lehanga. The sudden sensation of the filmy material pooling at her hips pulled a soft sigh from her.

"Now I intend to show you another method of pleasure." The rough edge of his voice rustled against her skin as he lifted his head to stare down into her eyes. It produced a delicious twist of excitement skittering down her spine.

He took her by the hand and pulled her over to the full-length mirror. Standing behind her, he rested his hands on her bare shoulders. The reflection sent an embarrassed flush of color through her cheeks. She watched as pink heightened the outline of her cheeks.

"There is no need to be embarrassed. You have a beautiful body. It was made for loving."

She shuddered at the words and met his gaze in the mirror. Jade embers skimmed over her with blazing need. His hands splayed against her waist heating her already warm skin that much more.

"Touch your breasts." His lips brushed over her shoulder, muffling the softly murmured words. Bewildered, she wasn't certain she'd heard him correctly. When he lifted his head, he smiled at her in the mirror. Taking her hand, he lifted it and placed it over her breast. With a gentle move, he reminded her how to tease her nipple until it peaked against her fingers. A quiet moan blew past her lips, and he nibbled at her neck. He then guided her other hand to the nest of curls between her full thighs. She gasped as he pressed her fingers against the nub beneath the curls. Following his husky instructions, she stroked herself to the soothing sound of the bells ringing lightly in the air.

His hands tightened on her waist, and he pulled her against him until he bore her weight, and she could focus on the pleasure her hands were evoking. Her eyelids hung heavy and she saw his image reflected in the mirror as he watched her fondle her body. The naked desire and excitement in his face sent a tremor through her. She found the faster she brushed her fingers over the sensitive spot between her legs, the higher the pitch of delight. Her fingers rubbed the small nub between her legs in a frenzied fashion, the bells singing an excited melody as the release she had experienced the night before crashed through her again.

The feel of his hands on her breasts heightened the sensation and with a wild cry, she arched back against him, her fingers growing wet with the juices that flowed from inside her. Spent from the pleasure she'd just received at her own hand, she rested her head against his shoulder, content to enjoy the gentle caress of his hands. He cupped her.

"Such lovely breasts. I grew hard watching you touch them."

Nothing he said could erase the lethargic warmth settling into her limbs. Bells jingled with every movement she made, and they soothed her senses with a sensuous stroke of the exotic. He straightened her upright and turned her to face him. Through droopy eyelids, she saw that he had removed his strange garment. The sight of his glorious body made her sigh with delight.

A smile curved his mouth, and he drew her back to the pillows. Together they sank down into the plush cushions, the richly colored hassocks forming a soft bed. His mouth brushed hers in a feathery kiss, and he slowly reclined into the pillows, pulling her with him. When his hand grasped her bottom, she quivered at the way his fingers kneaded the softness of her flesh.

Boldly, she pressed her tongue against his lips. A low chuckle greeted her action, and his mouth opened to give her access. In return, she pressed down against him, the wiry hairs of his solid chest tickling her breasts. Against her thigh, she could feel the hardness of him.

With a languid movement, she slid her hand along the hard length of his body to encircle him with her hand, and he released another groan. Aware that she could please him, she sat up to cup him as she had the night before. The bells on her arm resonated softly in the air.

Fascinated by the hard length of him, she studied him with intense curiosity. Her thumb edged over the top ridge just below the tip of his phallus. The caress made him jerk in her hand.

"Shall I please you as I did last night?" She tightened her grip slightly. He sucked in a sharp breath and she smiled with cunning amusement.

"To really please me, I require something different."

"Different?"

"Yes, the pleasure will be more intense if you take me in your mouth."

His words trapped her breath in her chest. The idea of kissing him so intimately made her quiver with excitement. She exhaled deeply, her body tingling with wicked delight at his request. He was leading her down a path of total destruction, and she admitted with reluctance that she wanted him to.

Still, she hesitated. A strong hand cupped her breast and she trembled at the deep need shooting through her as his thumb rubbed against her sensitive nipple. Warmth spread its way through her limbs, and she leaned forward to kiss the beautiful hardness of him.

With a life of its own, his phallus jumped with excitement. Playfully, she flicked her tongue across the rough ridge near the tip of him. A hoarse cry parted his lips, and as he jumped again, she embraced him with her fingers to hold him still. Again, her tongue feathered over him, delighting in his reaction. Noting the sensitive point near the swelled cap of his phallus, she wrapped her mouth around him and teased the spot with her tongue. Another husky groan escaped him.

Her gaze flickered to his face as she took him deeper into her mouth. His eyes were closed, but his features were taut with sheer delight. She tightened her lips around him noting how his jaw flexed in reaction to her touch. A wordless sound rumbled from his throat, telling her how much he was enjoying what she was doing to him. With slow deliberation, she trailed her tongue along the upper ridge of him. He tasted hot, salty and totally male.

Drawing him deeper into her mouth, her fingernails scraped lightly across his warm stomach, and the muscles flinched beneath her touch. In a leisurely motion, she eased him almost all the way out of her mouth before sliding back down over him in an abrupt move. His reaction was instantaneous. Strong fingers slid through her hair as he held her head in a gentle grip, his entire body rigid with a combustible tension.

"Sweet Jesus."

The hoarse exclamation scraped over her skin as desire swirled inside her. Surprised, she realized she was wet between her legs. Not only was she pleasing him, but it aroused and stimulated her too. He swiveled his hips slightly in an attempt to push deeper into her mouth. She let him do so before retreating again. With only the tip of him in her mouth, she circled the enlarged cap of him with her tongue. A groan of need escaped him as he inhaled a sharp breath. His green eyes flew open and locked with hers as she slid her mouth downward again.

"Christ almighty."

This time his voice held a small thread of desperation. It was a need she recognized from the way he'd brought her to a climax only a short time ago. A sense of mischief and power swept over her. Two could play the teasing game. He'd teased her earlier tonight with his erotic talk and touch. Now she intended to tantalize him until he pleaded with her. Her fingers stroked down a firm, sinewy thigh. It was such a contrast to the hard velvet she stroked with her tongue.

Again her mouth tightened around his phallus, maintaining a steady pressure as she suckled him much in the same way he'd suckled her. She slid up and down the length of him, her lips tight around his hardness while her tongue flicked and swirled around him. This time his groan was explosive with need

"God, yes! Suck me. That's it ... suck me."

His words incited her to move up and down his thick, hot length with increasing speed. His hips moved in rhythm to each laving swirl of her tongue, and she matched his beat with each caress of her mouth. He groaned again, his phallus jumping inside her mouth. The knowledge that she pleased him excited her, and her nipples grew taut with each groan that rolled past his lips.

Gently, she nipped at the roughness of him. The deep growl that emerged from him made her smile against his rigid phallus. Her mouth tightened again on his hardness, sliding up and down with rapid thrusts and she heard his pants of excitement. A moment later, a deep groan rolled out of him and his phallus stiffened before it rippled against her tongue. With a suddenness that startled her, he jerked away from her.

She watched as his seed spewed over his stomach. Her gaze shifted to his face. His eyes closed, a contented expression tipped the corners of his mouth at a slight angle. Glancing at the table a few feet away, she crawled forward and retrieved a napkin. She returned to his side and gently cleaned his skin.

At the touch of her hand, his eyes flew open and he studied her in silence. There was a possessive gleam in his gaze, and it pleased her. Finished cleaning him, she tossed aside the cloth and leaned down to kiss him.

"Did I please you?"

With a quick movement, he rolled her onto her back. His forehead resting on hers, he groaned. "Yes. In truth, you drove me over the edge far more quickly than I expected."

"But, isn't that the point of pleasure?"

"Minx." He laughed and rolled away from her onto his back. "I admit that you give me great pleasure, but I was hoping to relish each sensation gradually so we both experience it together."

Filled with the heady knowledge that she had the power to give him pleasure, she turned onto her side and reached for him again. The quiet groan rumbling off his lips made her laugh.

"God, woman, I've not yet recovered."

She pushed her hair out of the way and stared down at him, her eyes drowning in the jade depths holding her hostage.

"So what new sensation do you propose to show me now?"

"Dawn is near, and you should return home. But tomorrow night, we'll indulge ourselves further." The glint of deviltry in his eyes made her draw in a quick breath.

How had she come to such ruin? With just one look, he could reduce her to a quivering mass. She wanted to make him feel the same way. Did she dare to continue playing this dangerous game? She needed to take care or the wicked sensuality of the man would ensure he owned more than her body. Perhaps she was her father's daughter after all. The only difference was she was gambling with her heart.

Chapter 5

Charles hurried up the steps of Sheridan House. He was eager to see Ophelia. Embroiled all day in an urgent business transaction for his brother, he'd been unable to go riding in the park with hopes of seeing her. Over the past week, he'd discovered Ophelia and her sister were in the habit of walking along the Serpentine each morning.

Some days he would simply watch her from a distance, and at other times, he'd make it appear that happenstance had brought him to where she was. The fact that she occupied so much of his thoughts vexed him, but he attributed it to the lust her voluptuous body aroused in him.

Their love games over the past week had heightened his senses to such a state that on more than one occasion he'd almost given in to his desire to bury himself inside her. Yet, something held him back. Despite his confidence that she'd had a lover before, the ingenuous air about her restrained him.

It was the same innocent quality that stirred his cock each time she was near him. He found it difficult to understand what kept her from sliding down onto him and riding him with the passion he knew she possessed. The evocative image made him grow hard, and he grimaced at the uncomfortable tightness of his trousers.

What puzzled him most was her contentment with the erotic touches they exchanged. Did she not want to feel him buried inside her? Feel his cock throbbing inside her velvety heat. It perplexed him deeply. Even more disturbing was the tenuous lock he held on his own state of barely checked passion. He wasn't sure how much more he could withstand, given her aptitude for quick learning.

Leaving his hat and cane with the footman at the door, he moved through the crowded doorway and up the main staircase. Tension assaulted his stomach as he entered the ballroom. What the devil was the matter with him? He was acting as if Ophelia were the first woman he'd ever bedded. With a disgusted shake of his head, he moved to a secluded spot along one wall of the ballroom.

The large fronds of a potted palm partially hid him from prying eyes while affording him an excellent view of the room's entrance. He didn't have to wait long. Ophelia and her sister soon crossed the threshold. The tightening in his groin reminded him all too well how much the sight of her tormented his cock.

Tonight a peach silk gown hugged her luscious curves. The sleeves of the dress caressed the sides of her shoulders, verging on her breasts in a downward vee. Devoid of the normal fripperies and ruffles, the gown swept back around to the bustle she wore. She was voluptuous, sensual and wonderful to look at. In fact, she looked as intoxicating clothed as she did when she was his naked concubine among the pillows of his brother's den of pleasure.

The sight of Nickens greeting them sparked a jolt of satisfaction inside him. The man obviously coveted the sister. Playing on his brother's acquaintance with Nickens meant he could be near Ophelia without fueling gossip. It was fortunate the man wasn't one of Robert's close friends. Otherwise, he'd be unable to keep Nickens from knowing he wasn't the real Rotherham.

To his credit, Robert was extremely generous, and he always paid for his friends expenses when they traveled with him. As controller for the estate, he'd always raged about his brother's extravagant generosity. For once he was grateful for the extra money his brother spent taking so many friends to the continent. It left no close acquaintances in London who could accidentally unmask his deception.

Damn it, Robert. Couldn't you have been a bit more discreet so as to avoid owning the reputation of a profligate rake? How the hell am I suppose to enjoy myself without dragging Ophelia's name through the gutter.

The taut sensation in his chest was uncomfortable. Hands clenched behind his back, he flexed his fingers out of the tight fists then curled them up again. He wanted to throttle his brother. His lips tight with annoyance, he chided himself for the thought. Blaming his brother for his current predicament was useless. It had been his choice to play this game, and he alone must deal with the consequences.

He watched the trio move deeper into the room. Losing sight of them for a moment, he tensed as they came back into view.

Resentment churned in the pit of his stomach. Lord Albertson was leading Ophelia out onto the dance floor.

What the hell was she thinking? Albertson was a twit. His hands flexed then curled back into tight fists as he watched her laugh up at the oaf. Had she lost her mind? He struggled to remain in place, when what he really wanted to do was stride across the ballroom floor and punch the fellow in the nose.

She was his and no one was going to take her from him. The rush of possession that swept through his body made him swallow hard. God in heaven, he couldn't actually be falling for the woman. Forcing himself to relax, he folded his arms and leaned back against the wall. He watched the way she smiled at the man with growing irritation. The grimace he felt tugging his mouth annoyed him as well. One would think he could control himself better than this. After all, it wasn't as if he intended to marry her. Still the idea of Ophelia with another man filled him with an overwhelming sense of disquiet.

The music floating through the room reminded him of how beautiful she looked the night she had danced for him in her sari. He'd never seen anything more seductive or exquisite in his entire life. Mixed in with the orchestra's rendition of a popular waltz, the low voices of two women on his right intruded his thoughts when he heard the name Rotherham.

"One would think she'd have better sense than to be seen in that rake's company. After all, her father's gambling has placed the family in bad straits as it is. The man will never marry her."

"True, not even if they're caught in a compromising position. Surely, Rotherham knows about that scandalous incident with Blackburn last season."

"Oh, I didn't hear about that. Do tell, Millicent, do tell."

"Well, gossip has it she pursued Blackburn the entire season. When he didn't come up to scratch, she supposedly allowed her father to find Blackburn kissing her. Naturally, the man didn't marry her, but I did understand that Blackburn wiped out Sheffield's debts overnight."

"I'd heard Sheffield lost their estate to the earl some weeks ago. Do you think she's trying to win back their home from Rotherham?"

"I wouldn't doubt that she's trying something just like that, my dear. After all, what has she left without a home? Her reputation is already in serious doubt. Why else would the earl have anything to do with her at all?"

Disgusted with the vicious conversation, he pushed himself away from the wall. Brushing past the fronds of the potted palm, he eyed the women coldly. "Why indeed, madam? Why would I want to have anything to do with such a lovely young woman as Miss Sheffield when I hear such ridiculous allegations against her character? I fear you must forgive my skepticism, but I find the young lady's motives far less suspicious than those shared by other addlebrained members of society."

The stunned expression on their pinched features filled him with warm satisfaction. With a sharp bow, he turned and walked away. Damned prudes. His Ophelia was worth more than a hundred such repressed viragos. He quickly swept aside the possessive thought, refusing to consider the origin of such emotion. Instead, he focused on making his way through the crowd to where Nickens and the youngest Sheffield daughter stood.

"Nickens, a pleasure to see you this evening." He shook the younger man's hand, then turned to the woman beside him. "Miss Sheffield, you look lovely this evening."

"Good evening, my lord."

She bobbed her head in greeting and glanced toward the dance floor. Following her gaze, his lips tightened with irritation. "Your sister seems to be enjoying herself a great deal. Has she known Lord Albertson long?"

"I believe they met last year. He's quite taken with her."

"Indeed." Jealousy stirred his gut once again, and he turned his gaze back toward Ophelia's sister.

"Why, yes indeed." Mischief lit her face. "I've been meaning to inquire about your health, my lord."

"My health?" The question puzzled him and he watched the humor disappear from her face.

"Why, yes. I was given to understand that you suffer from severe migraines."

Baffled, he stared at her for a moment in complete confusion. At the look of horror creeping into her gaze, he realized that Ophelia had lied to her sister about why she was visiting his home at night. You, fool! Why would she tell her sister the truth about how she recovered their home? Bloody hell.

Unaware that he had uttered the curse aloud, he flinched at Nickens rebuke.

"My lord! You forget yourself."

"I do indeed." He bowed stiffly. "My deepest apologies, Miss Sheffield."

The sound of male laughter behind him made him turn his head. Lord Albertson was leading Ophelia off the floor, and when his eyes met her brown ones, he saw them flicker with a warm welcome. No doubt, that welcome would become anger when she discovered her sister believed the worst about their relationship. Especially when it was true.

As the couple reached the edge of the dance floor, Charles nodded in Albertson's direction. With a quick bow, he brushed his mouth over Ophelia's gloved hand. "Miss Sheffield, it would give me great delight if you would honor me with this next dance."

"Oh, but, I--"

"I'm sure Lord Albertson doesn't mind at all. In fact, I'm sure he'd agree that more than two dances in a gentleman's arms implies a most serious relationship."

"Why ... I, of course..." Albertson took a step back in fear as Charles glared at the man.

"Excellent. You see, Miss Sheffield, Lord Albertson is more than happy to share your delightful company." He offered her his arm with a smile, but sent her a hard stare daring her to refuse him.

With reluctance, she accepted his arm and sent Albertson a small smile of apology. It shot a stream of anger spiraling through his blood. His free hand covered hers in a crushing grip as they moved toward the dance floor. He struggled to keep a smile on his face. Confronted with the knowledge that he had betrayed her, innocently or not, he resented having done so. She should have told him. He would have happily protected her reputation.

When they reached the dance floor, he swung her into his arms and guided her across the floor. "Why didn't you tell me your sister knew about your visits to Rotherham House?"

She stiffened in his arms. "Dear Lord. What did you say to her?"

"I didn't. She asked me about my migraines."

"Oh, God. I told her you suffered from migraines, and that in exchange for Sheffield Park I was to visit you at night and relieve you of your headaches."

"Smile for God's sake," he bit out with a grimace. He could see the effort it cost her to smile and it tore at him. He'd brought her to this. It mattered little that she'd offered herself in exchange for the return of her home, what else could she have offered a notorious rake? He should have found something else for her to barter with other than her reputation.

A soft sigh parted her pink lips, and he wanted to kiss her until the troubled look in her brown eyes evaporated into an expression of soft desire. "I suppose I should have expected this. I'm surprised I managed to keep it from her for so long."

"And now?"

"Now?" She eyed him curiously, as he whirled them around another couple.

"How will you fulfill your part of our agreement?" The callousness of the question made her blanch, and he cursed inwardly at his oafish conduct. But he needed to know. He had to be certain she would return to him.

"I will meet you at the usual time, my lord. I shall fulfill my obligation to you."

The flatness of her gaze struck at him like a knife. His behavior was beastly, but he didn't know how to control the fear winding its cloying vines around him. The idea of never seeing her again attacked him with vengeance.

"Ophelia..." Whatever he thought he wanted to say died in his throat at her impassive expression. He averted his gaze and when the dance drew to a close, he halted their graceful movement. In silence, he escorted her back to her sister. Bowing, he thanked her for the dance, and with a sharp nod to the others, he walked away.

Why the devil did it matter that the woman's sister knew of their agreement? Ophelia was a grown woman, more than capable of making her own decisions. Still he'd recognized the abhorrence in the younger Miss Sheffield eyes. In all likelihood, Ophelia had kept her first lover a secret from her sister as well.

Bile rose in his throat as he acknowledged his own contribution to the situation. The fact he'd deliberately sought her out in public lay squarely at his doorstep. He'd already heard the gossips at work this evening, and his defense of her would only inflame those vicious tongues. He was to blame for her current predicament, and he didn't know how he could remedy the situation. Pushing his way out of the ballroom, he admitted he'd never felt so ashamed in his entire life.

* * * *

Hands clasped behind his back, Charles paced the floor waiting for Ophelia to arrive. While part of him prayed she would stay away, the other half of him prayed fervently that she would come. Rational behavior no longer applied where she was concerned. But tonight, if she came to him, he would free her from the agreement they'd made. Perhaps her reputation was still salvageable if he stayed away from her. The real question was, would he be able to stay away from her?

He stopped in front of the mirror and frowned darkly at his reflection. The man facing him bore too close a resemblance to the reputation his brother held. Perhaps Robert had good reason for acting the notorious libertine, but he had no such reason. Being cynical about women and their designs on his brother's title was one thing, but to act the rake and scoundrel at Ophelia's expense was inexcusable. Glaring at the image before him, he cursed beneath his breath.

"You're contemptible Lynton. A rake and scoundrel of the worst kind. You're going to let her go, because it's the honorable thing to do. If you don't you're worse than any label your brother owns."

A selfish voice flashed an image of Ophelia in front of him. The strength of the vision was so strong he could almost taste the tangy sweetness of her skin. The self-serving voice urged him to reject his decision, but he ignored it. No, he would set Ophelia free despite the price it would cost him. He only wished the entire affair finished. Waiting was not something he did well.

The knock when it came was soft against the wood. He strode to the door and threw it open. The sight of her nearly undid him. She was wearing the sari he'd given her last night before she left. Crimson silk of the sheerest weight covered her from head to toe. The transparent material revealed that she did not wear a choli beneath the sari, and the dark tips of her nipples pressed seductively against the silk.

His cock jumped to attention immediately. He wanted nothing more than to throw her onto the bed and sink into her heated depths repeatedly until they were both sated.

"Did Bateson see you dressed like that?" The idea of any man seeing her in this state of undress filled him with a jealous anger.

"No, I left my cloak at the top of the stairs as usual." She tipped her head at him, her smile not reaching her eyes. "Are you displeased?"

"Not at all." He forcibly swallowed the knot in his throat and stepped aside so she could enter the room.

Closing the door behind her, he paused to gather his wits before turning to face her. When he did so, a strange look flickered over her face. It did not last long enough for him to decipher it.

"You act as if you didn't expect me to come tonight."

"I admit to thinking you might not."

"I told you I would, and I never go back on my word."

"Damn it, you don't have to make it sound like this is some duty you've to perform. I had come to believe you were finding pleasure in our association."

A long silence filled the air, as he studied her serene features, but she didn't respond. When she remained silent, he dragged in a harsh breath. Stalking past her, he headed toward a small table against the wall. He poured a healthy dose of brandy and tossed the liquor down his throat.

"Why are you so angry?"

The softness of her voice caressed his ears and he looked at her over his shoulder, ignoring the question. "I'm freeing you from our agreement, Ophelia. Sheffield Park is yours free and clear."

Confusion danced across her face, and he turned away. God help him find the strength to let her go. Pouring another drink, he tossed the fiery liquid down. If he didn't look into those warm eyes of hers, he might just succeed in getting her out of the house before he lost all his willpower.

"I don't understand," she said.

"I thought I was perfectly clear, my dear. I'm freeing you of our agreement without any penalty. Sheffield Park is yours."

"I understand what you've said, but not why."

"It's not necessary for you to understand why."

She watched the muscles in his arms clench and bulge beneath her fingers as she touched his arm. "Yes, it is. I want to know why you've suddenly developed a conscience where I'm concerned."

"Because tonight I failed to protect your reputation. My public pursuit of you has put you at risk for complete ruin if we continue with these nightly trysts."

"And my reputation is important to you?" Her heart skipped a beat. He cared.

"Of course it's important to me. I might be a rogue, but I'm not about to shirk my responsibility when it comes to protecting you from comments about our association."

The words pricked at her heart like a needle. He only cared about her reputation. He didn't love her. But she loved him. A tremor shot through her. Sweet heaven, she loved him. Somehow she'd known all along she was in love with him. She'd hidden from the truth, knowing that any admittance of affection would be her downfall. None of that mattered any more. Not even the cost of loving him. She drew in a deep breath.

"Your gallantry is appreciated, but when I leave London, it will be permanently. Any gossip about me will be quickly replaced with the next scandal the moment I'm gone."

"Nonetheless, you'll go." Jerking free of her gentle grasp, he strode toward the door. "Come, I'll see you to your carriage."

"And what if I don't wish to go?" The moment she spoke, she knew she couldn't leave him. Her heart wouldn't let her do so. She loved him. She loved him enough not to care what others thought. It seemed so simple now. Her heart had decided her fate for her. She watched his hand slowly leave the door handle before he turned to face her.

"What are you saying?"

"Don't send me away, Charles. I want to stay here with you. When I'm with you, I feel ... I feel alive. Don't take that away from me." Would he reject her? Would he remain unmoved by her plea? She needed to move him into action, and her hands trembled as she slowly unwrapped the sari.

His mouth went dry at the sight of her movements, and he shuddered with the need to sweep her into his arms. Unable to speak, he watched as the sari's long length of material slid to the floor. Then her beautiful fingers taunted him with the unhurried manner in which she untied the drawstring of her lehanga. His cock pressed against his flesh like a rock.

The moment the flimsy petticoat drifted to the floor, he erased the distance between them in two strides. Beneath his fingers, her silky skin heated his hands. Her brown hair flowed over her shoulders like a warm curtain.

"Far be it from me to refuse you another night of pleasure." His voice was a hoarse whisper as he dipped his head and crushed her mouth beneath his. All thought of honor flew from his head. She wanted him. The need to fill her made him sweep her up into his arms and carry her to the bed.

Chapter 6

Stretched out on the bed before him, she was the most beautiful woman he'd ever seen. The soft candlelight danced across her skin in a sensuous caress, luminescent fingers encircled her breasts like a tender lover. Hard with the need to spill himself inside her, he suppressed the urge to take his pleasure immediately.

He wanted to see her writhing beneath him as he plunged into her repeatedly. Seeing her reach a fevered pitch as his cock throbbed inside her would intensify his own pleasure. The thought of her animated features lost in the throes of passion, increased his excitement. His fingers drifted over her belly in a feathery stroke.

Lowering his head, he pressed his lips where his hands had just been. A deep sigh echoed out of her, and he smiled against her sweet-smelling skin. Unable to help himself, his hand slid down over her hip and across to the apex of her thighs. Her hips bucked against the touch, and he inserted his finger inside her enjoying the warmth of her. His mouth nipped gently at her navel, then slid slowly downward.

A soft cry of surprised delight sprang from her lips as he slid his tongue between her sleek, velvety folds. The taste of her on his tongue made him nearly delirious. Her hands sank into his hair, and one leg drew up alongside his cheek. Delighted with her response, he allowed one hand to slide along a silken thigh, then up to knead the nipple of one breast.

He did not wait long for her quick release, and he tasted her exploding over his tongue. Nipping her inner thigh with his teeth, he slid his body up across her belly until he could capture her mouth with his. The quiet cries of rapture pouring from her throat pitched his excitement to a fevered state. He poised himself above her, then plunged deep into her. The sharp cry she made pierced him in the same way he pierced her maidenhead.

"Bloody hell." Shock lashed through him as he froze, buried deep inside her.

Her eyes flew open to meet his, and she quivered at the glazed look in the jade orbs staring down at her. His throat convulsed with emotion as he shook his head in disbelief.

"Why the devil didn't you tell me? I would have done more to try to ease your pain." The sight of his tortured expression tugged at her heart.

"Would you have taken me if I'd told you the truth?"

"No ... Yes ... I don't know."

"Then it doesn't matter. I wanted this as much as you did, and it doesn't hurt anymore."

She had done it. She had gambled everything she held dear to experience this one moment with the man she loved. Earlier tonight, his vivid, green eyes had been dark with torment for his part in making her a source of gossip. It had been that anguish that urged her to risk all she held dear.

The stiffness of him fit snugly inside her, and with the initial pain gone, she found the tight fit erotic and arousing. Her body had expanded to accept all of him, and when she shifted her body even the slightest amount his phallus throbbed inside her. The resulting sensation created a fiery need to experience it again. She shifted her body beneath his, and he groaned.

"For God's sake, will you remain still?"

"Are you in pain?"

"No." Something in his growl made her smile. Oh, to have only a few more nights like this and she would be content to live out her days in obscurity. She flexed her hips against him once more and elicited another low cry from him.

"Then as a master of pleasure, would you care to resume instruction." She teased. He throbbed inside her, and she shuddered with pleasure at the sensation. Instinct made her shift her hips upward and a deep groan rolled out of his throat.

He withdrew slightly then eased himself back inside her. Slowly he repeated the motion. The friction he created warmed her entire body. The hard heat of him caressed her insides with rivers of sheer delight. Her hands slid around his waist, and each time he lowered himself into her, she thrust her body upward to meet him. The corded muscles on his back rippled beneath her fingertips. A musky heat emanated from him, and she drank in his male scent. Bergamot mixed with spice filled her nostrils, and she gasped as he increased the speed and rhythm of his strokes.

Arching her back, she matched his movements with the same fervor he displayed. Caught up in the mind-numbing tempo, her hands clutched at him, her fingertips digging into his hard flesh. The sensations whirling through her grew until she exploded with a shattering spasm that gripped his hard length tightly. She cried out as she shot up to a pointed peak then surrendered to a delicious descent as her body shuddered beneath him.

Despite her explosive reaction, he continued the steady rhythm of his phallus, and pulled her up the mountain again. Writhing beneath him, she experienced another rush of vibrations in fierce succession. As she peaked again, he thrust into her deeply and uttered her name in a hoarse cry.

The sensation of him throbbing violently inside her made her muscles clench tightly, and he groaned at the tight grip of her body. The pace of her heartbeat slowly eased and she welcomed the warm weight of him as he sank down on top of her.

Only their ragged breathing broke the silence, and the thud of his heartbeat against her breast mixed with hers. There was something warm and comforting about the sensation. Contentment sank into every fiber of her being, and she sighed softly. Raising his head, he studied her with a somber expression.

"What the devil possessed you to stay here tonight? I told you to go."

"You've told me repeatedly since we first met to stop thinking and simply feel. I did that. Tonight I chose to feel instead of think."

"Then I told you wrong."

He gently extracted himself from her embrace and rolled onto his back. Losing his warmth made her shiver, and he reached for a light blanket at the foot of the bed. He covered her with the soft lambs wool cover before he slid out of bed. As he walked away, she sat up. Greedily she watched him stride across the room, and she uttered a quiet sigh. He was beautiful in shape and form. While he poured himself a brandy, she studied his lean, muscular body. A fine dusting of golden hair layered his strong, sinewy legs, which rose to meet firm buttocks. His back muscles rippled as he tossed down his drink. The glass clinked sharply against the tabletop as he slammed it down.

Sliding from bed, she moved to stand behind him. She embraced him from behind, and pressed her mouth against his back. He stiffened in her arms, but did not move. Her cheek resting on the hard muscles of his back, she ran her fingertips over his stomach.

"You're angry again."

"Not with you, with myself."

"But why?" Troubled by his aloof manner, she stepped around to face him. Her hands rested against his chest, and she stared up at him, waiting for an answer.

He closed his eyes briefly before looking away from her. "I should have realized how much of an innocent you were from the start of this mad game."

"I came to you of my own free will. What does it matter now?"

"It's one thing to make love to a woman already familiar with a man, but it's another matter altogether to lead an innocent along the same path. There are pitfalls on either side, but more so with an innocent."

The bitter resignation in his voice scraped across her heart. She stiffened and threw her head back with annoyance. If he wanted to feel remorse for initiating her into the pleasures of lovemaking, so be it, but she would have no part of it. For her part, she had no regrets. She'd experienced a delight that exceeded her wildest imagination.

"I see. And exactly what are these pitfalls you're so worried about?" Her tone deliberately light, she sent him a skeptical look. In response, he grasped her chin firmly in his fingers and frowned.

"There are consequences with everything one does."

"I knew the consequences when I gave myself to you. I've asked nothing more of you, and will not do so."

"You say that with great finality."

"Well, didn't you release me of our bargain earlier?"

Scowling, he planted a hard kiss on her mouth. She melted into him, responding to his harsh caress with a tender one of her own. Beneath her fingertips, his heart pounded wildly against his chest. With a sharp gesture, he pushed himself away from her. Grabbing his trousers up off the floor, he covered himself.

"Things have changed," he muttered.

"Have they? How?"

"Damn it, Ophelia. Don't play games with me. Do you think after tonight I can just let you go?"

"But you were willing to earlier, why should it be different now?"

"Because it just is."

"That is not an explanation," she said with exasperation. Following his example, she retrieved her lehanga and sari.

"Well it's the best I can do at the moment."

"Then it seems we have nothing more to say to each other."

"What the devil does that mean?"

"It means exactly what I said. We have nothing more to say to each other."

"God damn it. This is exactly what I meant by pitfalls. You're not making any sense at all."

She stopped in the middle of dressing and stared at him with her mouth agape. When he arched a questioning eyebrow at her, she laughed aware of the bitterness in the sound. "I'm not making any sense?"

"Well, if you're hoping that I'll offer for you, think again."

"My lord. If you were to get down on your knees and beg a hundred times over, I would not marry you."

"And why not?" His vanity pricked, he glared at her.

"You're a rake and a scoundrel, which makes you ill-suited for marriage." Finished adjusting her sari over her shoulder, she darted a quick look in his direction and glared at him. "Oh for heaven's sake, don't look so surprised."

She looked around for her slippers, and catching sight of them near the door, she crossed the floor to recover them. Hopping on one foot, she performed a small dance as she tugged on first one slipper and then the other.

"I don't think I can let you go so easily, Ophelia."

The quiet steel in his voice drew her up short, and she turned to face him. His chin rigid with determination, he folded his arms across his bare chest. The powerful magnetism emanating from him sent a shiver through her. Letting go would not be easy, but to tarry would mean the possible loss of her soul, since she'd already given him her heart.

* * * *

Ophelia descended the stairs the following morning, her body aching from the previous nights events. There was a pleasantly tender ache between her thighs, a poignant reminder of her evening with Charles. The deep sigh parting her lips became a yawn. She had slept little after getting home.

For most of the night, she'd lain staring up at the ceiling. She had known her heart was in danger from the first moment she'd set eyes on him. But she had never expected to find herself so deeply embroiled in a love affair that could only end one way.

The thought of losing him made her heart thud painfully against her breast. In the early light of dawn, she'd watched the sun slowly rise and vowed to cherish every moment she spent in his presence. When they parted, she would have beautiful memories to ease the pain of his absence.

At the foot of the steps, she turned toward the breakfast room. Behind her, a door crashed open violently. Jumping, she whirled about to see her father standing in the doorway of his small study.

"I want to talk to you, Ophelia."

Tension tugged at her muscles immediately, and controlling her features, she nodded her head. "Of course, Father."

She stepped past him into the room, and stopped as she saw Patience seated in front of Sir Sheffield's desk. Her younger sister did not look up, but kept her face averted as Ophelia sat in the chair next to her. Hands behind his back, her father strode around the desk and turned to face her. She studied him cautiously. He'd once been a handsome man, and it was understandable how his looks had swept their mother off her feet.

Now the dissipation showed heavily in his features. The unnatural ruddiness of his complexion cried of too much drink, and his bloodshot eyes announced his late nights at the gambling tables. Jowls heavy from too much food and drink, he was the epitome of a jaded nobleman content to do nothing but bury himself in self-indulgent behavior. She pitied him.

"Patience tells me that you are on the brink of ruin, girl."

"Then she is mistaken." Ophelia met her father's gaze steadily.

"How long have you been meeting the earl of Rotherham in secret?" His harsh voice whipped across the desk, and she stiffened at the angry question.

"Since the night I convinced him to return Sheffield Park to us."

"What in the blue blazes are you talking about, girl."

"Our home, Father, Sheffield Park. I persuaded the earl to return it to me."

"Whored your way to it most likely."

The crude accusation stunned her worse than a hand across her face might have. Tension racked her body and she slowly rose to her feet. "I had little else to offer in exchange for his returning the home you disposed of in such a cavalier manner."

"Damn it, Ophelia. Do you realize what you've done?" The pain in his voice did not mollify her.

"I did what was necessary," she said in a cold voice. "I restored Sheffield Park to our family."

"Was it worth it? Was it worth giving yourself to the man just to have Sheffield Park back?"

"Yes."

"Well, all is not lost. We'll make sure the earl gets his comeuppance, we will. Tonight, you're going to meet him in private at the Lansdowne affair. At which time, I'll put in an appearance and the man will be forced to marry you."

"I won't do it." Balling her hands into tight fists, she pressed them into the folds of her skirts.

"You will do it. I'll not have a daughter of mine associated with that bastard in anything other than the most respectable manner. Your poor mother, God rest her soul, would be heartbroken by your actions."

"My mother," she said through clenched teeth. "Would not have understood how her husband could be so dull-witted and dishonorable to gamble away a home that she treasured."

"Enough!" The roar of his anger only increased Ophelia's own fury.

"No, it is not. I will not let you blame me for any of this. I didn't lose Sheffield Park to a notorious gambler in a drunken fit of betting. Instead, I won our home back from the earl. I bartered with the only thing I had available. The earl and I made an honorable agreement. His Lordship has already returned our home to us, and I intend to fulfill my half of the agreement."

"Do you dare to defy me, daughter?"

"Yes." She turned and walked toward the door.

"If you walk out that door, I'll disown you, Ophelia. I'll have nothing to do with you. You'll have nothing."

Her movements deliberate, she faced him. "You have nothing left to barter with, Father."

"Oh, don't I? Sheffield Park is ours again. If you think to live there with your sister and me, you'll do as I say."

"No, Father. You don't understand. Sheffield Park is mine, and mine alone. The earl saw to it that my name is on the deed. He knew you would only gamble it away again. At least Patience and I will have a roof over our heads."

The stunned look of defeat on his flushed face filled her with sorrow. Clearly, he was grappling with the knowledge that he had tossed his life away. Perhaps in time, they would come to an understanding, but for now, she wanted nothing to do with him. His actions over the past two years had destroyed the trust she'd placed in him as a child.

Without another word, she left the study and climbed the steps. Her appetite for food had disappeared, and she wanted nothing more than to sit peacefully in her room. As she reached the middle of the staircase, Patience's voice bid her to wait. Pausing, she turned to see her younger sister staring up at her with an anguished expression on her face.

"Forgive me, Ophelia. I didn't know what to do. I only wanted to protect you."

"I know that, Patience. I don't blame you. You did what you thought was right." She descended the steps to brush her lips across the younger girl's cheek. "There's nothing to forgive, dearest. I have no regrets."

"None?"

Confidence flowed through her as she nodded her head. "None. Now, I wish to rest. I'll see you at midday's meal."

"And tonight? Will you go to him again tonight?"

Anticipation threaded her body with warmth. The thought of being in Charles' arms once more filled her with happiness. She nodded her answer then retreated up the steps.

* * * *

The humid warmth of the ballroom clung to her skin in an oppressive manner, and Ophelia regretted her agreement to attend the Lansdowne ball. But Patience's urgent pleas had persuaded her to accompany her sister as she had told Mr. Nickens they would be present. The young man had captured her sister's heart and Ophelia saw he returned those feelings. It would be a good match, and he was well on his way to becoming a respectable lawyer.

Her fan stirred the air in front of her face, but it failed to offer a cool respite from the heat. From her position on the edge of the dance floor, she smiled at the happy picture Patience made with her young man. At least one of them would make a respectable marriage, something that would not be possible for her. She experienced no remorse at the thought. The time spent with Charles had been one of the greatest adventures of her life. It was something she would not trade for anything in the world. Even if Sheffield Park were suddenly pulled from her grasp, she would still feel no regrets.

The familiar tingling brushed across the nape of her neck, and her fingers reached to touch the sensitive spot. There was no need to turn around. She knew he was watching her. A tremor shook her body, as she struggled to keep her eyes focused on the dancers in front of her. The prickly sensation grew until the warmth of his breath blew across her neck.

"Good evening, Miss Sheffield."

With a nonchalant smile, she turned her head slightly. "My lord."

"I want to speak with you. Meet me on the terrace at the top of the hour," he whispered before raising his voice. "Give your sister my regards, Miss Sheffield. A pleasure to see you again."

She lifted her fan to hide her smile and nodded her reply before he moved away. How long had it been since the last chime of the clock? The orchestra finished its song, and when Patience and her escort joined her, she inquired about the time.

Nickens pulled out a pocket watch. "It's five minutes before the hour of ten, Miss Sheffield."

A thin sliver of anticipation tickled her skin and she forced herself to act as naturally as possible. After a minute or two, she pleaded the need to visit the ladies room. When Patience offered to accompany her, she encouraged her sister to remain. With a smile, she tried to hide her eagerness and walked slowly away. The crowded room made it difficult to reach the doors leading out onto the terrace, but it also hid her from Patience's concerned eyes.

The cool summer air brushed her heated skin with a refreshing breeze. Stepping deeper into the darkness, she moved along the edge of the stone walkway. From out of the night, a strong hand gripped her wrist. Startled, she gave a small yelp as a pair of powerful arms wrapped themselves around her waist. The frisson of the experience made her shiver as she lifted her face to see Charles' rugged features shadowed by the moonless night.

"You took long enough," he growled. She breathed in his sandalwood scent as she pressed into him, wishing she could feel the heat of his skin beneath her fingertips.

"And you're far too demanding. I'm not at your beck and call, my lord."

"Perhaps we need to reconsider our agreement," he murmured.

"Whatever agreement you propose, I'm certain it will be heavily weighed in your favor."

"Naturally."

Lowering his head, he drowned out her gasp with a hard kiss. His hand brushed across the exposed skin near her breast, and a tremor of delight whipped through her. Nestled against him, she kissed the line of his jaw, while one hand traced the line of his hip then slid its way to the swiftly growing bulge in his trousers.

"Did you really want to talk to me, or was it just an excuse to get me alone so you could tempt me."

"Tempt you? You're the one who's doing the seducing." He uttered a low groan and she laughed softly against his mouth.

"Do you wish me to stop?"

"God no, my sweet, no I don't."

Her hand continued to rub him in a slow circle as she laughed. Boldly, she kissed him, lost in the delight of the moment. In the next instance, pleasure disintegrated into horror.

"Get away from my daughter, Rotherham."

Charles grew stiff in her arms, his muscles hard and inflexible. Glancing over her shoulder, she saw her father and Mr. Nickens standing a few feet away from them. Appalled, she shuddered as Charles pushed her away from him in a violent shove. Mute with disbelief, she reached out her hand to him, but he slapped it away.

"Well, Miss Sheffield. You disappoint me. Surely you could have arranged to have your father find us in a much more compromising position than this." Jade eyes colder than ice raked over her.

"No, I--"

"Spare me your platitudes, my dear. I have no use for them." The suppressed fury in his voice was a frigid blast of air lashing through her. Desperate, she clutched his arm.

"But, you don't understand."

"I understand clearly, madam," he snarled as he shook off her hand in a vicious gesture. He turned toward the two men standing nearby. "Send me your price tomorrow, Sheffield, but do not expect an offer of marriage."

Without another look in her direction, he walked away with a stride that betrayed an anger of immense proportion. Watching him go, she pressed her hands tightly against her stomach. The sight of him disappearing from view wrenched at her soul with an anguish she'd not even experienced at her mother's death. The muscles in her chest tightened, and she tried to breathe, but could not. In a daze, she heard her father speak to her.

"Come, Ophelia. We'll go home." The moment his hand grasped her elbow, she came alive with anger.

"Don't touch me."

"Damn it, Ophelia. The man's not worth getting worked up over."

"You planned this. You made Patience beg me to come tonight. How could you? Isn't it bad enough that your actions forced me to barter myself for our home, and now you use me to line your pockets? You're despicable." With a violent shove of her hands, she pushed her father out of her way and swept past Nickens.

Returning to the ballroom, she saw Patience waiting with an anxious expression near the terrace door. Unable to bare her soul without falling to pieces, she moved in the opposite direction. All she could think about was escape. She hurried to the manor's front door to wait impatiently for her carriage. When the vehicle finally arrived, she climbed into the dark interior with a sob of relief. She wanted nothing more than to crawl into a hole and die. Charles despised her.

She had never held any illusions about his intentions. When he married, she knew it would never be to a nobody such as herself. But she had prayed fervently that the blissful nights spent in his arms would last far longer. When she'd declared him ill suited for marriage, she had done so to protect her heart. The cruelest blow was that he believed her capable of such duplicity as her father. How could she make him understand she'd never agreed to her father's devious behavior? With a grimace, she opened the coach window and ordered the driver to take her to Rotherham House.

Moments later, she stood at Charles' front door. As Bateson opened the door, she slipped inside. The butler immediately became agitated.

"Miss, I'm sorry, but his Lordship has instructed me not to let you into the house."

The words cut deep into her heart and she flinched. "Would you at least tell him I'm here and ask only a moment of his time?"

"I've no wish to see anyone, Bateson." Charles' voice drifted from the top of the stairs like a cold wind. She whirled around, her heart growing still at the forbidding look on his face. "And I especially have no wish to speak with any Cyprian who dares to show up here uninvited."

The icy blast chilled her skin as she felt the color drain from her cheeks. He'd called her a whore. Blinded by pain, she slowly turned away. As Bateson opened the door, she stumbled through the opening. The night enveloped her in its sultry embrace, but it failed to warm her. This was what it felt like to be dead.

Chapter 7

Clouds drifted over the sun, reducing the intensity of the heat. Charles adjusted his perch atop his horse as he studied the trio walking in the distance. His eyes studied Ophelia's lush figure as she walked with her sister and Nickens. A frustrated sigh escaped him, and he turned and rode off in the opposite direction. Two bloody weeks, and he was no nearer to forgetting her than he had been the night she'd destroyed his world.

He had sent a draft note to Sir Sheffield, but it came back without a note of explanation. Not knowing what to make of the refused payment, he'd pondered it for a time. Then with a flash of cynicism, he realized that they were holding out for him to propose marriage. It had infuriated him that Sheffield would think he could coerce him into marrying Ophelia. But when no messages came the first week after the Lansdowne affair, he'd become puzzled. What were they waiting for?

The clip clop of Ares' hooves penetrated his consciousness and he realized he had already ridden almost completely around the park. In front of him, he saw Ophelia moving toward him. Something deep inside gnawed at him to stop. He needed to hear her voice again. The closer he rode to them, the more rattled he felt. His hands clenched the reins, and Ares tossed his head in protest.

Almost on top of them, he reined his horse to a stop. Nickens was the first to see him, and the man frowned darkly, bending his head toward Ophelia's sister. Instantly the youngest Sheffield lifted her head to glare at him. His jaw tightened with tension at the look. Ophelia seemed oblivious to anything. Her features were pale and drawn. Was she perhaps pining for him? Is that why she looked so withdrawn?

He lifted his hat, and bowed his head. "Good morning, Nickens. Miss Sheffield. Ophelia."

"Rotherham." Nickens nodded his head sharply.

For the first time, Ophelia seemed aware of his presence. When she lifted her eyes upward, his heart slammed into his ribs like a hammer. He'd never seen such a lifeless expression. She immediately looked away, continuing her walk without a word of greeting. Recoiling from the pain lashing at him, he tightened his lips into a grim line. With another bow of his head, he bid them good day and moved on.

"Damn her," he muttered. "Why the devil do I feel like the villain here?"

He didn't like the answer his conscience offered in reply to his self-doubt. With a sharp jab to Ares' girth, he cantered toward home. Could he have been wrong? She looked miserable, and instinctively, he knew it was his doing. Sweet heaven, what if she were with child. The thought made him rein Ares to a halt.

Twisting in the saddle, he watched Nickens help Ophelia and her sister into an open carriage. If she were to have a babe, why hadn't Sheffield been to see him? Demand payment? No, she couldn't be with child. Sheffield would not let that go. Shoulders sagging, he turned around and set off for home once more.

Tonight was the Farington ball, and it was his last official appearance as the earl of Rotherham. Robert would be home tomorrow and he would be free to visit Roth Manor. The need for escape had grown over the last few days. Troubling dreams filled his nights. In his nightmares, Ophelia pleaded with him only to walk away into the darkness like a ghost. He would run after her, but she was nowhere to be found. In his dreams, she looked just as she had the night of the Lansdowne affair.

Her boldness in following him home had astonished him. But he'd been even more astounded at how she had responded to his harsh words. Her face had paled to a translucent white before she turned and stumbled out of the house. It had taken every ounce of willpower he possessed not to run after her. Now he wished with all his heart he had. Perhaps he might have had the answers to his questions. He'd been brutal in his treatment of her.

"No," he whispered fiercely. "She tried to catch herself an earl."

The sharp response from his conscience made him flinch. Yes, he'd lied to her, but he'd never expected to fall in love with her. He jerked Ares to a halt. The animal whinnied a loud protest. God help him, he was in love with Ophelia. The knowledge wrapped a cord around his chest, constricting it. How the devil had he fallen in love with her? She had tried to entice and trick him into marriage.

He prodded Ares forward into the mews and dismounted. Still grappling with the idea that he loved Ophelia, he strode into the house. Inside, he passed the kitchen and caught a whiff of Cook's crumpets. A loud guffaw of laugher rolled through the door, and he stopped abruptly. The familiar laugh came again, and Charles entered the kitchen.

Robert sat at the table eating a crumpet, while conversing with Cook. The moment he entered the room, his brother turned toward him. With a cry of delight, Robert sprang to his feet. A moment later, Charles was enveloped in a warm hug.

"Well, little brother, let me look at you." Robert pushed him back to look at him. Hands still on Charles' shoulders, the earl of Rotherham frowned. "By God, you look a mite peaked, old man."

"I'm fine, but now that you're back, I'll be leaving for Roth Manor." He stepped away from his brother and moved back into the hall. Robert followed.

"What the hell for? How can you possibly find anything to do in the backwaters?"

"Unlike you, Robert, I never have enjoyed town life."

"True, but you've never acted this despondent before either."

"I am not despondent."

"Of course not. But then gossip holds that you're pining for a certain young lady."

Drawing up short, Charles wheeled to confront his brother. "What the hell are you talking about? What gossip?"

Robert frowned. "Word reached me in Paris that the earl of Rotherham was deeply involved with a new ladylove. Naturally, since I was in Paris, I could only hold the gossip was about my little brother."

"Forget the gossip. There's nothing too it," he said bleakly and continued toward the main hall.

"Are you in love with her?"

Charles glanced over his shoulder as Robert trailed after him. "What kind of question is that?"

"A simple one, I thought." Robert chuckled. "Come on, tell your big brother all about it. Did she break your heart, or did you break hers?"

"Go to hell."

The amusement on Robert's face evaporated as he followed Charles into the study. "I say, that's rather harsh."

"The subject is no longer relevant."

"Bloody hell. You are in love with the girl."

Robert's soft exclamation made Charles clutch the edge of the desk. Ignoring his brother's comment, he nodded to a stack of papers.

"These are ready for you to sign. While you were gone, I did dispose of a piece of property, but I shall pay you for it."

"What property."

"A small estate called Sheffield Park."

"Sheffield Park ... hmmm ... ah yes, I won that a couple of nights before I left for the continent. What did you do with it?"

"I gave it to Sheffield's daughter."

"You did what? Damn it, Charles, that was prime property. It abuts Roth Manor, and I thought to expand our holdings in the country with it. I don't understand ... By God, she's the one, isn't she."

"As I said, I'll pay for the property."

"To hell with the property, if you're in love with the woman, why don't you marry her?"

Charles flinched at his brother's words. God, he'd made a bloody mess of things. About to fend off another onslaught of questions from his brother, Bateson's entrance saved him from any further inquisitions.

"What is it?" When they spoke in unison, Charles grimaced at his brother. With a gesture of surrender, he turned back to the papers on the desk.

"There's a young lady to see Mr. Lynton, my lord."

The announcement crackled the air with tension, and Charles turned slowly to face the butler. The unspoken question hung between them, and Bateson gave an imperceptible shake of his head. Disappointment weighed his shoulders down and he frowned.

"Did she give a name, Bateson?"

"Yes, sir. She says her name is Miss Patience Sheffield, and a Mr. Nickens is with her."

Hope cascaded through him, and he grasped his brother's arm. "Robert, stay here. I'll greet our guests, find out what they want, then send them on their way."

"I would like to meet this Miss Sheffield."

"No, I've enough trouble as it is, I don't need you to compound matters for me."

"Very well, little brother, but remember, I expect a full report when you return."

Ignoring Robert's sly tone, Charles hurried from the room. His guests stood quietly in the main hall. They both turned toward him as he approached.

"Miss Sheffield, Nickens. Won't you come in? I will arrange for something to drink."

The young woman frowned. "No, thank you, my lord. Anthony tried to keep me from coming, but when I threatened to come alone, he wisely chose to be my escort."

"I see."

"No, you don't see at all. At least you don't see what's right in front of your nose. My sister is slowly wasting away because of you, and if I could, I'd call you out for the way you've treated her."

Charles stiffened at the sharp words. Clasping his hands behind his back, he frowned. "I'm not certain I understand you, Miss Sheffield. How have I wronged your sister?"

"By accusing her of setting a trap for you. Only a fool and his money could be parted faster than you allowed yourself to part with my sister. She had nothing to do with our father's attempt to blackmail you."

Rigid with tension, he narrowed his eyes at the young woman. "Explain."

"I told our father about your arrangement with Ophelia, and he ordered her to arrange it so he could accuse you of ruining her. But Ophelia wanted nothing to do with his plan. She refused to do anything that might injure you."

"Then how did your father know we were on the terrace together?"

"Because I told him you were." Nickens jerked at her words, and she turned to him. "I'm sorry, Anthony. I should have told you."

"We'll discuss this later, my dear," her companion said. "Now please continue with your explanation to his lordship."

Patience nodded her head as she squeezed Nickens' arm. Turning back to Charles, she eyed him with a somber expression.

"My lord, my sister is wasting away as we speak. She refuses to eat, drinks little and on the occasions we convince her to go outside for fresh air she manages to retreat to her room shortly after her excursion outside. I've never seen her so heartsick, and I want to know what you intend to do about it."

"Me? I don't see where I have any control over your sister."

"For heaven's sake, are you that blind? Didn't you see her today?"

"She looked a trifle pale, but hardly on the verge of collapse."

Patience blew out an angry sniff before turning to the man beside her. "Anthony, I'd like to leave. I was wrong to come here. How my sister could possibly be in love with this man is beyond my comprehension."

The room spun around him and Charles inhaled a deep breath. Uncertain he'd heard her correctly, he shook his head. "What did you say?"

She sent him a look of contempt. "I said I can't comprehend why my sister has feelings for you."

"How do you know she loves me?" The hoarse whisper barely passed from his lips. His mouth had gone dry and his throat was tight with emotion.

"I know my sister, my lord, and even if she's not admitted it to me, I know she's in love with you." Patience tucked her hand inside her companion's arm and they turned to leave.

"Miss Sheffield." A shudder reverberated through him. "Will you and your sister be attending the Farington event this evening?"

He watched her spine stiffen in a fashion similar to Ophelia. When she turned, her gaze was cool and stern, yet he could see a slight softening in her face. "She has refused to go. While it will be a difficult task, I believe I can persuade her to attend."

"Then I hope I have the pleasure of seeing you and your sister this evening."

"We shall see." She proceeded to walk toward the front door with Nickens at her side.

"Miss Sheffield."

"Yes?" Glancing over her shoulder, she sent him a questioning look.

"Thank you." His quiet words softened her features further and with a nod of her head, she left the house with Nickens following close behind.

As the door closed behind them, Charles released the tension holding his body hostage. She loved him. A rush of exuberant emotion plunged through him and he smashed his fist into an open palm with immense satisfaction. She loved him, and tonight he would convince her to marry him. Happier than he'd been in more than two weeks, he turned toward the study.

Robert, leaning against the doorjamb of the office, watched him with a solemn expression.

"You have a problem, little brother."

Charles groaned. "Bloody hell! She thinks I'm you, and when she finds out I've been lying to her all along...."

"The woman will not want anything to do with you."

"She loves me," he ground out. "She'll forgive me."

"And if she doesn't?"

"Then I'm damned." Without another word, he climbed the stairs leaving his brother in the foyer.

* * * *

Ophelia's feet hurt. At least two of her partners had stepped on her toes, and she was irritated at how easily she'd given in to her sister's pleas to attend tonight's affair. She wanted to go home. Anything to avoid the sound of laughter, when all she wanted to do was cry. Tomorrow they would return to Sheffield, and she was glad of it. The sooner she left London, the better. She couldn't bear the thought of accidentally running into Charles again.

This morning when he had spoken to her, she'd sensed his anger. Why had he bothered to speak to them--to her? The sound of his voice had reminded her of the nights spent in his arms when he'd teased her, caressed her and made her feel, not think. Oh, it was pointless to think about the man. He had thought little of her when he refused to let her defend herself to him. His unbending attitude had crushed her. A tiny needle of anger spiked her heart. He didn't deserve her love. The man had only pretended to be honorable. She'd known from the start that he was a rogue. Why had she expected it to end any other way than with her tending a broken heart. Worse yet, she continued to torture herself with thoughts of him.

Her neck tingled, and she reached up to rub the skin at the nape. The warm breath against her fingers made her stiffen.

"Meet me on the terrace in fifteen minutes."

Wheeling about, she watched Charles walking away from her. The curious looks she received from two matrons standing nearby filled her cheeks with heat. Flustered, she averted her eyes.

He was here. He wanted to talk to her. What could it mean? Did he want to torment her further? She wanted to run home as fast as her feet could carry her. How could she face him again? Did she want too?

Her stomach churned violently as indecision made her tremble. She struggled to control her shaking hands by stirring the air with her fan. The orchestra finished with a flourish, and dancers moved off the floor. Patience came to a halt at her side, a slight pant signaling her recent exertion.

"Are you feeling all right? You look terribly pale."

"Yes, I'm fine," Ophelia nodded briefly and glanced away from her sister's observant gaze. "I'm simply feeling warm. It's quite hot in here."

Patience eyed her closely for a moment, and then nodded. "Why don't you let Anthony get us some refreshments?"

"No, I think I'll go stand at the doors leading out to the terrace. I heard someone say there's a pleasant breeze out there." Her sister's frown pulled a small smile to Ophelia's lips. "You're a worrywart. I'll be fine."

Without waiting for a reply, she moved away. It took several moments to reach the terrace doors, and by the time she'd reached the opening, she was trembling. One hand resting on her stomach, she struggled control her emotions. Why was she doing this? What demon prompted her to open up her heart to the possibility of more pain? She stepped back from the doorway, a mixture of anger and fear driving her heart into a frenzied pace.

"Enough," she said beneath her breath. "He's a rogue, not a devil." She stepped into the darkness.

The summer night air was a gentle caress across her skin. From where she stood, she could see couples strolling through the softly lit garden. Moving to the stone wall overlooking the grounds, tension tightened her muscles at the realization she wasn't alone.

"Good evening."

It was Charles' voice but there was something odd about it. She couldn't put her finger on it, but he sounded different. Unwilling to have him too close, she whirled around so she could keep him at a distance. Even in the near darkness, she could make out his beloved features. The sight of him sent a chilly finger down her spine. Something was wrong.

He stepped toward her, and she immediately retreated. Light from the ballroom lit his features and as she gazed into his eyes, she grew cold. This wasn't Charles. This man had crystal blue eyes. She trembled. Who was this man?

"I can see you realize I'm not Charles."

With a slight shake of her head, she tried to rationalize how two men could look and sound so much alike. He smiled. It was a weary smile, but filled with kindness.

"If I had known Charles had agreed to meet you out here, I would have avoided taking in the fresh air."

"Who ... who are you?" she whispered hoarsely.

"Perhaps I should let Charles explain."

"No. I want to know who you are."

He frowned and shook his head. "I really do think it would be best if I left you alone. I'm sure Charles will be here any moment."

Ophelia tensed as he brushed past her. Fear drove her to clutch his arm. "Tell me who you are."

"He's my older brother." The sound of Charles' voice floated across the patio. "He's also the earl of Rotherham."

Immediately, she jumped away from the man whose arm she grasped. She turned her head to see Charles standing a few feet away. But he was the earl of Rotherham. He'd given her Sheffield back. He'd given her the deed. She raised a trembling hand to her forehead.

If Charles wasn't the earl, then that made the deed she held, worthless. She'd sold herself for nothing. Sheffield Park was gone and she had fallen in love with a rake. A rogue in disguise she'd called him that first night. She'd no idea how true that statement had been. The depth of his betrayal sliced new wounds in her heart, twisted her soul with an agony that sickened her. Swaying at the pain racking her body, she swallowed the bile rising in her throat. She wanted to gag with the despair that was choking her.

When Charles strode forward to steady her, she pulled back with revulsion and a white fury enveloped her unlike anything she'd ever felt before. "Do not touch me, sir."

"Ophelia, I want to explain--"

"Explain what?" she bit out. "That you took the opportunity to enjoy a twisted little game with me. I thought my father was despicable, but you have fallen to the same level of debauchery."

"Damn it, I didn't realize--"

"Do not play me for a fool! I'm no longer an innocent, but of course, you know that, don't you." Hatred as stark as her love roiled through her. It burned its way through her limbs, until it engulfed her heart searing it black.

"If you would just let me explain."

"I recall another night when I tried to explain to you. If you'll recall, you denounced me as a Cyprian." All she wanted was to get as far away from him as she could. She swept around him toward the terrace doors. When he caught her arm and restrained her, she tried to jerk herself free of his harsh grip.

"God damn it, Ophelia. Will you at least try to listen to me?"

"Take your hands off me," she bit out in a low voice. "I never want to see you again. You're a liar. You've lied to me about everything. Oh no, not everything, you once said you were a rogue in disguise, and that is the truth."

With a vicious wrench of her arm, she pulled free of his hold and sprinted toward the door. Behind her, she heard him growl her name. Loathing ate away at her soul, as she plunged back into the ballroom. The sudden change in light blinded her, and she blinked rapidly trying to see where she was going as she stumbled forward.

Whatever presence of mind she still possessed guided her to her sister's side. Numb with shock, she accepted Patience's hand as the younger girl rushed forward.

"Ophelia, what is it? What's wrong?"

"I'm feeling quite ill. Would you mind if we went home."

"Of course we can. Won't you tell me what's wrong?"

"There's nothing wrong," she snapped. The familiar tingle scraped the back of her neck, and she turned her head. Charles stood in the terrace doorway watching her with narrowed eyes. Animosity numbed her and she turned her head sharply away. She loved a man who had used her and left her to pick up the pieces of her soiled reputation and broken heart.

Chapter 8

"What the hell are you doing out here?" Charles bit out in a fierce tone.

"I didn't know you'd arranged to meet Miss Sheffield here. I'm sorry."

Charles pressed his palms on the patio wall's stone surface and stared out into the darkness. The granular feel of the stone was as abrasive as the emotions scourging his heart. What was he going to do? He'd lost her. Lost her and any semblance of honor he'd ever had. He was exactly what she'd called him. A rogue in disguise.

For the first time in his life, he didn't know how to fix a problem. He'd always taken care of Robert's affairs with great success. It was the first time he'd ever looked defeat in the face. The bitter taste in his mouth was not to his liking. Gripping the stone wall, the rough surface bit into his skin. But it didn't begin to assuage the pain in his heart.

"Go after her, Charles." His brother's quiet words broke through his painful musings.

"No." He released his tight grip on the rough wall and straightened. Shaking his head, he swallowed the self-disgust pressing upward in his throat. "You heard her. I used her for my own selfish reasons before I discarded her. And God help me, she's right. I lied to her."

Robert grasped his arm and shook him. "Christ! Are you really that stupid? Fight for her. If you love her, you'll fight for her. Grovel, beg, plead. Do whatever it takes to win her back. Don't let your life become a meaningless existence because you made the mistake of not fighting for the woman you love."

"Who the hell are you giving me advice on how to win her back?" he said in a savagely bitter voice as he jerked his arm free of Robert's grasp. "As I recall, I tried to convince you to go after Christina all those years ago, but you didn't. Why shouldn't I follow my brother's example? I've already taken the first few steps by having my way with an innocent."

Robert's features paled as an expressionless mask settled over his face. "Say what you will about me, Charles, but know this. I made a grave error by not going after Christina. I've found that life without her is far from pleasant. It's downright hell. So choose, little brother, but remember that you've no one to blame but yourself if you don't fight for her."

Spinning on his heel, Robert left him alone on the patio. Although the sounds of the ball drifted out onto the terrace, he experienced a sensation of silence. The weight of it crushed him. It was the silence of his soul condemning him.

He walked to the terrace doors and searched the room. Ophelia was nowhere to be seen. Why would he expect her to still be here? A grimace tugged at his lips. The tight cord around his chest had not eased, and he growled beneath his breath. He needed to get out of here, do something to shake off this weighty burden of anger and pain.

With a quick stride, he left the ballroom. Collecting his hat and walking stick, he charged out into the warm night air. He had no destination in mind, he simply walked. Each step he took brought him no closer to a solution to his dilemma. Robert was right. He needed to fight for Ophelia, but how?

In the street, a carriage rolled by, its wheels clattering against the cobblestone. Ahead of him, he saw a drunken young man arguing with a constable. A moment later, the policeman grabbed the inebriated gentleman and hauled him off to a waiting wagon. Watching the small scene, he shook his head. He ought to be the one stone drunk. At least he might possibly find relief from the pain he was dealing with now. Continuing on his way, he strode past the minor drama playing out as the drunk tried to argue with the bobby.

How could he get Ophelia alone so he could try to explain his actions? Getting her to listen would be hard enough, but he needed to find a quiet place for them to talk. He grimaced. It was doubtful they'd talk. She was furious with him, and if she didn't try to fight with him like the drunk had with the--

The idea hit him with the force of a boxer's blow. Wheeling about, he watched the policeman lock the drunk into the jail wagon. What if he found a way to ensure that Ophelia listened to him? The idea continued to evolve in his head. He would need help though. Patience Sheffield had helped him once before. Would she be willing to do so again? A tiny flame of hope warmed his heart as he turned and headed home. Tomorrow he would put his plan into action.

* * * *

"God damn it!" Charles slammed his fist against the top of the desk. "Where the hell is she?" The morning after Ophelia had learned the truth about him, he'd planned to kidnap her and keep her with him until she listened to his explanations. But his plans shattered the moment he discovered the Sheffields had left town. For the past week, he'd scoured the town looking for Ophelia and her family. He'd even sent a man to Sheffield Park to discover if they'd gone home.

"I'm sorry Mr. Lynton, but we're doing everything we can to find the young lady."

"Well, you're not doing enough, Robson," he snapped.

"Perhaps you're going about this the wrong way, Charles." His brother's calm voice broke through the tension hanging in the air.

"What the devil is that suppose to mean?" Charles swung about to face the man who could have been his twin. "If you've got a better idea, then tell me. At least it would be more than what Robson has offered."

"Use logic, Charles. You've searched the town to see if they've acquired new lodgings. You've had someone visit Sheffield Park, they're not there. So that means they've had help from someone. Relatives? Friends? Have you checked that?"

The invisible rope of frustration tying his hands made him clench his jaw. He'd had the private investigator search for relatives, but he'd not considered friends as a possibility. "Robson?" He growled the man's name like a hungry tiger.

"Well, Mr. Lynton, I did check on relatives, but Sir Sheffield has no living relatives and his wife was an only child. As for friends, well I...."

As the man's voice trailed off Charles restrained the urge to pummel the man. "Get out of here."

The private investigator needed no further instructions as he raced from the room. Charles began to prowl the office with a savage stride. From behind the desk, Robert sighed. "Will you stop that pacing, Charles. You're acting like one of those lions I've seen in the zoological collection over at Regents Park."

"The man's an imbecile. What am I paying him for if he can't provide me the information I need?"

"There has to be something you're overlooking. Some friend she has. They can't have just fallen off the face of the earth."

Despair tightened its grip around his chest. "Do you think I don't know that? Even Nickens denied knowing where they were."

"Hmm ... are you sure he was telling the truth?"

"Of course he was. The poor bastard turned green when I threatened to grind him to a pulp if he didn't tell me the truth."

"Nickens?" Robert said with a heavy note of surprise in his voice. "Nickens is rarely rattled by anything. The only time I've ever seen him disturbed was when he lied to Lord Malventhorpe to protect a young pickpocket. Saved the lad by saying the boy had found Malventhorpe's wallet on the ground. Damnedest thing I've ever seen. Malventhorpe knew he was lying by the man's cold sweat, but Nickens stuck to his guns and didn't give the pickpocket up. One has to admire any man who stands up to Malventhorpe, the bastard."

Charles grew still. "Are you telling me that Nickens might be lying? That he might actually know where Ophelia and her family has gone?"

"It's possible, but if I were in your position, I'd have someone watch him. See if he goes anywhere, if he sends messages out by post, things like that."

"I don't have time for that. I'll go see Nickens again, and this time he's going to tell me everything he knows."

Charging into the foyer, he viciously swiped up his hat and walking stick before he exited the house. If Nickens had been lying to him, he'd throttle the man. His pace furious, he'd covered a great deal of ground before a heavy hand fell on his shoulder. Robert forced him to stop. "You're in no mood to talk to Nickens. If he knows anything, threats aren't going to help you. This calls for diplomacy, and that's something you don't possess at the moment. I'll talk to him."

Despite the need to get his information quickly, he had to admit his brother was right. In fact, for the past week, Robert had been the voice of reason. With a sharp nod, he slowed the pace of his walk. With his brother's help, he'd find Ophelia, and then he'd convince her of his love and his need to spend the rest of his life with her.

* * * *

Ophelia stooped to pick another bunch of gooseberries off the prickly bush. Placing them in the basket she carried, she stood upright and with her hand on her back, flexed her muscles. For a moment, she surveyed the lush landscape stretched out before her.

With Patience now engaged to Nickens, he had expressed his wish to welcome all three of them into his household. She had been equally grateful when the young man had suggested his aunt would welcome them for a visit at Epping Manor.

Their father had protested, but Nickens had once again come to the rescue. He'd scathingly reminded her father that if he didn't do as requested he would not be welcome to live with Patience and him after their wedding. The honorable behavior had impressed Ophelia, revealing the depth of his feelings for her sister. It had endeared him to her.

Now, as she stood atop one of the small knolls surrounding Epping Manor, she stared out at the beautiful scenery with sadness. Recognizing it was lovely did not erase the empty, dark hole in her heart.

She closed her eyes and shuddered. Would the pain ever ease? It had not even been two weeks since she'd discovered Charles' betrayal. The heat from the day made her skin tingle at the back of her neck. She lifted her hand to rub her skin. The frisson didn't disappear, but grew stronger.

Whirling around, her gaze met a familiar pair of jade eyes dark with a mixture of pain and something else she couldn't define. The sight of his drawn features squeezed her heart viciously. Remembering his treachery, she closed off the feelings of desire and love threatening to overwhelm her. She faced him quietly, refusing to say anything, although what she really wanted was to shout her anger at him.

"Good afternoon, Ophelia."

When she merely arched an eyebrow at him, his firm mouth tightened into a grim smile. The memory of how wonderful those lips felt against her skin sent a shiver skipping down her spine. She watched him clasp his hands behind his back and stare out over the landscape.

He'd lost weight, and there was a haggard look to his features. *Enough, I will not allow myself to feel anything for him. To do so only created great pain.* Whatever the reason for his rumpled appearance it was of little concern to her. A small voice whispered, 'Liar.' She ignored it, waiting for him to speak.

"I'd like to talk to you, but not here. I need to explain."

Gripping the handle of her basket with both hands, she flinched as she heard the wood snap beneath her savage grasp. "We have nothing to say to each other, sir."

Without waiting for his reply, she swept around him to head back toward the house.

"For God's sake, Ophelia. Look at me," he said hoarsely. "Give me a chance to explain, please, I'm begging you."

The raw agony in his voice struck a chord with her. She stopped and turned around. The sight of him on his knees drew a fiery hand across her heart. Her hand flew to her throat as it closed up. The basket she carried fell to the ground and the green carpet beneath her feet was strewn with gooseberries. Frozen by the poignant expression of despair on his face, she could only stare at him, her voice gone.

A flicker of hope brightened the glaze of pain in his eyes when she didn't move. Slowly, he rose to his feet. "What I did was wrong. I thought you were after Robert's title, and I've always protected him from women who might try to trap him into marriage. Then when I discovered you weren't after his title, I'd already gone past the point of no return."

He stepped forward and gently took her hand. "By the time I realized you deserved the truth, it was too late. I knew you would hate me. I couldn't face that."

The warmth of his hand on hers frightened her. It reminded her too much of how he could manipulate her to the point of distraction. His touch had always made her quiver, and it did so now. Frantic, she jerked away from him.

"I understand you wanted to explain yourself, sir. However, it was unnecessary."

"It was necessary."

"And what do you hope to gain from this confession? My forgiveness?"

"No. Your love."

His response punched its way through her stomach. How could he possibly know she was in love with him? Panic-stricken, she struggled to keep her composure. She could not let him see the truth.

"My ... You astound me, sir! What on earth makes you think I feel anything for you other than contempt and loathing?" She whirled around to stalk off, but his hand prevented her from leaving.

"Damn it, Ophelia. I love you. And I think you love me too. I've existed in hell for more than a week, and I can't bear to be without you another day."

Joy fluttered its way across her skin in a feather-light caress, but it was crushed beneath his expectation they would continue as they had before. No doubt, he would provide her with a small house of her own. She'd be at his disposal anytime he had need of her. But, she refused to be his mistress. It would be heaven until the day arrived when he'd leave her to face a hell far darker than the one she existed in now. He was a rogue, and to expect him to change was asking too much.

Her willpower wavering, she trembled as he grasped her hand again. "I ... I cannot ... you ask too much of me."

"Can you stand here and tell me you don't love me?"

"I ... I will not allow you to confuse me."

"I love you, Ophelia, and I know you love me. Say you love me. Tell me you'll marry me."

His words washed over her with the strength of a terrible wind and she didn't protest when he pulled her against him. With a quick move, he lowered his head and kissed her. The taste of him was tangy and filled with spice. Lethargic warmth filtered into her bones and she did not resist. The scent of leather filled her nostrils, and she shuddered.

Her mind reeled against the assault on her senses. She had misunderstood. He could not have proposed. He was mistaken. No, it was another trick. She didn't believe him. He'd lied. He was the worst kind of scoundrel, and he would lie again to get what he wanted. Horrified, she jerked free of his hold and retreated. He followed and she braced her palm against his chest.

"Do not come near me."

"For God's sake, Ophelia. If you don't love me, I can live with that, as long as you marry me. Love will come in time."

"Stop," she cried angrily. "How can you ask me to love you? You destroyed me and now you want me to forgive you? Love you?"

"Yes ... no. I don't expect you to do so right away." His hands closed over the one she pressed against his chest. "I just want you to think about it. I love you. I want you for my wife. All I ask is that you consider my offer."

"Please let me go, I don't ... I must ... go."

Despondency swept over his features, and she winced at the need to soothe his pain. She took a quick step away, then turned to flee. His voice held her back.

"I'm staying at the Rose and Crown. I'll stay until day after tomorrow. If you don't come to me, I'll leave you in peace and never bother you again. Come back to me, Ophelia. Let me love you as only I can love you."

A breathless sob parted her lips as she fled. Stumbling over the uneven ground, she raced back to the house. Once inside she ran up to her bedroom, locking herself inside. She sank down on the bed's mattress and buried her face in her hands. He'd declared his love and proposed marriage.

But could she trust him again? Trust him with her heart. And did she love him enough to forgive his deceit? She pondered the questions for a long time. After more than an hour, she still had no answer.

A soft knock sounded on the door and she rose to turn the bolt. Opening the door, she stared into her sister's concerned eyes.

"Are you all right?"

"Of course, just a bit tired."

"Where are the gooseberries?"

"Gooseberries?" She raised a hand to her cheek. "Oh, I stumbled and the basket just flew out of my hands and the berries went everywhere. I was too tired and hot to hunt for more."

"Are you certain you're all right? I don't want you to miss the social at the Merricks this evening."

"Is that tonight? I'd forgotten."

"How could you forget? When I saw Miss Merrick and her brother in the village, Mr. Merrick specifically inquired whether you would be coming this evening. It seems he is quite taken with you."

Ophelia cringed at the thought. She had no wish to encourage any man. When she didn't answer, Patience leaned forward and kissed her cheek. "I'll leave you to rest now."

As she closed the door behind her sister, Ophelia hugged herself about the waist. She had no idea what to do about Charles. The thought that he was so close and yet so far out of reach rent her heart in two.

* * * *

The Merrick house was large and comfortable, and as they entered the main salon, Ophelia was surprised by the number of guests. Mr. Merrick had immediately taken it upon himself to introduce her, and he stayed close by her side as they continued around the room.

A small group stood near the fireplace, and as they opened their circle, she inhaled sharply. Charles stood in the midst of the group, a small smile on his face, which didn't reach his eyes.

"Lynton, I'd like to introduce you to Miss Sheffield," Merrick said with a broad grin. "She's new to the area, but I hope to convince her to stay indefinitely."

The openly displayed interest startled Ophelia, and she could only smile at the man, her ability to speak gone. She darted a quick peek in Charles' direction. The expression on his face was dark, his fierce anger just beneath the surface. Before she realized what she was doing, she tapped Merrick's arm playfully with her fan.

"You're far too kind, Mr. Merrick. As to Mr. Lynton, we are old acquaintances. I wasn't aware that you knew each other."

Merrick laughed. "I went to school with his brother. I just happened to see him in the village this morning and insisted that he join us this evening. Isn't that right, Lynton?"

"A most fortunate encounter," Charles said with a hint of sarcasm. He offered her a slight bow. "Miss Sheffield. I trust you still maintain your daily habit of walking?"

"Indeed," she said with a bright smile. "Although today, I did not enjoy myself as usual. Perhaps I need you to accompany me in the future, Mr. Merrick."

She turned to smile brilliantly at the man next to her. Out of the corner of her eye, she saw the look of agony slashing across Charles' face. A sliver of satisfaction edged through her. It would do him good to experience a small taste of the pain she'd experienced at his hand. It wasn't her nature to taunt and tease, but he'd made her heart bleed with an agony that blinded her to any anguish he might be experiencing now. Despite the thought, her heart wrenched at the torment haunting his gaze.

Merrick beamed at her statement, and nodded. "Walking with you would give me immense pleasure, Miss Sheffield."

Clearing his throat, Charles bowed again. "If you'll excuse me, my throat is dry and I require refreshments. Could I bring you something, Miss Sheffield?"

"Oh that's not necessary, I'm sure Mr. Merrick will be kind enough to bring me a glass of punch."

"But of course, Miss Sheffield. I shall return momentarily," Merrick exclaimed. "Shall I bring you something as well, Lynton?" When Charles gave him a brusque nod, the man moved away with an eager step.

The remainder of the original group surrounding them had moved off to another portion of the room, leaving Ophelia alone with Charles. He glared at her. "If you are deliberately trying to make me jealous, it's working."

She bit her lip. Was she trying to make him jealous or was she simply trying to make him hurt as he had hurt her? The motives were too closely linked to give her a clear answer.

"I think your jealousy is like the reaction of a spoiled child who's upset at being denied a plaything."

"Damn it," he muttered. "Do you have any idea what it does to me when I see you flirting with Merrick?"

"I am not flirting."

"You forget who taught you how to seduce a man, Ophelia."

The flagrant reference to their lovemaking made her cheeks blaze with heated color. Wishing to be done with him, she turned her head, looking for Merrick. Where was the man? Didn't he know she was in need of rescue? Rescue from the clutches of the man she loved. The thought tightened her chest and her breathing increased significantly.

"If you'll excuse me, I think I'll go see what's become of Mr. Merrick and my punch."

"You do that, and while you're in his company, think on this. You're mine, Ophelia. You have been and always will be."

Her limbs were lead weights as she moved away from him. The realization that he was right sank into her heart. Her love for him was stronger now than it had ever been. If she were to believe him, she would have to forgive and trust him. She didn't know if she had the ability to do so.

Throughout the evening, she found her eyes drawn to Charles and the angry despair in his face. Each time her eyes met his, she could see his suffering, but as the evening progressed, anger mixed with the pain. It was an undeniable emotion of the darkest nature. She had wanted him to hurt as she did, but the path she had set out on this evening seemed destined to destroy the man she loved.

Merrick's attention to her only seemed to make Charles retreat deeper into the shell of the man she knew. The spirited life she'd always seen in him was dying a slow, painful death. Aware that she had encouraged Merrick, she could no longer deny her behavior as petty and childish. Tomorrow she would go to the inn and ask Charles' forgiveness.

Engrossed in a conversation with Mr. Merrick and his sister, she stiffened as the now familiar frisson scraped across her neck. She lifted her head and stared into her lover's stony expression. Beside her Merrick spoke.

"Surely you're not leaving us so soon, Lynton."

"I'm afraid I must. I'm returning to London at first light."

His words struck her with the force of a slap. He was leaving tomorrow. But he'd told her he would not leave for another day. Panic rose in her throat and her hands trembled. With a slight bow, he said his good-byes to the Merricks then turned toward her. Her throat closed and she struggled to speak. She stretched out her hand, but he did not take it. Instead, he sent her an abrupt nod. "Miss Sheffield. I hope the country air continues to agree with you."

The bitter glare he directed toward her made her drop her hand back into her lap. The force of his anger and pain engulfed her, and she realized she had pushed him too far. He wheeled about and strode from the room, taking her heart with him. Merrick uttered a soft exclamation of surprise, but Ophelia ignored him. She had to go after Charles. No matter what the cost to her pride, she knew she could no longer live without him.

Chapter 9

Ophelia waited impatiently at the front door of the Merrick's house as her sister said her good-byes. From the moment Charles had left, she'd been frantic to follow him. When they finally moved into the night air, Ophelia hurried down the steps to the waiting carriage. Nickens was talking with the driver as Patience joined her in the vehicle. She clasped the younger girl's hand in a tight grip.

"We must go to the village inn at once."

"What on earth for? Why would you need to go at this time of ... Oh, you mustn't Ophelia. If you go back to him now, you'll only be hurt that much more."

"I don't care. I love him," she whispered.

Nickens climbed into the carriage, closing the door behind him, before sinking into the seat next to Patience. He took her hand and raised it to his lips.

"Well, my love, did you enjoy yourself this evening?"

Ophelia watched her sister send the man a distracted smile. Then he turned his gaze on her.

"And you, Ophelia, did you enjoy yourself?" Unable to lie, she could only stare at him. He nodded his head. "I didn't think so. I would imagine Lynton's presence was a bit uncomfortable for you. I suppose I erred in telling him where to find you."

"You told him where Ophelia was?" Horror filled Patience's voice. "Oh, Anthony, how could you?"

"Because the man was demented with grief, my love. He swore to me his intentions were honorable, and I believed him."

"I know that now," Ophelia whispered. "And if I don't go to him now, he'll leave tomorrow morning, and I'll never see him again. I won't let that happen."

"But it's improper, the entire village will--"

"I don't care what anyone thinks. I only know I won't lose him."

With a nod, Nickens tapped the roof of the vehicle. "Take us to the Rose and Crown, Jack."

Ophelia swallowed the apprehension rising in her and leaned forward to squeeze her future brother-in-law's hand with gratitude.

* * * *

The Rose and Crown's stable yard was bustling despite the late hour. As the carriage rolled to a stop, Ophelia sprang toward the door. She was halfway out of the vehicle, when Patience's hand delayed her. "We'll wait for you."

She shook her head. "No, if the worst happens, I shall find another way home."

Standing on the ground, she shivered despite the warm night air. Would the worst happen? She prayed fervently that he would not reject her. The door to the inn swung open under a slight push from her hand. Inside she looked around for the proprietor. She did not have long to wait as an older man approached her, wiping his hands on a dirty towel.

"Might I be of service, miss?"

"Show me to Mr. Lynton's rooms, please." She flinched at the smirk that slid over the man's coarse features.

"And is Mr. Lynton expecting you, miss?"

"Whether he's expecting me is none of your concern. Now I suggest you show me to his rooms, or my husband is likely to thrash you for your impertinence."

The man paled at her words, his attitude suddenly obsequious. "Of course, Mrs. Lynton, my humblest apologies. If you'll follow me."

His stride quick and furtive, the innkeeper led her up to the second floor. Stopping about midway down the hall, he was about to knock, when she delayed his hand. "That will be all. My husband is not expecting me, and I wish to surprise him. You may leave."

The man nodded and with a quick bow disappeared down the stairs. Tremors shook through her body, and she pressed her fingertips to her forehead. Gathering her courage, she knocked on the door. Charles' commanding voice ordered her to enter.

She entered the room, and quietly closed the door behind her. His back to her, Charles was packing a leather saddlebag. The white shirt he wore pulled tight across his shoulder muscles, outlining the hard sinews beneath the material.

"Well, what is it now?" he growled. "And if you tell me my bath water won't be ready for another hour, I'll string you up by your ballocks."

"Since I am not the innkeeper that would be rather difficult to do." She tried to keep her voice light as he whirled around to face her.

"What the hell are you doing here?"

For a moment, she could only stare at him. His shirt was splayed open to the waist, and she trembled at the thought of touching his beautiful chest, kissing him until she heard him cry out with need for her. His eyes narrowed and he folded his arms.

"I asked you a question, Ophelia. Why are you here?"

"I ... I ... you told me earlier today that you loved me."

He shrugged, his mouth tightening into a relentless line of anger. "I said a lot of things today, which would have been best left unspoken."

"Then you were merely toying with me again," she whispered as despair cut a vicious wound in her heart."

Turning away from her, he went to stand at the room's sole window. His hands braced against the portal's frame, he bowed his head. "No, I was not toying with you. I meant every word I said, but it's obvious to me that you do not return my feelings."

With a soft cry, she flew forward. Wrapping her arms about his waist, she sobbed, "No. I do love you, and if you leave me behind, I'll die because life is not worth living without you."

Beneath her hands, she could feel his muscles grow rock hard as tension flooded his body. He did not move, and she quivered with fear. "Charles, please. I love you."

She rested her check against his back, her arms tight around him. With a suddenness that surprised her, he unclasped her hands and whirled to face her. He cradled her face in his hands as his jade eyes raked over her face.

"God help you if this is some trick to humiliate me further, Ophelia. I reached my limit earlier this evening watching Merrick fawn all over you."

"I know, I was wrong in trying to make you jealous. I only wanted to make you feel the pain, I'd experienced. It was childish."

"Be certain of this, my love, if you stay, I'll never let you go again."

Her hands pulled his face down to hers, and she brushed her lips across his mouth. "I love you, Charles. I only want to be with you."

A deep groan rushed from his throat, and he crushed her to him. His kiss heated her with a consuming fire. Her hands slid inside his shirt and traced across his skin lightly. The muscles under his supple skin jumped beneath the touch of her fingertips. The familiar spice scent of him tantalized her nostrils, while he singed her mouth with his kiss. A shudder ran through him, and his fingers undid the back of her dress with haste as their kiss deepened. She felt his tongue against hers, and she whimpered at the delight tickling her skin.

Desperate to have nothing between them, her hands pushed her gown off her hips. She nipped at his bottom lip as he drew back. Passion darkened his face as he turned her around, his hands racing to undo her corset. A prisoner of her own desire, she struggled out her clothes as quickly as she could. Her stockings slid off her legs and as her drawers pooled at her feet, she felt his warm hands slide over her buttocks to grasp her hips. He pulled her back against him, his arousal pressing into her through the material of his trousers.

An urgent need surged through her veins, and she twisted in his arms to face him. Raw desire tightened his jaw, as he stared down at her. Without taking his gaze from her face, he removed his shirt, followed by his trousers. A burning need to melt into him tugged at her as she ran her fingertips over his upper lip.

Strong hands gripped her waist, and he pulled her against him. She gasped with pleasure at the hard length of him pressing into her tight curls. His head bent to her breasts, she moaned at the feel of his tongue grazing across first one nipple and then the other. Her hand reached between their bodies to stroke his phallus.

She felt him shudder against her. With a sharp move, he lifted her in his arms and turned so her back pressed into the rough wood of the wall next to the window. Grasping her thighs, he forced her to wrap her legs around his waist. His fingers bit into her skin as he thrust himself up into her.

The hot surge of him into her tugged a cry from her lips, and he captured her mouth with his, stifling the sound. She clung to him as he tasted the softness of her neck. The feel of her beneath his hands made his cock throb inside her. Slowly he ground his hips against hers. The low moan of delight parting her lips and the look of pleasure on her face tightened his chest with the need to plunge into her over and over again. He watched as the tip of her tongue darted out to wet her lips. The seductive move drove him over the edge.

With a sharp inhalation, he pulled away from her slightly, and then plunged back into her. This time, she pushed against him, and he inhaled the sweet fragrance of her desire. She was slick with need, and yet she encircled his cock with a tight grip. He'd never felt so wild and out of control in his entire life. Her velvety folds trembled and clutched at him in a wild spasm, and he rocked back and force at a fierce pace. Another cry broke from her lips, and he growled at the way her wet folds squeezed against his cock, rubbing it, pulling on it until he felt the familiar surge of the muscle, and he spilled his seed with a loud cry of satisfaction.

For several long moments, they remained where they were, their ragged breaths mixing together. Slowly the residual effects of their lovemaking eased, and Charles gently lowered Ophelia to her feet. Her arms linked around his neck, she smiled up at him.

"That was an unusual lesson in the art of pleasure, Mr. Lynton."

"Do you object?" he smiled as he nuzzled her shoulder with his mouth.

"Not at all, but I must confess that my derriere is protesting somewhat."

"Turn around then and I shall tenderly kiss the pain away." The gasp of appalled surprise parting her lips made him laugh. "There is still more for you to learn, my love, but we have other matters to settle before we continue our lessons in pleasure. I refuse to let Merrick, or any other man, come near you, so we'll marry at the earliest moment possible."

"You are certain that's what you want?" The note of hesitancy in her voice made him tighten his arms around her.

"I'm certain. I love you Ophelia, and I'll never let you go."

"I love you too."

"Then come to bed, so I can take my time loving you." He brushed his fingertips over her breasts and smiled as she sucked in a quick breath. Already he could see the desire building in her once again. The thought of pleasing her elated him. Her hand in his, he drew her to the bed. He sat down and she nestled her soft bottom in his lap. The lush feel of her stirred his cock sooner than he'd expected.

She wrapped her arm around his neck and buried her face in his neck. "I never thought loving a rogue in disguise would bring such happiness."

"But the rogue is unmasked, my love, and his heart is in your hands from this moment forward." With a swift movement, he spun her around so she lay on the bed beneath him. "So shall we advance to the final lesson of pleasure?"

"And what lesson is that?" She laughed quietly.

"The lesson of two hearts exchanging their love for all time, my sweet."

He nibbled at her bottom lip, delighting in her low moan. She was his. Now and forever. Their lives stretched before them, and he knew he would never tire of showing her the ultimate lesson of pleasure for the rest of his life.

The End

TUTORING LADY JANE

By

Charlotte Featherstone

DEDICATION:

Many thanks go out to my critique partners, Monica Burns and Kristina Cook for their unfailing support and enthusiasm. Where would I be without you?

To my husband and daughter, who support my writing and share my goal of being a published author, despite the take out dinners and the messy house, thank you, and I love you.

And lastly, to every woman out there who has ever thought she didn't have what it takes…. I dedicate this book to you.

Chapter One

London, 1780

The cracking of a log in the hearth sounded over the crinkling rustle of French silk. In the distance, the muffled rhythm of the minuet could be heard beyond the paneled door of Lord Lennox's study. Senses attuned to any sound that might lead to someone discovering him and ultimately an inconvenient dawn appointment, Gavin Reynolds, Viscount Grayson, spread his arms wide on the back of the brocade settee, watching as his latest conquest--Lady Lennox--worked to unfasten the jade buttons of his waistcoat.

Surely the languid warmth of the fire and the view of Lady Lennox's breasts, which he'd recently freed from her bodice, were the reasons his senses were slow to process the fact that they had a visitor, and a decidedly female one at that.

From his peripheral vision he saw the door inch open, revealing a sliver of a heavily embroidered eschelle corset, above which sat the creamiest bosom he'd ever seen--and he'd seen plenty.

"Oooh," his conquest purred as she parted the lace ruffle of his shirt. "I've wondered what your dark skin looks like. Sarah was right; it does resemble coffee with cream."

He stiffened, unable to stem or hide the impulse. For some damnable reason his eyes automatically searched the opening in the door, checking to see if the female ensconced behind it had heard Helena's words. He didn't give a bloody farthing what Lady Lennox thought of him, he knew what all the women of the *ton* called him. But for some elusive reason, he did not want the voyeur behind the door to hear the comment and thinly veiled reminder that he was nothing but a filthy half-breed.

He knew who watched him, knew and sensed as he always did whenever she strolled into a ballroom or happened to glance his way. His body always reacted to Lady Jane Westbury in such a curious way.

The woman was not the type he normally cavorted with. It was said that she was rather plump and unremarkable. Plain, he'd heard countless men describe her. Yet he, a self-confessed connoisseur of female flesh found her utterly intriguing. He supposed she was plain when compared to some of the beauties of the *ton*. But there was something about her that captured his attention in a far deeper and more meaningful way than the buxom lovelies he spent his evenings with.

Lady Jane was buxom, of that he was certain. But it wasn't only the sight of full breasts and lushly rounded hips that drew his eye. No, it was a quality he had never experienced in his legions of paramours. Lady Jane was a true lady. A paragon of womanly virtue. A woman of taste, refinement and kindness.

That she should be here now, watching as Helena Lennox tore open the flap of his silk breeches while he reclined on her husband's settee, was impossible. Impossible and highly arousing. His reputation as the whoring India Rat would be firmly implanted in Jane's mind. He didn't know quite what to make of that.

"My lord," Helena, cooed, her lips a scant inch from his cock. "My work seems to be cut out for me this evening."

Gavin glanced down to see his limp member in Helena's beringed hand. She looked up at him imploringly through painted eyes. Her face was powdered white with the exception of two rouged circles on her cheeks. At the corner of her right eye sat a black beauty patch in the shape of a crescent moon. She was the height of fashion. Every man in London thought her beautiful, and yet he couldn't get up the desire--literally--to take her.

He blinked, trying to clear the vision of Helena's head with its gray curling wig covered in pearls and a ridiculously large blue plume lowering to his lap. A fleeting vision of a fresh, country faced countess flashed before him and he groaned. His mind supplied the visual of firm, large breasts and plump thighs, not to mention his dark hands covering every inch of her milk-white skin. Even now he could imagine the feel of her body, could conceive of the way his fingers would trace the curves of her figure. She would be ripe and full beneath that rose-colored gown and he knew, as sure as he knew his name that she would be possessed of a derriere he could cup and knead while she lay atop him.

"Ah," Helena murmured between flicks of her tongue. "This is what you're in need of."

"Perhaps." His answer was vague and noncommittal as he

rested his head back against the settee, letting his body go limp as he tried to push the sound of his uninvited guest's hushed intake of air out of his mind. He'd shocked her, no doubt. She shouldn't be here. She shouldn't be witnessing the extent of his wickedness. And she should damn well not be privy to him allowing a married woman such as Helena to take his cock greedily into her mouth.

"My lord," Sarah Manchester said huskily as she strolled from where her gown and petticoats lay in a heap on the floor. "Are you ready to play?"

That damnable sound of hushed shock again resonated through his brain. He instantly regretted agreeing to meet with the two friends who apparently enjoyed sharing everything. Thankfully his body was now working on instinct alone and would not disgrace him.

It had never been a trial for him to perform the sex act while thinking a myriad of thoughts--hell, as he'd been tupping Sarah last night he'd pondered what his cook would be making him for breakfast.

But he couldn't seem to get these thoughts--thoughts of Lady Jane out of his mind. He imagined her working his cock with her pink mouth, visualized her naked on her knees before him looking up from a cloud of honey brown hair. On a whim he conjured up the feel of her breasts, full and heavy, the nipples erect and searching as his lips fastened onto them, suckling her, making her moan and pant beneath him.

"Mmmm," Sarah purred, standing behind the settee and lowering her breasts to his mouth. He leaned his head further back to take one erect nipple between his teeth, pretending the husky desire he heard belonged to Lady Jane, not Sarah, the man-eating Duchess of Manchester.

Already tired of Sarah, he pulled away, fixing his gaze on the door. *She* was still there, watching, her bosom rising and falling rapidly above her tight corset. He could smell her, the scent of sweet country flowers. And he could still see her as she glided into the ballroom not more than two hours ago and smiled at him. It had not been a smile of invitation for an illicit rut in a study, nor a mocking grin because she had heard the gossip that his mother had been nothing more than a Bombay whore, but a smile of genuine kindness and warmth. A smile that had unexpectedly and confusingly, invaded his dreams.

She was a lady, true as well as bred. *He* was the son of a scandalous liaison and marriage between a half Indian, half English concubine and her lover. A lover who had, unexpectedly, inherited a viscountcy.

His parents' torrid love affair, and the fact that his proper English father had not only married, but procreated with a courtesan who was at one time in the keeping of a Sultan, was the bane of Gavin's existence. He'd lived his whole life fighting the stigma of his mother's heritage and her illegitimacy, while enduring the cruel taunts of the children at school. The sly comments had not ceased at Eton, but continued on in the form of the callous remarks of men and women who were no more moral or pious than himself.

But *she* had never looked at him in such a way. He had always fancied that the intelligent and somewhat plain Lady Jane had seen more to him than his legendary sexual propensity and colorful breeding.

"Grayson," Sarah scolded, brushing her nipples against his lips, coaxing him to suckle her. "Your reputation is tarnishing by the second. I enjoyed this much better last night. You were much more exuberant."

Damn her, he thought, suddenly feeling sick. He meant nothing to them; he was just a prick to play with. He would only ever be the half-breed with a large cock, hard body, and strange, dark skin that every woman of breeding fancied a go with. In the light of day he would forever be the dirty half-breed whose only claim to fame was that he'd fucked half of the ladies in the adjacent ballroom.

Clearing his throat, he sat forward, removing Helena's hand from his rigid length, a rigidity caused not by Helena, but by the woman who was hidden behind the door. "I grow bored, ladies. Excuse me."

Ignoring Sarah and Helena's shocked expressions and pleas that he stay, he refastened his breeches and shirt before knotting his cravat. Without a glance, he donned his waistcoat, buttoned the jade closures that everyone said so resembled his eyes and shrugged into his frock coat. With a curt bow he turned and stalked to the door, grinning as the sliver of bodice instantly disappeared. It had been one of his best conquests--to have the very proper Lady Jane Westbury's full attention. Now it was just a matter of finding the enigmatic countess amongst the guests and discovering just what made her seek him out, as he knew she had. He'd felt those chocolate brown eyes following him throughout the night. Perhaps, he thought, as he reached for the door latch, she wished to experience the delights of his bed. The very idea made him pleasurably aroused.

"Filthy Indian," Sarah cried, as he stepped into the shadowed hall. "You'll never be anything more than an oddity to take to bed."

"But not your bed," he quipped without looking back. No, the only bed he envisioned himself falling into in the foreseeable future was Jane Westbury's. A daunting, but thoroughly arousing thought.

* * * *

Jane picked up her skirts and raced through the darkened hall, her heels clicking against the wooden floor. She must have been absolutely depraved, not to mention desperate to follow the viscount. She'd known he was about to meet his latest paramour, but she had never, not in a hundred years guessed it would be Lady Lennox, not to mention the countess' good friend, the Duchess of Manchester. *Two women*, her mind screamed as she made her way to the ballroom of the Lennox country estate. His debauchery truly was everything she'd heard, and his mastery everything she'd dreamed of.

Damn her curiosity, she fumed as she stopped running and smoothed her skirt. She should never have accepted the invitation for a genteel country weekend at the Lennox estate, and she most certainly should never have entertained the notion of meeting with, much less propositioning the viscount.

With a flick of her hand, she opened her mother of pearl fan and forcefully beat the air before her. Damn her wastrel husband, too. For if Archie, the Earl of Westbury, had not abandoned her and their wedding vows for the far too young and lovely Arabella, she would not have found herself in such a predicament.

Nodding to a few acquaintances, Jane waded through the ballroom, heading to the terrace and the sanity of the cool night air. The ballroom was filled to overflowing and the evening was at its height. No one would notice if she stepped out for a brief minute. No one ever really noticed her. They hadn't before her marriage, and most certainly not since Archie had cast her aside, except, of course, to whisper behind their fans and cast looks of pity in her direction.

Stepping out into the darkness, she sighed, pondering her circumstances and her foolish plan to follow Lord Grayson. Had he seen her? No, she didn't think so. He'd been too involved in the beautiful women fawning over his body. A body, Jane had to admit, that she'd always admired.

Archie had been pale and thin, where Grayson was tall and broad and possessed of the most exotic skin she'd ever seen. He looked perpetually tanned, and when he grinned, flashing a set of brilliant white teeth, she felt weak-kneed. Her husband had been nothing like the viscount. Archie always shaved his hair, preferring wigs to his natural blond locks. But the viscount wore shoulder length black hair, tied in a queue with a simple black ribbon. And those eyes.... Jane fanned herself again. When he'd looked toward the door, those infamous green eyes pierced her. She'd sworn he could see her then and she had been unable to move. She'd been hypnotized, bewitched by turquoise eyes that she thought surely must resemble the waters of the Indian Ocean.

Foolish. She was being fanciful. Viscount Grayson would never look at her as she looked at him. She was plain and plump. So unremarkable, in fact, that she faded into the silk cloth that lined the walls of the Lennox's ballroom. She had always been, and forever would be the *ton's* wallflower.

She was glad she'd run away when she saw him stroll to the door. She had saved herself a cartload of the humiliation she would have experienced when she presented him with her outrageous idea. Surely he would have narrowed his gaze and grinned at her in mockery.

What would the handsome and notoriously experienced viscount say when the utterly proper and undesirable Lady Jane Westbury asked him to tutor her in the ways of pleasuring a man? Laugh, that's what he would do, then he would look upon her with sympathy. 'Poor, plain Lady Westbury,' he would mock, 'unable to find herself a man after being left by her husband.'

Damn Archie for succumbing to the wiles of a girl less than half his age. Archie had been forty, when he'd left her for the charms of Arabella. Arabella in turn had been only eighteen, and infinitely stupid. Although apparently not half as feeble-minded as herself--Arabella, had, after all, been able to attract and keep Archie's attentions. Something she had never been able to do.

How fitting that Archie should decide to cock up his toes in Arabella's bed. Archie had never exerted enough energy in their bed to even break a sweat, and Jane couldn't help but think that the blackheart had deserved everything he had gotten. Well, it meant nothing now--it did not matter a fig about Archie and Arabella. But Archie's death had left her in a bit of a fix.

She was now a thirty-year-old widowed countess without an admirer, a husband or children. It was all she had really ever wanted growing up--children of her own, a loving husband and a quiet but happy life in the country. What she'd gotten was a philandering spouse whose idea of loving was to come to her room at night, lift her night rail and plunge into her, spending himself in the hopes of siring an heir. Archie had been neither loving nor particularly caring.

He hadn't always been quite so cold, not in the first years of their marriage, but five years ago, all had changed. Archie had become moody and irritable, forever finding fault with a body that had, admittedly, changed in the years since she married him at the tender and impressionable age of seventeen.

She'd been but a girl when she'd wed him. A thin, straight figured girl with a flat stomach and narrow hips. It was only natural that she would one day turn into a woman, and a woman had curves. It was with the blossoming of her figure that she discovered Archie detested voluptuousness in women. Not only was it her body he found abhorrent, but it seemed he found her rather inconvenient as she could not even do her duty and conceive. 'And you're not even pretty,' he'd snapped as he stalked out of their bedchamber leaving her alone in the dark. 'Had it not been for your dowry you would've been utterly useless to me.'

Archie's taunts and sneers reverberated around her brain and she looked up, into the night sky, trying to erase the pain of her marriage. She no longer loved him, had not really loved him for the past five years. Still, she would not have left him as he had left her. She would not have shamed or humiliated him by dying in her lover's bed.

And that brought her up to her present circumstances. She had narrowly avoided humiliation once again. For degradation would have been her best friend had she the backbone to ask the infamous viscount to show her the way of getting a man's attention and keeping it too.

Fool, she muttered as she turned to walk back into the ballroom. She would leave for Kent tomorrow. She would return to the empty, lonely estate she had purchased with what little money Archie had bequeathed to her.

"Wait."

The voice was dark and sensual and Jane's skin came alive as the word caressed her neck.

"You've been spying on me."

Every nerve ending reared and tightened and she gasped, as she always did when she couldn't string two words together.

"I heard that very sound not more than five minutes ago and do you know what it did to me?" Hot breath caressed her neck, the ribbon securing her diamond choker tickled her skin. "It made me wonder why a *lady* such as yourself would be observing such a personal moment."

She licked her lips and willed her knees to stop trembling. Why, when she felt the first touch of his finger stroking her spine above her stomacher, did she have the impulse to confess all?

"Perhaps you were merely curious, hmmm? Wondering just what the India Rat does with all those women he has at his beck and call."

"N-no," she stammered, hating the name coming from his own lips. It didn't matter that the others called him that. He was not an India Rat. He was not, despite what the *ton* said. Feeling somewhat brave, she screwed up her courage, preparing to bare her deepest desires to a man who reputedly would do nothing but exploit them.

She was a woman of thirty. A woman who had experience of men and the marriage bed, although not nearly enough. Surely she could present her plan in such a way that the viscount would see fit to agree. Surely he would not humiliate her if he found her scheme laughable.

When the silence stretched on, she felt his muscled chest press into her back. "Perhaps you entertained the notion of joining us? Four makes for much more spirited play than three."

She gasped again. The idea was scandalous and the thought of sharing him with those two tarts, revolting. It had been a long time since she harbored secret fantasies of the viscount, and the very thought of sharing him was inconceivable. In her dreams, he had wanted no one other than herself.

"What is it you wish for? For I know you want. I am aware of it coursing through your veins. I can feel it on your skin; I can smell it." And as if to make his point, he leaned into her, his lips teasingly grazing her neck. "Most definitely I can smell it. Tell me, Lady Jane, is it desire I sense? Do you yearn to be seduced by the wicked India Rat, or is your penchant more voyeuristic? Do you want to watch me have sex with those women, then sneak out and rut with a more respectable gentleman, all the while thinking of me?"

"I want you to teach me to be the type of woman a man desires."

There, she'd said it. The only thing left to do was steel herself against the eerie silence and his ensuing mocking laughter.

But the laughter did not come. Instead, he placed his warm hands on her shoulders and turned her to face him. She was instantly met with his legendary eyes. They were not teasing and sensual, but dark and haunting in the dim candlelight that poured through the French doors.

"The tutoring of Lady Jane," he murmured his voice dark and dangerous. "I vow, I'm astonished."

"Well," she huffed, irked by his words and the reminder that she was unable to capture a man's attention. She didn't need any reminders that her body was not made to fascinate a man. "You needn't be disagreeable, sir."

"I have neither agreed nor disagreed."

"But you--"

"--was already preparing my lessons, I assure you."

She was speechless as she looked up into his handsome face. A face she had always been drawn to, and lips she had dreamed of kissing.

"I know what it is you want, and I assure you, you could not find yourself a better, or more knowledgeable teacher."

"Well, yes," she said, licking her lips once again, fear and uncertainty suddenly clouding her excitement. "However, I'm not at all certain that we will suit. Perhaps we should not proceed with this ... with this bargain."

"We will suit very well, never fear. I know what it is women want, but most of all, I know what it is *you* want, Jane. And believe me, I'm more than capable of instructing you."

"Capable, yes, but willing?"

He looked into her eyes and she swore he was seeing her deepest desires as well as her darkest fears.

"Willing? I'm more than willing to take you to bed and show you everything a man desires."

"And what do you wish for in return for your tutelage?" she asked. "I have some money and jewels."

His eyes darkened and his hands gripped her shoulders. The silence stretched on, and Jane fought the urge to squirm beneath his cold glare. "I don't give a damn about jewels and I have more money than I could waste in a lifetime. What else have you to offer, Jane?"

She felt her face fall. She could grant him nothing more than monetary rewards. She had neither her virginity nor a beautiful face or body to offer him--nothing else to tempt him. "I have nothing, my lord, that you would want."

"You're wrong, Jane. There is something I want. Your corruption--and all at my experienced, debauched hands. I shall tutor you, Lady Jane, in the pleasures of the flesh. And in the end, we will see who is the pupil and who the master."

Chapter Two

The rain streaked down the window in rushing rivulets as Gavin stared out into the black night. Howling wind sent the rain splattering against the glass once again, temporarily blinding him before a brilliant streak of lightning forked down from the heavens, illuminating the inky darkness.

Damn it to hell, what was he doing pining for Lady Jane? How long had it been since he'd taken up his post by the window, searching through the dark for a glimpse of a carriage lamp? *Too bloody long*.

She obviously was not going to meet him tonight or any other night, for that matter. Why the hell had he accepted her outrageous offer? He was setting himself up. He knew it. He should never have agreed to be her tutor in the sexual arts. And he damn well should not have invited her to Richmond. What the hell had he been thinking? That she was different? That she didn't think of him the way the rest of the *ton* did? When he'd penned his invitation to her, he'd had the foolish notion that perhaps this bargain of theirs might go beyond what either of them had planned. *Bloody fool*. It had no doubt been the lingering effects of too much claret and the empty-headed attentions of a notorious Cyprian that had sparked such a ludicrous thought.

"My lord?"

Gavin glanced over his shoulder, not bothering to lower his arm that rested against the window frame. "Yes, Prakash?"

"I have brought you your tea."

Nodding, Gavin returned his watchful gaze to the window and the black night beyond. He could see Prakash, his majordomo, in the reflection of the glass. He was a small man, short and narrow shouldered. His long black hair was concealed by a brown turban and he wore the muslin tunic and pants of India.

Prakash set the silver tray down upon the desk and straightened. "The rains are heavy tonight," he said in his Bengali-English accent. "It will not be easy to travel these roads. But your Dharma shall arrive nonetheless."

Gavin shifted from the window and strolled to the desk, helping himself to a steaming cup of tea laced with cinnamon and aniseed--a special brew common to India, and one of his favorites.

"And what do you know of my fate?" he muttered, sipping the spicy tea.

"You wait for a woman, yes?"

Gavin straightened and pierced the servant with a glare. "That is none of your concern. We might have grown up as friends, Prakash, but that does not mean you are entitled to know all of my business."

Prakash chuckled and his brown fingers, so much darker than Gavin's came up to scratch his beard. "Now I know it is important, this business that has you brooding and pacing. You only remind me of my place of servitude in your house when you are trying to play the arrogant viscount. This woman, she must be very important for you to be this unsure."

"I don't know what the devil you're talking about. Unsure of what?"

"Yourself."

"Don't be absurd," Gavin growled, replacing the gilt cup and saucer back on the tray. "I know perfectly well what I'm about."

"Do you?" Prakash asked. "You have been lost for a long time now."

"Because we've known each other since we were in swaddling clothes does not give you the right to talk to me in such a fashion. I pay your wages, if you will but recall--a very handsome stipend if the gowns on your wife are any indication."

Prakash laughed and bowed before him. "Indeed you do. Maya is kept in the finest silks and embroidered cloths. And you are a very a good employer, but a terrible friend."

Gavin raked his hand through his hair and fought the urge to shift his gaze to the window. "I should not have spoken to you so harshly. You've been my greatest friend and ally." My only true friend, he silently added.

"You are forgiven. I understand what drives you to speak such things. We are of like backgrounds, yet I am accepted much more readily than you. I am but a Bengali. Born of Indian parents and brought to England with my family to serve in your parents' home. I am respectable as long as I stay within my bounds of service. You, on the other hand, are neither English nor Indian. You are lost, *bondhu*, searching for the place in which you will fit."

Old wounds threatened to reopen. Not wanting to listen to or examine what his friend was telling him, Gavin returned to the window and peered out into the black nothingness. It was rather like opening the door of his soul--black and empty.

"You walk away from me because I speak the truth."

"Go back to Maya. She is no doubt waiting for you. I shall see to the candles and the locks."

"Maya asked that I see to you. She cares for you, too. She worries."

"She needn't. I have no need of her concern."

"You have only one need," Prakash muttered. "Your need is revenge and humiliation upon those who talk behind your back. You seek vengeance on those who cast aspersions on you and your parents."

"You know nothing of what I seek."

"I know what it is you search for, *bondhu*. This is the first time a woman other than your mother and sister has set foot inside your home. No woman has ever garnered such an honor. This woman must be very special. It is love like that which your mother and father shared that you truly seek."

"*This woman* has made a deal with the devil," he snapped before he could stop himself. "And I intend to hold her to it."

"All this pacing for a bargain? You're more foolish than I thought."

"Go to bed, Prakash. I have no need of your predictions or insights. I know perfectly well what I am, and what I want."

"I will not. Not until I see the lady who is making you suffer so. Ah," Prakash murmured, his dark brown eyes widening as he cocked to his head to the right. "A carriage, with at least two teams approaches."

Gavin peered into the darkness, searching for any sight of a carriage. There was nothing there, save for the swaying branches of the large willows that lined the drive.

"She will be approaching any time now. I must leave you, *bondhu*, and prepare to greet the lady."

He nodded, knowing that his friend's declaration would turn out to be true. Despite what he had told Prakash about his predictions, he knew beyond a doubt, that his friend, or *bondhu*, as they called each other, had the sight.

As the door closed behind Prakash, a black carriage led by four grays came into view. The full moon magically appeared between the parting clouds, the white light glinting off the top of the carriage. A carriage lantern swayed with the rhythm of the horse's canter and Gavin followed its yellow light like a beacon. The windows were draped in cloth, and the carriage door was free of a family crest or marker. *It was her.* He felt it in his bones, in the way his blood quickened in his veins. She had come at last, to be tutored in the art of pleasing a man.

The carriage rolled past the window only to stop before the entrance of the front door. The coachman jumped down from his perch and lowered the step from beneath the carriage frame. The door opened and strangely Gavin felt himself holding his breath. At last she appeared, swathed in black velvet, her face concealed by a long lace veil that billowed out when the wind caught it. The sight was arousing, in a mysterious, forbidden sort of way. A veiled woman, shielding her impeccable reputation in order to tryst with a rake such as himself. The wind caught the lace again, and he was helpless to stop from wondering what her face would look like behind a shimmering red face veil, her chocolate brown eyes outlined lavishly with kohl.

The wind howled louder as the front door flew open and Prakash rushed out, holding an umbrella above her and signaling the coachman to drive around to the stables and carriage house.

What was she thinking? Were thoughts of him running through her mind? Did the idea of sharing a bed and their bodies appeal to her as much as it did him?

Voices, low and hushed echoed in the hall and Gavin had no time to stalk to his desk before Prakash opened his study door. That familiar and arousing hushed breath sounded throughout the room, making his blood run hot. Glancing over his shoulder he met the pale, yet beguiling face of his pupil.

Jane couldn't help but gasp at the sight that greeted her. There, standing before her, arm propped against the window casing stood the Viscount Grayson. He looked dangerously handsome dressed in a black velvet robe with scalloped edges and elaborate gold embroidery around the cuffs and the collar. Beneath the garment he wore a white linen shirt, edged with a minimum of lace. Lace cuffs dangled from the sleeves, and Jane was struck by the beauty of his elegant hands as they rested against the window. He wore no stock and his shirt was opened, revealing a naked throat and a small, but intriguing glimpse of his chest. His black hair, thick and straight was unbound, lying against his shoulders.

Taking a deep breath, she swallowed hard and watched as he lowered his arm and slowly turned to face her. Turquoise eyes scanned her from head to toe, and when his gaze rested on her veiled face, he raised one inky brow.

"Good evening, Lady Westbury."

For some silly reason her breath left her lungs in a whoosh. Elation swept through her that she had actually found him home waiting for her. She forced her hands not to tremble as she reached for her veil.

"My pleasure," he said silkily as he strode toward her with predator-like grace.

There was something in the way he was looking at her that suddenly made her remember where they were and who was standing behind her. Lowering her head, she darted her eyes to where a turbaned man stood waiting. Grayson's eyes followed hers and he nodded to the servant.

"Thank you, Prakash. You may retire for the night."

"As you wish, my lord," the man said, bowing. "If there is anything you wish, you have only to ring."

Lord Grayson said nothing while the servant, obviously his butler, reached for the door. Before he closed it, the man spoke. The language was foreign, and the sound somewhat harsh to her ears. The viscount answered him, while never taking his eyes from her. His voice was deep and melodious, and the language, which was obviously Indian, rolled from his tongue with ease. The words sounded evocative, their exoticness intrigued her, and she was left feeling more breathless then when she first entered the room.

"Now then," he said when they were alone, his index finger tracing the lace that rested against her chin. "Where were we?"

A log in the hearth cracked. His eyes narrowed when she jumped, and he tipped her chin up with his finger. "You're no doubt rethinking this bargain of ours."

"No," she said, shaking her head. "I am not." Good heavens, she hadn't thought of anything other than this very night since receiving his summons. Indeed, her every waking thought had been consumed with images of him and what he was going to teach her.

"You do not lie, do you?" he asked, tracing her lips through the lace with the pad of his thumb. "You're not coy and artful like the other women of the *ton*."

Her belly tightened when his thumb passed over her bottom

lip. "I despise deceit."

"A novel attribute in a woman, and one I have never had the pleasure to encounter. I'm sure you're aware that the women of my acquaintance are the very definition of deceit."

"I'm sure I don't know what you mean, my lord."

"A lie. I can see it reflected in your eyes, Jane, and it displeases me."

Unable to stop the action, her lashes lowered, immediately shading her eyes from his.

"Open your eyes, Jane."

She could feel his finger tracing her brow then sliding down to her closed lids. With a soft brush, he fanned her lashes with his fingertip, the sensation heightened by the lace. When his finger rested on the small indentation at the corner of her eyelid, she opened her eyes and peered into his.

"Don't ever lie to me again, Jane," he whispered as his mouth lowered to hers. "I will not tolerate falsehoods from you. It is beneath you. I want only honesty from you, Jane." His breath caressed her lips through her veil. "Now then, I'll ask once more, does my touch disgust you?"

Her gaze flashed away from his lips only to land on his eyes, which were veiled by a long fringe of sable lashes. He was staring at her mouth, at his thumb as it pressed into the corner of her lip. "No."

His chest widened as he took a long breath. She could feel the heat from his body penetrating the dampness that had seeped through her silk gown.

"Do you know, Jane, I don't know that I've met with a more powerful aphrodisiac than truth." His eyelashes lifted and she met his gaze through the black lace. His lips curled in an arrogant grin and Jane felt her stomach clench in anticipation of whatever was to come. "I am quite undone, Jane."

With a quick swoop he took her lips, the lace buffering the feel of his mouth against hers. His hands framed her face and he kissed her softly, his lips nipping and tugging at hers.

It was over before she knew it, and as soon he pulled his mouth from hers, he reached for her veil. With slow determination, he raised the lace, inch by inch, his eyes scouring all of her as if he was seeing her for the very first time.

When her face was bared to him, he took his finger and traced the same path as he had when her face was covered. When he was done, he reached for her bonnet, tugging at the silk ties in a slow, hypnotic fashion. He pulled it from her head, dislodging pins from her hair. One by one, he removed the remaining pins, only to rake his fingers through her thick brown hair.

Twining a curl around his finger, he brought it to his lips. Closing his eyes he inhaled softly, kissed her hair, then lay the curl atop the mound of her left breast. His finger pressed the ringlet into her flesh, and his eyes slowly lifted to meet hers.

"You please me. And that, Jane, is the truth."

Chapter Three

Gavin looked down into Jane's upturned face. Her porcelain skin was flushed a pale peach and her lips, which had been thin before his kiss, were now plump and glistening. Her eyes had darkened to a richer shade of brown and he could see his reflection staring back at him in their dark depths. He was aroused--painfully so. When was the last time a simple kiss had made him hard as iron? When was the last time he had even enjoyed kissing?

His gaze lowered, past her chin, down the column of her throat where a black velvet ribbon encircled her neck. Below that, a lace fichu was tucked artfully into her bodice, barely concealing the large ivory mounds that edged above her gold brocade gown. He watched the slow rise and fall of her breasts, studied the way a charming freckle inched its way above the fichu as her breathing became deeper and more rapid. Unable to resist touching her, he reached out, trailing his finger down the cleft of flesh to the row of cream-colored bows that lined the front of her bodice.

She was every inch the lady, dressed as she was. The bodice was tight, molding her breasts into perfect peaks, shaping her waist so that he could see the womanly flare of her hips. Her breath caught as he reached out and trailed the back of his finger up along her bodice, directly over her breast to pluck the fichu slowly from her ivory flesh.

The scent of country flowers assailed his senses and he brought the lace to his face, inhaling softly. "Indeed, Jane," he murmured, tucking the lace into the pocket of his dressing gown, "you please me very much."

She wet her lips and he followed the path of her tongue, imagining the feel of it gliding against his lips and his cock.

"Does that mean you are still willing to go through with our agreement?"

"I have invited you to my home, have I not?" His finger traced the edge of the velvet choker and he swore he heard the faintest of whimpers whisper pass her lips. "I am to be your tutor, and you my pupil. Is that not right?"

She nodded and her lips parted but no words were spoken.

"What do you know of your tutor, Jane?"

"That you are very skilled in the art of love," she whispered, unconsciously tilting her head when his finger skimmed lower on her throat.

"Not the art of love, Jane. Never make that mistake. I'm skilled in the art of pleasure. Sex for sex's sake. There is a difference."

"Is there?"

Her dark eyes challenged him and he felt his blood still at the same time his cock swelled with raging need. "Didn't you learn that lesson during your marriage with Lord Westbury, Jane? Didn't Archie teach you the difference between love and sex?"

She shivered and he felt the faintest hint of regret that he had caused her discomfort, but it was needed. She had to know he would not love her. That sex was the mere melding of bodies-- nothing more. Nothing was more dangerous to a man than a woman who confused carnal pleasure with everlasting love and devotion.

Jane looked at him, her big brown eyes wide and curious. He had bedded many women much more beautiful than she, yet he'd never once been dangerously close to drowning in their eyes. Never before had he thought that if he did not take control immediately, he might find himself giving the upper hand to a woman. But Jane made him think these things. Only Jane had compelled him to warn her not to become emotionally involved with him. The others had never needed a warning--they had been merely vessels for his passion and his revenge. But Jane was different. Already she was something more to him, and he didn't like it.

She licked her lips again, then stared steadily into his eyes. "Are you warning me not to fall in love with you, sir?"

"That is exactly what I am saying, Jane. Do not confuse the delights of the bedroom for that of love. That is your first lesson in my tutelage. A man will look to bedding as a way to slake his needs. A woman looks at it as a way to bind a man to her. They are ever opposing goals, Jane, and I would have you know that what happens between us will be carnal and perhaps passionate, but never anything more meaningful than that."

"I understand perfectly, my lord," she said. "What I want you to provide me with are the skills needed to attract the attentions of men. Men who are not afraid to love."

Every muscle he possessed tightened. Damn the little minx, did she know what she did to him? Could she possibly have any idea that her words were like a sword through the heart? He didn't want to think of Jane with another man after giving herself to him. But damn it, he couldn't love. He didn't know how.

"Our agreement, my lord, was for you to tutor me. Nothing more. There is no need for you to worry."

"But you forget, my *shundori*, there was one more stipulation."

"And that was?" she asked over her shoulder as he stepped behind her and trailed his fingertips up her spine to the top of her bodice.

"Your corruption--at my hands. There is a price to pay, you see, for my tutelage. It will cost you a pretty penny, Jane, and will no doubt be more than you're willing to pay."

"And what are you suggesting, sir, that I will not be able to learn your lessons?"

"Oh, you'll learn them well enough," he whispered against her shoulder as his fingers worked to untie the bow that laced her outer corset. "But they shall be lessons of my choosing. Perhaps we should get started with the first one, Lady Westbury."

"By all means."

Her voice was assured, yet he heard the barest hint of huskiness in her words. She was becoming aroused and it made him feel reckless. As the bow came free in his hand, he hooked the tip of his finger at the top of the lacing and pulled the string from each eyehook with one continuous tug.

"Now then," he said as the corset fell to the floor. "The first rule to keep in mind when attempting to attract the attentions of a man, is exuberance. Do you know what I mean by that, Jane?"

"High spirits and liveliness."

"A very nice definition that you could find in Samuel Johnson's dictionary, but I was referring to the context in regards to men."

She shivered when his hands traced the square neckline at the back of her gown. With skill honed from too much experience, he deftly unbuttoned the pearls that held her dress secure and pushed the sleeves of her gown down along her shoulders.

"Exuberance is everything to a man, Jane. It tells him that the woman is more than willing. It tells him that she's participating. There is nothing more potent to a man than being with a woman who throws herself into sex. Are you one of those women, Jane?" he whispered in her ear. "Or are you the sort who lies quietly beneath a man, thinking of things other than who is on top of you, praying that his penetration will not hurt and that his passion will be expedient?"

He felt the pulse at the base of her neck quicken beneath his lips. "Never mind. I know the sort of woman you are, Jane. It shall only be a matter of time before my suspicions are confirmed." She whirled around and faced him, her eyes wide and perhaps worried. "Ssh," he said, placing a finger over her lips. "I am not through with my first lesson. When I am done, you shall have all the time you wish to ask me questions."

Her eyes narrowed at his tone, and his breeches tightened at the sight of it. None of the women he'd been with had challenged him--not physically, and certainly not mentally, but he could see that Jane would challenge him in both areas. He liked that she would not just bow to his wishes. She would make him work hard to please her and the thought, the very idea that he would have need of every skill in his broad knowledge of sex, aroused him greatly.

When her haughty look passed, he brought his hands around her waist and untied her corset, tossing it onto the floor. He stepped back and looked at her, her bodice hanging about her waist, her chemise, transparent and formfitting around her breasts. He could see the dark outlines of her areolas beneath the linen, and taut nipples that only became more erect the longer he stared at her.

"The second thing to remember in attracting the attentions of a man," he said, circling the shadow of her nipple with his finger, "is confidence." His eyes met hers and he felt her breast become full against his hand. "Are you confident, Jane?"

Her lashes partially lowered, shielding her eyes from him. "Of course."

She was lying. He saw it in her eyes, but more importantly he felt her self-consciousness flowing from her.

"Just how confident, Jane?"

"Very."

"Well, then," he drawled. "You may show me this confidence by disrobing until you are completely naked. Then, you shall come to me wearing nothing but that pretty black ribbon about your throat."

"But...." she stuttered, suddenly clutching her bodice to her breasts.

"That door, Jane," he motioned to the paneled door across the room. "Open it and come to me--naked, willing, confident. I want to watch you move. I want to see just how eager you are to learn and please. Unless of course, you lied to me, Jane." She stared at him but said nothing. "Did you lie, Jane?"

"No."

"Then the first lesson in the art of pleasing a man will commence in less than a minute. I suggest you ready yourself. It is never wise for a pupil to be tardy for her first lesson."

* * * *

Jane watched as Lord Grayson stalked to the door, his dressing gown swinging out behind him. Opening the paneled door, he stepped into the darkness beyond, leaving her alone in his study without a backward glance.

Damn him! What was he about commanding that she disrobe and walk naked before him? She was way out of her league. He was a master of seduction, and she had very little experience with such things.

Her fingers trembled nervously against her bodice as she paced before the fire. What was she to do? Run? Absolutely not! She would not have him think that he had scared her with his sexual mastery. But to disrobe and walk before him was unthinkable. It made her feel vulnerable and she would not allow the viscount to reduce her to such a state. She had vowed she would not leave herself open to any man. When Archie had left her, she had promised herself that she would not give any man the power to make her feel exposed and weak.

With a helpless cry, she forced the bodice down her hips, letting the full skirts pool around her knees. Forcing her eyes shut, she tried to block out the memories of the viscount's touch, the way his eyes locked with hers--the way his jade eyes turned to turquoise when he looked deep into her eyes. He was the most beautiful man she had ever met--and the most lethal. He was dangerous to her peace of mind, her body, and her precarious self-confidence. Not only was her heart slowly being lost to him, but her newfound resolve was also in jeopardy. There was no other man within the *ton* she wanted to please more than the viscount. But she knew she didn't have it in her to please him. How could she with her rounded belly and plump thighs? How could he want her after having nearly every desirable woman of the *ton* falling at his feet? It was utter madness to think that he would be drawn to her sexually.

And yet she still wanted him, despite the fact that the viscount had probably never looked at her before last week. From the very moment she had glimpsed him across Hyde Park during a ride with Archie, she had been taken with him. At first she was intrigued by his colorful background, enraptured by the tale of his mother and father--an odalisque in a sultan's keeping and the man who had stolen her from beneath the sultan's nose.

Soon she was watching him during balls, spying on him at the opera. She had even at one time pretended that Archie was the viscount, lying atop her, driving into her. She had waited over a year for this night, and now she was powerless to choose.

If she ran, if she lost what nerve she had, all would be ruined. She would never know what it was like to touch his bronzed skin, to feel his mouth on hers. But if she obeyed him, if she submitted to him and made herself vulnerable, she might never again be able to look herself in the mirror.

As the wire hoop frame that supported her skirts slid down her waist, Jane weighed what she was about to do. Submitting to him was the only way to gain entrée into his world. She might only ever have this one chance. Was she really willing to risk losing this chance at passion, a passion that she had dreamed of-- all because she was terrified to bare herself to his all too experienced gaze?

Her hand brushed her breast as she reached for the tie of her chemise, instantly reminding her of his touch. Not even Archie had sent such need spiraling within her. Her breasts had never tightened and filled the way they had with only the viscount's beautiful eyes for stimulation. She had braved his perusal once; surely she could brave it one more time.

Naked, she glanced about the room hoping to find a blanket in which to cover her body. There was nothing. She had only two choices left: don her clothes and flee from his house or open the door and step into the viscount's world.

She opened the door and was greeted with a third choice. On the threshold, folded neatly, lay the viscount's dressing gown. Without thinking, Jane picked it up and slipped her arm into the sleeve. It was heavy and warm and smelled of sandalwood and soap. His scent, as well his body heat lingered in the garment and she pulled the sides tight around her, burying her face in the velvet, the gold filigree rough against her cheek.

With renewed hope she walked down the darkened hallway to where another door was slightly ajar and the flicker of candlelight shone through the crack. It would work, she thought as she reached for the latch. He would teach her how to attract a man's attention, and then, she would use all his lessons, everything he had taught her--on him. For that was what she wanted most out of their agreement--to capture and hold the attentions of the notoriously unattainable viscount.

Chapter Four

Jane stepped into a garden sanctuary. As soon as she closed the door the scent of jasmine, sweet and exotic, assailed her senses. It was as if she was dreaming, leaving behind a room only to have it replaced by a Garden of Eden. Everywhere she looked palm trees towered above her. To her right were lemon trees with flowering vines growing up their trunks. The wind whispered past her through open arches and she looked up to see a glass dome, the stars twinkling brightly through the glass. It was then that she realized they were in a conservatory of some sort.

Padding barefoot, she walked silently along the fieldstone slabs, listening to the hum of crickets and the wind as it whistled by. The sound of water trickling and flowing in the distance called to her, and she followed the sound. Guiding her path stood torches, their flames flickering and hissing in the breeze. Braziers of incense burned. The tendrils of smoke, laced with the scent of sandalwood and myrrh, filled her head, and Jane felt herself slipping into a calm that she had never before experienced.

The water now sounded like it was rushing and tumbling over rocks and as she came to a circular clearing, she breathed in awe at the sight before her. There, in the middle of the conservatory sat a large waterfall surrounded by palm trees, their feathery fronds waving softly in the night air. Torches were positioned around the waterfall and Jane could see that the water emptied into a pond with pink and white lotus flowers floating lazily on top of the water.

A flicker of light to her left captured her gaze and her eyes widened when she saw what lay behind the pond. A beaded tent, made of the sheerest silk hung from a frame in the ceiling. The color was dark and sensual, reminding her of a rich claret. Through the curtain she could make out numerous pillows and the flickering of more candles. She took a step closer then gasped as a dark figure emerged from behind the waterfall.

"You are not naked, Jane."

She took a deep breath and prayed she was taking the right

path. "I am not all that confident, my lord."

"I know."

Her belly tightened and her pulse leapt. What would he do to her? He was looking at her in a way that made her uneasy. It was so hard to know what thoughts ran through his mind. She had never had to guess what Archie was thinking--he had never failed to tell her. But this man was different. He was secretive and mysterious and Jane didn't know how to proceed with him.

"Come," he commanded, beckoning to her. When she was standing before him, he tipped her face up to meet his eyes. "That is the second lie you've told me, Jane."

"I only wanted to please you." And it was the truth.

"Why did you have to lie, when I already told you that you pleased me?"

She shrugged and hugged the edges of the gown closer to her. "I did not want you to have cause to end our association before it had begun."

He traced her bottom lip with his finger and goose bumps erupted on her flesh. "I shall not be the one to end it, Jane. Unless of course, you lie to me again."

She nodded, understanding that he meant what he said. From now on he was in complete control and she was at his mercy.

He took her by the hand and guided her to the tent. "Tell me why a woman such as yourself is not confident. You have the world at your feet. You're rich--titled. What is it that makes you think less of yourself?"

"I do not know...." She trailed off as she stepped into the tent and came face to face with what a harem really must look like. She watched as the viscount sat on a thick cushion, then stretched out his long length against the jewel-colored pillows behind him.

Motioning for her to join him, she sat on the cushion next to his thigh. He reached for her hand, drawing her near him and positioning her to lie beside him. Brushing her hair from her face, he peered into her eyes. "You never knew the pleasures of the marriage bed with your husband, did you, Jane? He never caressed you and sung your praises. He never told you that your skin reminded him of fresh cream, or that your eyes are wonderfully large and dark. A man could drown in eyes like yours, my *shundori*."

"Tell me what that means," she asked, delighting in the exoticness of the word on his lips. There was something so powerfully mesmerizing in his voice. The foreign language combined with the way he said her name was making her melt in a way she had never experienced before.

"It means my beauty. That is what you are in Bengali."

Her breath caught, and when she shook her head in protest, he stopped her with the barest touch of his finger. "Exuberance and confidence are the first two things to draw a man's eye, Jane. A woman thinks she must be beautiful in order to attract a man, but that is not so. Beauty is different for every man. What one finds attractive, another finds only pleasing. There are many facets of beauty, Jane, remember that. Now then," he murmured, smoothing her hair back over her shoulder and allowing his finger to graze her chin. "Tell me why you are unable to bare yourself to me." She stiffened as his finger edged the gown away from her throat. "Tell me why you would not allow me to view your nakedness?"

"I am ... fuller in places than I wish to be."

"Is that so?" he asked, slipping his hand inside the velvet so that his warm palm rested on her waist. "I am sorry that you denied me the pleasure of seeing you. Unlike your husband, I prefer the attentions of women, not girls. I like voluptuousness in women." She squirmed beneath his touch as his hand slid up her side to graze the underside of her breast. "Tell me, Jane, are your breasts full and large?"

She nodded and closed her eyes. Lord, he was wicked and if he didn't soon touch her, she would die of sheer torture waiting for the feel of his hands on her.

"Allow me to judge." Nipping her lips he soothed them with flicks of his tongue. Then he parted the velvet, letting the one side slide over her hip and buttock exposing the left side of her body to his gaze. "They are indeed," he said, gazing up at her from beneath his sable lashes. "From what I can tell, Jane, you are not a bit too full. You are exactly what I wish you to be."

He ran his hand down her side and along her hip to her thigh, his gaze moving with the motion of his hand as it trailed along her pale skin, assessing her like a slave at a bazaar. His lashes flickered, then lifted to meet her face while his hand skated over her rounded belly. "Very lovely, Jane. Soft and warm all over. You'll curve into me perfectly when you are lying satiated in my arms." And then he slowly lowered his lips to hers, softly, soothingly, enticing her to return his kiss. She opened her mouth to him, allowing him entrance and he pushed her back into the cushions, crushing her with his weight, reassuring her with his heat.

She moaned when she felt the lace of his cuff tickle her chest, then whimpered as he caressed her breast with his smooth nails, all the while deepening the kiss, making her yearn for more of his lessons.

"You're showing exuberance, Jane." He grinned as he stared down into her eyes. "I can see you'll pass this first lesson with ease."

Unable to help herself, she raked her hands through his long hair as he bent over her, his tongue trailing a line from her navel to the valley of her breasts. Instead of licking her nipples as she expected and hoped he would, he nuzzled them with his lips, moistening them with his breath and then blowing gently against them until they were so tight and erect she moved restlessly against him. It was the most exquisite of tortures waiting for him to suckle her. Her breasts were very sensitive, and she had always wanted Archie to play with them--but he never had.

Her hands continued to slide through his silky hair while he held himself above her, bracing his weight on his forearms. He was still teasing her and Jane opened her eyelids a fraction--just enough to watch his bottom lip toy with the very tip of her nipple. His eyes, now more turquoise than jade, met hers, and with deliberate intent he nuzzled her nipple, then pursed his lips and blew softly against her.

Entranced by his mysterious eyes, Jane was helpless to do anything but watch as his tongue came out and gently, almost imperceptibly, flicked the very tip of her nipple. She groaned, needing more, yet wanting his torturous ministrations to continue. He continued to hold her gaze while his tongue crept out again. This time though, he circled the erect flesh in a slow, deliberate swirl.

"You have very lovely breasts, Jane," he said against her nipple. "I could play with them for hours. Would you like me to?"

She was panting beneath him, yet he didn't move. He maintained his position above her, caging her with his muscular arms while capturing her nipple between his lips and pulling, before letting it slip out of his mouth.

He shifted his weight to his side in order to cup her breast and Jane watched as he studied it, the flesh more than filling his large hand. He squeezed softly, molding it to his palm, circling the nipple with his thumb. Then he brought it to his mouth, teasing her nipple with his lips until she begged for him to suckle her, and only then, when he heard her pleading whimpers did he take her into his mouth and suckle her. Soft and rhythmic, he pulled her breast into his mouth while he massaged her with his long fingers.

Sinking further into the silk cushions, Jane let her fingers roam through his hair, clenching when arousal coiled and tightened in her belly. She watched him suck and lave her breasts, and whenever he looked up at her, he held her gaze while wickedly swirling his tongue around her nipple, sending sharp pains of desire deep within her.

After long moments in which Jane thought there could be no greater pleasure than having him pay attention to her breasts, he released her, placing a kiss on her reddened nipple.

"Now then, Jane," he murmured, his voice dark and husky. "Do you want to know the last two things that will keep a man coming back for more?"

She nodded, feeling nervous and needy all at once. She watched as his gaze slowly lowered to where his linen shirt met her bared breasts. Lowered still to her belly. Lower ... until he reached the apex of her thighs and she raised her knee, unconsciously hiding her sex. She had been naked but twice before with a man, and that had been with Archie on their wedding night. Archie had not taken the time to look at her or woo her with words. He'd climbed atop her, spread her thighs and drove into her. He had released his seed in a matter of seconds and promptly rolled off, snoring within minutes. The second time was when he had cast criticism on her and left in a fit of disgust after seeing that her breasts and thighs, not to mention her bottom, had curved and filled out, replacing her childish figure.

"There are two things a man truly desires, Jane," he said, drawing her out of her memories. His fingers stroked her thigh before they moved to her knee where they continued to graze her sensitized skin. With little encouragement, she let her leg drop so that her mound was exposed to his gaze. "What a man wants, Jane, is a lady to keep his house and converse with. She should be a paragon of devotion to show to his friends at balls and the opera. But his other desire, Jane, is a whore. An accomplished courtesan who will succumb to his every desire. Who will join him in bed and match his enthusiasm for sex. Can you be that,

Jane? Can you play the whore as well you play the lady?"

Jane lay beneath him, frozen. Could she do that? Could she pretend she was a lady by day and a Cyprian by night? Could she let loose her tightly held inhibitions and pleasure the viscount in any way he asked? Could she shed her insecurities about her body and pretend she was beautiful and desirable?

"Let us see, shall we, Jane?" he said, lifting himself off of her and pulling his shirttails from his breeches. He flung his shirt beside them and loosened the flap of his breeches. She met his gaze, then leisurely let her eyes roam the expanse of his chest which was broad and heavily sculpted. The muscles of his belly were taut and chiseled. A silky line of black hair swirled around his navel only to disappear below the waist of his breeches. He was beautiful and handsome, with light brown skin that was shiny in the candlelight. He was everything she had ever dreamed about, and she was very willing to play the part of the whore if only for a chance to make this man see her as more than just a pupil.

"You are very handsome, my lord," she said, noticing how his erection thickened and swelled behind the fabric. "And I can see that the rumors about your size are not exaggerated."

A small grin passed his lips, and he cocked one brow. "Why do you not see for yourself, Lady Westbury? It is always prudent to examine a tutor's credentials before taking him into service."

She had never done anything like this with Archie. Once or twice she had inadvertently brushed against his manhood, but it had been flaccid and lifeless. But Lord Grayson's manhood seemed to be stretching with a life all its own. She reached out and stroked her fingers down the front of his breeches. He was large and thick and she had the uncontrollable urge to tear open the flap.

"I think all your credentials are in order. I'm ready for my first lesson."

He smiled then and slowly pushed aside the fabric. Grasping his erection in his hand, he stroked it before her. Jane felt her eyes widen at the size of him, but also at the way he intimately and shamelessly stroked himself. Impossible to believe, his shaft actually thickened and widened, and Jane looked up to his face and saw that his gaze was riveted on her.

"Watch me, Jane. Study the way I hold and stroke it. Learn the way to arouse and entice a man's desire with only your hand."

With a deep breath she lowered her eyes, watching as his

erection slid between the space between his thumb and index finger. Slowly at first, he stroked, up and down, reaching only as far as the pink tip. His grip was loose and slow, his hips moving in time with his hand. But soon his breathing increased, as did his hold. Soon he was gripping his engorged shaft, working it hard and assuredly, watching her as she studied him.

Suddenly he stopped and stood, removed his breeches and stood naked before her, his shaft thick and throbbing between his thighs.

"Sit up," he commanded before walking behind her. When he was seated on his knees, he whispered against her hair. "Now, my *shundori*, you will show me how you like to be touched."

He brought her knees up so that her feet were resting flat on the cushion. With his palms on her knees, he spread her thighs wide and placed their entwined hands on her sex, sliding their joined hands along her flesh. She gasped and pressed her legs together.

"No. You will not hide from me. Show me what I want to see."

"I-I can't," she blurted, squeezing her eyes shut. She didn't want to do this. She didn't want to be exposed before the viscount.

"What are you ashamed of?" he asked, kissing the hollow below her ear. "Are you ashamed because you are here with me? Do I shame you, Jane?"

She was mortified by the very thought and she moved her head on his shoulder so that she could look up into his face. "I would never be ashamed of you."

"Then tell me why you are afraid, Jane. What do wish to hide from?"

"Myself," she whispered, looking away from his far too knowing gaze.

"I see." He parted her thighs and pressed his fingers into her plump flesh. "That is something we shall have to work very diligently against, Jane, for I do not wish to be denied a glimpse of your delectable body."

She stiffened, feeling more vulnerable than she ever had before. She was naked in his arms, and she could feel his gaze scouring every inch of her. It made her wish to cover up with anything she could find, to hide her imperfections from him, to prevent him from thinking ill of her.

"I will see you, Jane," he commanded, pressing her thighs further apart. "You will not hide when you are with me. I want all of you, Jane, and I will not compromise on that."

With that, he slid his fingers along her sex and parted her. She felt his hot gaze there and she fought the urge to press her thighs together. He must have known what she was thinking for he slid his finger up the length of her and said very softly, "The most beautiful pink silk I've ever touched. Can you feel me growing harder against you as I watch my fingers stroking the honey from you?"

His words made her squirm for more, but he deprived her of that wickedness when he brought his finger to his mouth and licked it.

"The scent and flavor of a woman, there is no other taste on earth like it. A man craves it during sex, Jane. He wants to run his tongue along her lips, her nipples, the very rim of her body that trembles for his cock." She moved her bottom restlessly against the cushion. He pressed his chest against her back and cupped her breasts, pushing them together then parting them, all the while rubbing her nipples with his thumbs.

"Tell me your secret fantasies, Jane. What is it you crave?"

"To be desired."

"At whose hands, Jane? Any man's?"

"Yours," she couldn't help moaning and arching her back as her body tightened.

"Do you want to know what I desire, Jane?"

"Hmmm?"

"I want to watch you as I make you come. You've never climaxed, have you, Jane?"

"No," she whimpered.

"Then I shall be the first. That is my desire."

Before she knew what he was about, he was lying on his back and urging her on top of him. When he kept pushing her hips higher onto his chest, she protested, confused as to what he wanted her to do.

"Lower yourself onto my mouth, Jane, and let me taste you."

"Oh, I couldn't."

"A man wants to feel his lady's sex against his mouth, Jane. Replace the lady with the wanton. Let yourself go and see what it is like to be sinful."

And then she did. With shaking fingers she clutched onto his shoulders, his hands anchored her hips, tilting them until her mound was angled toward his mouth. Then the sensation of his hot tongue brushing the length of her made her moan long and deep.

"That is it, my *shundori*, show me that you want this."

And then he stopped whispering to her and instead moved his tongue in enticing, erotic, not to mention almost painfully slow circles around her sex. The light dusting of whiskers on his cheeks and chin abraded and sensitized her skin, making the sensation so much more consuming. Soon her fingers were pressing into his shoulders as she moved atop him, showing him with her hips the direction she wanted his tongue to move. The pressure was building deep within her when suddenly she cried out and pressed her sex to his mouth, trembling as he sucked--drinking in all of the wetness she felt seep out of her body.

"Gavin!" she cried, not caring that she was using his Christian name. She rocked shamelessly against him and moaned a deep, guttural sound from her chest. Good lord, she shouldn't be doing this; it was shameful and wanton to be doing this, but she couldn't stop it--her body had a mind of its own and it would not allow her to curb its pleasure.

When at last she stilled, she pulled away from him, sliding down his body and burying her face in his hard chest.

"Jane," his voice was soft and soothing, much like his fingers as they raked through her tousled hair. "Do not be ashamed, Jane. You were beautiful and passionate, and you have given me a gift that no other shall ever have."

She looked up at him through a veil of hair and smiled uneasily. "I am afraid I am more wanton than you thought."

"No, Jane. I knew what your response would be. You only needed the encouragement to let yourself experience it. You might have lain still beneath your husband, but you will not do so for me. Now go to sleep, Jane. You will need your rest for the next lesson."

Chapter Five

Looking out the window, Gavin marvelled at the sunrise and wondered why he'd spent so many mornings of his life tucked in bed suffering from the ill effects of whatever overindulgence had consumed him the night before. How many dawns just as spectacular had passed him by with no thought or care? And why the hell was he musing about it now? Because he'd experienced something earth shattering with Jane? Many women had cried out his name during the peak of their passion. It was only ever his title, but it was his name nonetheless. He'd pleasured legions of women, all of them succumbing to his ministrations just as easily as Jane had last night. So what the bloody hell was wrong with him this morning? Why was he up at the crack of dawn, listening to birds chirping and watching the brilliant, orange sun rise above white fluffy clouds? *Because, fool, you experienced something like never before--something that has always evaded you.* Last night, he had felt more than a physical connection to Jane, and the very idea that he was admitting it to himself scared the hell out of him.

It wasn't that her breasts were the loveliest he had ever seen, or the fact that she responded to the faintest touch of his hands--it was something more, something simpler. When he had looked at her, her dark eyes staring vulnerably up at him, he had felt like giving a piece of himself to her. As his eyes locked with hers, he'd felt the overwhelming need to tell her that he wanted what was going to happen between them to be much more than an empty mating of bodies. In that moment, their eyes locked, their breaths mingling, he'd wanted to tell her that he needed someone like her in his life.

Bloody ass! Who the devil was he fooling? He was a tutor--nothing more. A means for *m'lady* to perfect her skills in order to dazzle the more palatable men of the *ton*. She didn't want the half-breed, not in any permanent sense, she only wanted his skills, and even that would be short-lived. Damn it to hell, he hadn't been thinking straight when he'd agreed to tutor her. No--that wasn't true. He had been thinking--thinking of himself between her ivory thighs. What hadn't occurred to him was the possibility that his way of life, his very heart, might be in jeopardy.

"Good morning, my lord."

Gavin glanced over his shoulder to find Prakash carrying a washbasin and towels as he sauntered into his chamber.

"I trust you slept well?"

"Not a wink," Gavin grunted before returning his gaze back out the window. "I've been up all bloody night." And, he silently added, he didn't even come during the long night. Instead, he had carried Jane to a chamber, tucked her in bed and left her alone. He hadn't trusted himself with her. Not after she had fallen asleep on his chest and he started thinking of how very nice it was to lie beside a woman and do nothing but feel her breath against his neck and her soft skin beneath his fingers. It was when he decided that Jane had the sweetest face when sleeping that he knew he was treading treacherous waters and thought it far safer to be rid of her.

"Your mind is troubled."

"I'll thank you to stay out of my mind, Prakash."

"Your lady, she did not please you?"

"That is none of your affair."

"I see. She pleased you too much."

"Bloody hell," he roared, swinging away from the window. "Will you cease your meddling?"

The damnable man had the nerve to grin and bow mockingly to him. "You think you hide what you feel, but I know better. I saw your face when you first saw her last night. Your feelings are engaged."

"Just my usual feelings, Prakash, the ones that involve getting between a pair of plump thighs and having my way." But then he thought of Jane's lovely thighs and the taste of her arousal on his lips and he knew then that these were not just ordinary feelings of desire. The way he had pleasured Jane last night was far more intimate than the way he had pleasured any of his other conquests. With them they had pleasured him, stroking his cock and fulfilling *his* yearnings. Last night he had barely thought of his own needs--instead he'd thrust aside the desire to have her mouth around him and instead thought of nothing other than pleasuring Jane as she never had been before.

"Maya is with her now," Prakash muttered as he set the basin onto the commode. "Where do you wish to meet your lady?"

Forcing away the image of Jane naked and atop him, Gavin strolled over to the commode and pulled his shirt over his shoulders, baring his chest. Bending over, he splashed his face, running his hands through his hair. "The terrace, I think," he said at last, drying his face with a towel. "You may serve breakfast there."

Prakash bowed. "I shall tell cook."

Gavin flung the towel aside and soaped his arms. "Inform cook that I shall require a basket be packed for a midday meal."

"A luncheon in the open air." Prakash grinned. "Will wonders never cease?"

Glaring at his friend's retreating back, Gavin continued soaping his body, not wanting to think of the madness that had prompted him to be so impulsive. It was all for the purpose of instruction, he reminded himself--for Jane's edification, nothing more.

* * * *

"Tell me about your parents."

Jane watched as Gavin stiffened and slid his gaze to the blue horizon. "I do not talk about my family," he said at last. "It's something I do not care to share."

"It's not as though I haven't heard the story," she said, meeting his gaze. When his face turned hard and unreadable, she reached for his hand, stroking his knuckles with her finger. "I'd like to hear it from you. I've always thought it the most romantic tale I've ever heard."

Gavin reached for a pear inside the basket and bit off a large chunk, watching her thoughtfully. "You find the story of my concubine mother and the fool who risked certain death to rescue her romantic? I call it foolish and not worthy of the time it would take to tell it."

"Are you ashamed then? Is that why you refuse to discuss it?"

"I am not."

"Then why won't you tell me?"

"I thought you different, Jane. But I see you're like all the others, you only want to hear the scandalous details of their illicit love affair."

"No." Jane placed her hand on his arm and forced him to look at her. "I ask because I find your culture exotic and romantic. It is so different from English culture and I cannot help but be entranced by the idea of being in the keeping of a very dark and powerful man."

He raised a brow and stared at her. "The tale my mother told of her servitude to the Sultan was neither romantic nor passionate. She was sold, Jane, by her own mother at a bazaar. Mother was sixteen then, and the bastard daughter of an English peer. Her mother's father was an influential Bombay businessman, and when he found out she was carrying a babe without benefit of marriage, he tossed her out into the street. My mother never knew her father, and my grandmother struggled through many hardships to raise her. When she arrived at the Harem, she became the Sultan's favorite and served him as his whim decreed. When my father arrived he was a guest of the English ambassador to India. My father told me that when he first saw my mother, her wrist was chained to the Sultan's chair. She was wearing a red sari, and her face was partially veiled with gold silk. Father said her green eyes followed him wherever he went, and he was so taken with her that he fell immediately in love with her."

"Do you share the same color eyes with your mother?"

He looked away from her and bit fiercely into the pear. "A trait, bestowed by my English grandfather. Whenever I look in the mirror I am reminded of my tainted, bastard blood. My father had blue eyes. I used to pray when I was a little boy that my eyes would somehow change and be more like his. My prayers were never answered, Jane."

"I've seen the blue in them," she whispered, unable to stop herself from brushing back the hair from his face. "I imagine that the Indian Ocean is turquoise like your eyes."

His gaze flickered to hers and she saw the slow change in his eyes. Yes, there was most definitely blue in his eyes. His lids lowered and he looked away from her, up at the sky where some birds were circling overhead.

"My parents became lovers while my mother was under the protection of the Sultan," he said quietly. "Under dangerous conditions, my father secured her passage to the outside and together they ran away, into the Bengali region where they lived until I was six."

"That is when your father inherited the title."

"Yes. He never expected to. When his brother died childless, the title fell to him. He packed up my mother and me, and we sailed for England. We were not greeted with open arms, Jane. Indeed, we were despised, my mother most of all. But she suffered through the humiliation and the insults for my father, and for me. My parents were devoted to each other, and my mother still mourns him after all these years."

"And you still feel like that lost little boy, do you not?"

He tossed the pear to the ground and refused to look at her. His shoulders were tense and a muscle in his jaw worked furiously. "I have a title and a fortune and women constantly falling at my feet. What more can a man ask for, Jane?" His gaze swung back to her and she startled at the barely concealed anger she saw in his eyes. "Now then, it is my turn to ask you a question."

"If you'd like."

"Tell me, Jane, do you know how to flirt?"

She picked at the fringe of the wool blanket and searched the tops of the trees. "I'm afraid I have never learned the art."

He reached for her hand and stroked her palm with his fingertip. In the sun, his hands looked so much darker than her pale ones. Jane studied the way his fingers, elegant and long--like an artist's, stroked her skin. Suddenly he replaced her hand on her lap and looked away, plucking a blade of grass and twirling it between his fingers.

"Don't ever try to learn, Jane. It's something a man detests."

He was different today. Aloof, almost cold. When she had greeted him that morning over breakfast he had bowed formally and said very little. She wondered at the change in him and surmised that she had failed miserably in her first lesson of pleasing a man. How could she have pleased him? She'd fallen asleep after indulging her own pleasure. She had most certainly been selfish last night.

"A man despises the coy art that women employ, Jane. They blanket their motives under the guise of flirtation, but it is much more complex than that."

She wondered at the conversation and his obvious lack of desire to continue where they had left off in the conservatory. But instead of guiding the conversation to what he was attempting to avoid, Jane placated him. "Then why is it women are encouraged to flirt?" she asked, surprised and confused. Every woman of her acquaintance knew how to use her eyes and fan as a weapon in the art of flirtation. She had been a miserable failure, of course, never learning the subtleties, but that had not prevented her from watching the experts in the *ton*.

Watching flirtations in the ballroom had always fascinated her. Men succumbed to the wiles of the women who could wield their eyes and their bodies with ruthless determination. It was utterly impossible to believe that the viscount wished her to think that men did not fall in with the practice of flirtation.

"It has always amazed me," he sighed, tossing the blade of grass from his fingers, "to see what lengths seemingly intelligent women will go to in order to seduce a man through vanity. Behind their wavering fans and painted eyes lay evil machinations. I for one have never been taken in by their coquetries."

"Are you speaking for all men, then?" she laughed, trying to cajole him from his blackening mood. "For this is the purpose behind your lessons, is it not? To make me understand the mystery behind the male mind."

Tearing his eyes from the horizon, he levelled her with his glare. "You laugh, and that disappoints me, Jane. Somehow I thought you were above batting your eyes and pouting your lips. However, if that is the sort of fool you wish to attract then all by means, Jane, wave your fan and have your maid squeeze your breasts together into a corset that makes you unable to breathe. You'll no doubt have an easy time of it. There are any number of idiots in the *ton* that would fall for the meaningless wiles of a woman such as that."

"But you're not one of them, I assume?"

His face paled and his eyes narrowed as he continued to glare at her. "I hope that is not your feeble attempt at flirtation, Jane. For I fear if it is, you do indeed lack the talent. I have had experience resisting the flirtations of women who are much more skilled in the art than you, Jane. It will take more than a feminine laugh and the heaving of bosoms to make me blind to a lady's motives. You needn't think that I told you about my parents because you smiled and looked shyly up from your lashes, Jane. No, I told you because you asked me forthrightly and you spoke with honesty of your curiosity. Had you simpered, I would have ignored you and finished my pear. But because you looked me in the eye and asked me, I told you. Never confuse honesty with artful flirtation, Jane--flirtation will get you nowhere."

He was extremely intelligent, Jane realized. He was seasoned and knew everything about women and their desires and their machinations. She would have to tread carefully where the viscount was concerned. One misstep and he would cast her out of his life. Her precarious situation was even now in jeopardy. She sensed she held his attention by the thinnest thread, and she knew she would have to be just as intelligent and evasive as he if she was to arouse his interest to more than that of the jaded tutor of the sexual arts. She hadn't the looks to capture him, but she did have intellect, and from what she had learned today, intelligence in a woman was something the viscount admired.

"And what have I said that amuses you so?" he asked, his voice deep and laced with a hint of danger.

"I thought it diverting that you sought to warn me about flirting with you," she said, hoping to detract him from discovering her designs on him. "I have made it quite clear, my lord that you are but tutoring me to lure some other unsuspecting member of your sex. You're supplying me with the lessons to keep my future lover enthralled with only me."

He frowned, looking ferocious and hard. "Glad to be of assistance, Lady Westbury. I was certain that I was going to prove of some use to *someone.*"

"I seem to have hit a nerve, my lord. I did not mean--"

"You have hit nothing, I assure you. I'm quite beyond your reach, madam."

"Quite," she said, looking away and hiding her grin. The viscount might be extremely intelligent, but so too was she. Perhaps she was plain and unassuming, but she more than made up for her appearance with her acute mind. And her intelligence told her that the viscount was being unnecessarily haughty because she had touched him. In what way, she did not fully understand, but something told her that he did not let anyone see his temper. He chose to hide that particular emotion with his rakish behavior, but she had seen beneath the veneer and discovered something new about the viscount.

"We have wasted the afternoon, Jane. We should have started our lessons an hour ago."

"And what is lesson number two?" she asked, wishing he would let her into his heart--even if it were only for a brief minute. How was she, unskilled and plump, ever going to tempt the man who could have whatever woman he wanted?

"The art of patience," he murmured, gazing down at her breasts that edged above her bodice. "A woman must make a man yearn. She must strive to haunt his every thought and consume him with burning need."

"And how is that done, my lord?"

His finger lightly traced the freckle that marked the top of her left breast. "Evasiveness, Jane," he whispered as he lowered his mouth to her breast. "A woman must only give a man a tantalizing taste. It is the chase, you see, that fuels hunger and need." His lips kissed her freckle before he began to nuzzle the valley between her breasts. His warm palm that rested on her belly slowly slid up her bodice to capture her breast.

She understood what he was saying. A woman needed to draw out the tension, bringing the man to his knees before giving in and letting him between her thighs. Had she tantalized him last night? Was he even now burning for her?

Was he hinting that she should leave so that he could think of her and want her? She could be evasive, and God willing, she would have him burning with need by the next time they met for her lessons.

"Show me your breasts, Jane," he said against her skin. "You've tantalized me long enough with glimpses of your décolletage. I want to see your pale skin in the sunlight. I want to see your pink nipples harden in the afternoon breeze."

"I do so hope we might continue this discussion another day, my lord," she said, removing his hand and shimmying her body away from his searching mouth. "I'm afraid I must be getting back to Town," she said, trying to hide the tremor in her voice as she stood and shook out her skirts. "I had not planned to dally long in Richmond, you see, and unfortunately I have made plans for this evening."

His face pinched and tightened. Anger, immediate and dark, filled his eyes. "Where are you going, Jane? Surely you are not relieving me of my post after only one lesson?"

"Of course not, but I cannot spend all my days on lessons. One must have some recreation outside the school room, is that not right?"

His looked of stunned stupefaction made her smile. As she made her way to her mare, Jane had the sudden thought that she might do very well in her dealings with the viscount. Already she was discovering just what triggers to press to make the prickly viscount lower his mask of mystery.

She would use these next few days to make him burn, she thought as she allowed him to help her onto her side-saddle. With any luck, their next meeting would involve the viscount learning a new lesson.

Chapter Six

Saddle leather creaked as Gavin repositioned himself atop his stallion. The black's ear flickered before he snorted and stomped in frustration. With pressure from his thighs and a firm grasp on the reins, Gavin subdued the beast's irritation, but the action did nothing to abate his own.

The beast tossed his head and snorted insolently once again. Leaning forward, he ran his gloved hand through the horse's mane. "I know it has been too long, Rama, but I'm afraid I cannot leave."

Secreted amongst the trees, Gavin focused his attention on the cozy scene before him. He'd been there for an inordinately long time, just staring and watching, waiting to feel his irritation subside. But with each passing moment he felt his irritation turn to something far more unsettling.

As he watched Jane and her friends frolic and laugh on the blanket in the middle of Hyde Park, the Serpentine glistening in the sunlight behind them, he felt the first stirrings of jealousy. He had never before experienced the emotion--certainly not in relation to a woman with another man. He had never given a farthing about the women he had been with and whom they might also be sharing their favors with. But obviously it was not so for the woman in the pink striped gown and wide brimmed straw bonnet.

It had been an hour at least since three gentlemen had joined them. An hour since he'd sat hidden amongst the trees, watching as Jane smiled and glowed under male perusal.

Damn him for coming today. What sort of fool had he been to search her out? And why the bloody hell was he unable to signal his mount to move forward and announce his presence? Why couldn't he take his eyes off the fetching figure in pink and return to the riding path?

The wind gusted, unravelling Jane's already wildly flapping bonnet strings. With a laugh that was carried on the breeze, he saw her smile as the wind lifted her bonnet from her head and carried it to the grass. He watched with growing unease as one of the gentlemen jumped up to retrieve it. He returned it to her with a flourish, bowing before her, presenting it proudly to her like a faithful spaniel would present a grouse to its master.

His fingers tightened on the reins when the man insisted on helping her retie the bonnet strings and he swore viciously when he saw her lower her eyes and smile shyly. Bloody hell, the rogue was taking his time about securing the damned bonnet. He was probably leering down the front of her bodice. Damn it, but he hadn't ever noticed just how scandalously cut her gowns were. He looked to her friends and saw that they wore the same neckline, but their breasts were not anywhere near as lavishly displayed as Jane's.

Rama snorted and pranced as the bit dug into his mouth. "Sorry, my friend," he muttered, loosening his hold. "You see, I am much like you when you sniff another male around Sita."

The horse's black head turned, considering his master with his large brown eyes. Despite his foul mood, Gavin grinned, amused that the only word Rama understood from him was Sita--the name of his future breeding mate. He'd had to move Rama to a different stable owing to the fact the stallion was crashing down walls to get to the mare. Bloody hell, he scoffed, he was talking to his horse and drawing analogies between the two of them. What the devil was the matter with him?

Giggling once again drew his attention to the happy party, and he shifted and tensed when he saw the gentleman grasp Jane's hand and raise her from the blanket. Who the bloody hell was this upstart with Jane? And why the devil was she allowing him to guide her to the water's edge? She shouldn't be leaving with the man. It wasn't a damn bit proper, and Lady Jane Westbury was the epitome of everything proper. Wasn't she?

His mouth twisted in disgust as the young man he knew to be Lord Winterbourne raised her gloved hand to his mouth and lowered his lips to her knuckles. Bloody hell, what was this? Was *he* the reason she hadn't been able to meet with him to continue their lessons? Was he the *'obligation she must see to'*?

Grinding his teeth in order to prevent himself from savagely gripping the reins, Gavin watched the interlude with something akin to murderous rage. Damn her and her beguiling smiles. Damn her for awakening a part of him he never knew existed and didn't particularly care to have.

It was all happening too fast; the butterfly was emerging from her chrysalis much too precipitously. He hadn't wanted it to be this way. He had wanted to draw it out, to spend more than a night with her. He wanted her emergence to be with him. He wanted to be the first to see her wings flutter out of her cocoon.

What did it matter to him if he wasn't the one? It wasn't as though she owed him anything, nor did he owe her a thing. He wasn't going to marry her, wasn't going to give her children. What did it matter that she had set her sights on someone else, someone who would give her what she wanted? After all, she had made her desires perfectly clear. She wanted a lover who would be captivated by her. A lover who would turn into a husband and a father.

He thought of Jane full and heavy with a babe as he watched her standing beside the Serpentine. He envisioned hands, large and dark, stroking her swollen belly. They were not the hands of the young lord smiling wistfully beside her. They were his hands. It was *his* fingers possessively sliding along her belly. *His* child in her womb. Bloody hell, he had gone daft. As sure as the sun was in the sky, he was bloody well mad.

He didn't want a wife. He didn't want children. Why would he bring children into the world to suffer the stigma that he had suffered? He wouldn't do it. He would not subject an innocent babe to the taunts of bastardy and savage blood.

He had made the decision and never given it another thought. So why today, when he was watching Jane with another man did he imagine her carrying his babe? How had an image so vivid and clear invaded his waking mind?

He knew the reason. He refused to credit it, but it lingered nevertheless. He wanted to mean something more to Jane than just a tutor in the sexual arts.

A snort sounded from the bridal path, sending Rama's ears flickering. Before anyone could happen upon him, he motioned Rama around and headed back to the path. As he emerged from the trees he was met with a pair of lovely grey eyes.

"Good day," Lady Catriona Hamilton smiled invitingly. "I thought I saw you there. There's no mistaking you, after all, is there?"

Gavin stopped his mount and blinked. Lady Catriona was looking him over like a prize ham at the butchers.

"Good day, Lady Hamilton," he nodded, removing his hat and inclining his head.

"Your mount is extremely beautiful," she said, coyly appraising Rama. "He is a stallion?"

"He is."

"So broad in the shoulders," she murmured, assessing the width of him in his riding coat when she should have been gazing at his mount. "I'll wager there is no end to his stamina, is there?"

"He is very strong," he said with lack of interest.

Catriona smiled and moistened her lips. "Why don't you come closer and introduce your stallion to my mare? I think he's already caught the scent of her, don't you?" She flicked her eyes along him, letting her gaze rest at the juncture of his thighs. When her eyes came up to meet his, they were sparkling with amusement and desire. "Yes, I most definitely think your stallion is eager to meet my mare. I can see," she said, boldly returning her gaze to his breeches, "that you might think it just the thing to join the two of them together."

The double entendre made him grow cold. The lady's intention could not be more blatant. And contrary to what she might think of the bulge in his breeches, it had nothing to do with her flagrant suggestion or her very lovely person. But it did have everything to do with the woman sequestered behind him, the image of her smiling and naked beneath him still flashed through his mind making him swell uncomfortably beneath his fawn colored breeches.

"I'm afraid I must be going," he muttered, nodding once more. "Enjoy your ride, my lady."

"I'd enjoy it much more if you were sharing it," she said huskily, reaching for Rama's reins as he nudged the horse forward.

"I have an appointment."

"Yes you do," she purred, before leaning forward and whispering to him. "Tonight, Lord Grayson, in my bed. I'm looking forward to finding you there."

And then she cantered off, headed toward the bridle path to join the rest of her party. A husky laugh invaded his shock, and he realized that he only had to think of Jane in order to be aroused. Not even the notion of sleeping with Lady Hamilton, the woman acclaimed to be the most beautiful in the *ton*, could arouse him as thoroughly as Jane's innocent laughter.

The devil take it, he was in a bad way. Perhaps he should take her ladyship up on her offer. Maybe a night spent between Catriona's thighs would rid him of the niggling anger he felt at seeing Jane with another. But when he closed his eyes and envisioned a night spent in dissipation, the only person he saw was Jane, her plump thighs spread for him, her arms welcoming him, her smile warming him.

Good God, what had the chit done to him?

Chapter Seven

Jane steadied her hand, careful not get a drop of red punch on her gown. Her hand was shaking so severely she thought she might disgrace herself by spilling the entire contents of her glass. It was all because of him, she muttered to herself.

"Look at that," Emily Beaumont, her very good friend whispered to her. "Lady Hamilton has done everything but offer herself on a platter to the man."

Jane took a delicate little sip of her punch and willed her stomach to stop churning. What was the matter with her? It wasn't as though she hadn't seen Gavin cavorting about ballrooms with women before. Good Lord, she'd watched him more times than she cared to admit as he danced and strolled about with his conquests. She had even spied on him with his doxies, for heavens sake. But it had never felt like this. Like having a sword slowly thrusting through her heart.

"He is outrageously handsome, isn't he?" Emily sighed. "That hair, it's so black and shiny. Like silk, don't you think?"

Jane nodded and took another sip. If felt like silk, too. She remembered the feel of it sliding through her hands. Recalled how he had looked with it unbound as he pleasured himself. It was unbound tonight. He had defied every polite dictate of dress and wore his hair long and untied.

Her gaze flickered to where he stood in the corner of the room where Catriona Hamilton monopolized his attentions. He looked breathtaking dressed in gold silk breeches and a black velvet frockcoat with a restrained amount of gold threading around the cuffs and collar. While other men wore coats heavily embroidered with gold and gems in glaring shades of pink and green and lace cuffs as thick as hers, Gavin looked regal and subdued in black and a minimum of lace.

"He really does have the most intriguing eyes, don't you think?" Emily whispered. "His gaze has a queer intensity to it, like he's undressing you and seeing what's beneath all the corsets and petticoats." Emily took a sip of her punch and licked a drop from her lips. "He's looking at you, you know."

Jane promptly choked and began to cough. Gavin was looking at her? He hadn't even glanced her way all evening. Discreetly she tilted her head in order to see him better. Their eyes met over the pink plume perched in Lady Hamilton's white wig. His expression was implacable, unreadable. His green gaze was hooded but she felt the heat from his eyes cutting into her. Was he undressing her? Was he recalling just how unfashionable she was when she was naked in his arms?

And then he very slowly lowered his gaze to his companion's face and smiled. The glass slipped from Jane's hand, shattering into thousands of twinkling shards beneath the candlelight. He had never smiled at her. The thought reminded her of just how undesirable she truly was.

"Good heavens," Emily gasped, pulling her out of her shocked state. "Jane, are you well? Jane?" she asked again, shaking her arm.

"What have I done?" she whispered, coloring profusely as people began to stare at her. "I don't know what happened," she muttered, lowering herself to her knees.

"For heavens sake, Jane," Emily hissed, grasping her elbow. "Don't pick it up, everyone is watching."

Was he watching? Or was his gaze still firmly fixed on the outrageously beautiful Lady Hamilton?

"Come with me," Emily said, leading her to the refreshment table. "Act as though it slipped from your hand and you're returning for another. Smile, Jane," her friend commanded.

Pasting a false smile on her face, Jane allowed Emily to manoeuvre her to the buffet. She darted her eyes to the corner where Gavin and Catriona had been standing seconds before, but they were no longer there. They had probably left, searching for an empty room to carry out their amorous congress. The thought made her feel ill. She wanted to be the only woman in Gavin's life, but how did she stand a chance against someone as perfect as Catriona Hamilton?

"Here," Emily commanded, shoving a plate in her hand. "Put something to eat on this and pretend that nothing is wrong."

She reached for a pastry, filled with rich cream and smothered in chocolate. The delightful morsel would do the trick. Food had always comforted her when Archie would not. Surely it would soothe her now. Her gloved fingers reached for the pastry at the same time a pair of dark fingers did. She pulled back and looked up into a pair of familiar jade eyes. They studied each other and

Jane felt the beating of her heart in her throat.

"Oh, let her have it," simpered Catriona who stood beside him, batting her lashes and fanning herself. "I don't eat sweets. Look what they do to you."

Jane felt her face flame and she automatically dropped the éclair back onto the silver platter. His lips parted, as if he were about to say something but then he closed them, remaining silent. Jane lowered her lashes and blinked away the tears that were steadily forming behind her lids. She went to snatch her hand away when Gavin reached for it and pressed her fingers in his. He kissed her hand then, a polite, solicitous kiss before slowly raising his gaze to hers. "My apologies, madam."

She watched him closely, wondering who he was apologizing for, himself, or the ignorant doxy who stood beside him heaving her bosom and her fan.

"Accepted, sir," she said, forcing her lips to stop trembling. She really needed to leave the room before she disgraced herself. She didn't want to cry before the *ton*, and she most especially didn't want to cry in front of Catriona. To let Lady Hamilton know her comment had achieved its mark would be unbearable.

"May I?" Gavin asked, taking her plate and motioning to the platter the éclairs were on.

"Thank you, no," she said, smoothing her hand down her bodice. "I fear I have lost my appetite. Please excuse me," she mumbled, wishing she could run from the room before he noticed her tears. "I believe I require some fresh air."

"Would you like me to join you?" Emily whispered.

"No, I just need a few minutes," she whispered back before heading off for the safety of the terrace.

Once outside, she lifted her skirts and ran for the maze that loomed opposite the terrace. She would have all the privacy she craved amongst the immaculately trimmed cedars.

Nearly blind with tears, Jane rounded the corner and found a bench. She sat on the cold marble and stared impotently up at the moon. Why did she let comments like that from Catriona hurt her? She'd heard thinly veiled insults before and had brushed them aside with ease and the knowledge that the person was an ignorant fool. But she could not brush aside Catriona's insult because it had been said in front of Gavin. And that, Jane admitted, as the tears began to roll down her cheeks was what was so painful. In some wistful part of her heart, she had pretended that Gavin's agreement to tutor her stemmed not from his rogue appetites and his desire to corrupt her as he had so straightforwardly put it, but rather he had agreed because he had desired her. Because he found her beautiful and voluptuous and because he *wanted* to bring her to his bed. And Catriona's ridicule had dashed away all hope that Gavin would remain ignorant of her shortcomings.

"Jane." The warm hand on her shoulder was his. She turned away from the concern she heard. "Look at me, Jane," he said quietly as he sat down on the bench next to her. She lowered her head, fighting back more of the tears. She didn't want him to see her this way, weak spirited and self-conscious.

"Don't do this, *shundori*." He hooked his finger beneath her chin and forced her to meet his gaze. His eyes softened when he saw a tear roll out and trickle down to her lip. "Jane," he said tenderly, wiping the wetness from her mouth. "Let me take the pain away."

Then his lips were soft against hers, his fingers strong as he wrapped them around her nape and brought her closer to him, deepening the kiss. Her mouth parted on a protest, but he took it as an invitation to slide his tongue inside. His kiss was slow, thorough, drugging in its intensity. Slanting his mouth against hers, he deepened the kiss. His tongue became more forceful, and he groaned.

She didn't want him to kiss her out of pity. She was not so lost in passion that she forgot his words seconds before his mouth descended to hers.

"Don't run away from me, *shundori*," he commanded, bringing her closer so that the tops of her breasts grazed his lace cravat. She tried to pull away again, but he anchored his fingers on her neck and tilted her head so that he could penetrate her mouth deeper.

"Don't," she whispered, wrenching free of his embrace. He held her tighter, refusing to let her move away from him.

"Beauty is in the eye of the beholder, Jane. Surely you haven't forgotten that."

And what beauty had he beheld tonight? It certainly wasn't hers. No, it all belonged to Catriona Hamilton. How would she ever compete with her stunning beauty? How could she ever rival her for Gavin's attentions?

"You have something she will never have, Jane. You're kind and thoughtful. You bring joy to people's lives."

"Those are qualities that you would attribute to a faithful dog," she spat, rubbing her arms against the sudden chill that hung in the maze. She had never before considered herself vain, but damn him, she wanted to be more to him than kind and loyal. "I don't need your empty attempts at consolation, my lord. Nor do I desire to be kissed out of pity."

"I wasn't kissing you out of pity," he said, rising from the bench and pulling her up against him. "I kissed you because I wanted to."

"You cannot possibly look at me and tell me you desire me over ... her."

"You would not believe me even if I did."

She knew it. She couldn't compare to Lady Hamilton, and he had tried to salvage her ego by turning the tables on her. She was a fool to have entered into this bargain with him. How could she believe that after evading him for two days that he would come to her on bended knee? That he would be on fire for her. Desire her? All this time she had thought she was being so clever. What a fanciful simpleton she was. He hadn't been yearning for her, because he'd been slaking his desires with Catriona.

"I must leave."

"Why, Jane?"

"I have something to do."

"Is it that irritating obligation again?" he asked mockingly. She ignored him and raised the hem of her skirts before stepping around him. He reached for her arm and held it firmly in his grasp. "Winterbourne is not the sort of man you want, Jane."

She glared at his hand around her arm, then met his gaze. He was right. Winterbourne wasn't the type of man she wanted. There was only one man for her, and he couldn't be further from her reach.

"Winterbourne is an insolent pup. The lad is so green behind the ears that he couldn't organize a piss up at a Public House."

She steeled herself against his mockery. "He is young, but what does that matter, he's still able to give me what I need."

"Oh?" he asked, his voice lethal. "And what would that be, Jane?"

"He gives me something you never could."

His eyes narrowed and his fingers bit into her arm. "Why don't you explain that enigmatic statement, Lady Westbury?"

"Every time I'm with him, he gives a piece of himself. He is not afraid, Lord Grayson. And that is all I desire."

Chapter Eight

He is not afraid. He gives a piece of himself to me and that is all I desire.

Jane would never know how her words had haunted him. He had spent the last week in agony, pondering her statement and chastising himself for not being what Jane had needed the night Catriona Hamilton slighted her.

Bloody hell, he was an ass. Why couldn't he have comforted her and told her what she needed to hear? Why was it so bloody hard for him to let her glimpse his desire for her?

Bloody right it was difficult. She might discover what truly lay in his heart, and that he could never allow. She could never learn that in his cold, unfeeling heart she had warmed and softened a corner and made it just her own.

As he stalked along Oxford Street without any thought of where he was going or what he was about, Gavin allowed himself to remember the night he had held a crushed and weeping Jane in his arms. She could have no way of knowing that his kiss had been heartfelt and the only time he had ever pressed his lips to a woman's mouth without expecting anything in return. In his own awkward and inexperienced way, he had tried to comfort her. How was he to know that Jane was beyond his miniscule skill? Why hadn't he seen that kissing Jane had only ignited the rampant insecurities that coursed within her?

If there was one thing he was an expert at, it was women and their emotions. He had learned to read the signs and retreat when he didn't like what he saw. There was not a woman out there who made him unsure of his skill. But Jane had. He had missed the fact that what she had needed was more than his kiss, or his hand against her breast. She had needed words and words were admittedly something he didn't do well.

She was right, he was afraid.

If he told her how he felt about her, she would hold too much power over him. While he knew Jane was kind and for the most part not conniving, the fact still remained she was a woman, and women were the masters of emotional manipulation. He had never been in danger of succumbing to their wiles, but he had come damn close when he had seen tears spill from Jane's lovely eyes.

He stopped and looked around at his surroundings, taking stock of where he was and just how far he had wandered from his home in Portman Square. He looked up and saw the black and gold sign of Thompson jewellers. He'd travelled a great distance with only his thoughts of Jane for company.

He looked at the sparkling gems shining in the window and then he saw her, a more brilliant diamond than any displayed in the glass cases. His body tightened and his eyes hungrily scoured her from head to foot. He could not stop himself from stepping into the shop.

"Good day, Jane."

Jane hid the tremor that lanced through her when she heard the viscount's deep and melodious voice address her. Replacing the lapis lazuli bracelet she had been admiring back into its nest of white silk, Jane turned and smiled politely. "Good day to you, Lord Grayson. Out for a stroll?"

"Indeed." He grinned, but it was not warm, it was rather forced and tight on his beautifully sculpted lips. "And you?"

"Oh, just waiting for Lord Winterbourne and his sister," she said, motioning to where they stood talking with the shopkeeper. "It's their mother's birthday and they are buying her a pair of ruby earrings."

She watched as he turned his head to study the pair, noticing how his eyes turned a frostier shade of green when his gaze raked Lord Winterbourne. "And you prefer lapis?" he said turning his gaze back to her, then picking up the bracelet and watching as the gold streak in the stones flashed in the sunlight.

"Why yes. I think lapis is a most startling gem. The blue is like nothing I've ever seen before."

"Lapis is the gem of the Sultan, did you know that, Jane?"

"I did not. Another lesson, perhaps? I vow, you are a most knowledgeable tutor."

He reached for her hand, and his finger traced her skin below the cuff of her glove and slowly, with his back concealing his actions from Winterbourne and the shopkeeper, he slipped the bracelet around her wrist. "Lapis, Jane, was the most prized jewel in the harem. It represented passion and lust, and when the Sultan gave it to one of his odalisques, it was assumed that she had become his favored concubine."

"How very interesting," she breathed, watching as his fingers closed the clasp of the bracelet.

"The Sultan only gave lapis to the women who pleased him, who fulfilled every one of his whims. The symbol became one of ownership and desirability. Every time the woman wore it, everyone in the harem knew she had pleased as well as pleasured the Sultan."

"This is really very interesting," she said, attempting to slide the bracelet from her wrist. "But I'm afraid that I shall have to defer this lesson until another time. I have promised to attend Lady Carstairs' salon with Lord Winterbourne and his sister, and I see that they are preparing to leave."

He ignored her and slid the bracelet further down her wrist. "Lapis from the Sultan meant the slave belonged to him and only him. He did not share her with any man, Jane."

"Really, sir, this is most inappropriate--"

"The woman wore the lapis because she was proud to have caught the attentions of the Sultan, and she was not ashamed to have everyone know she had shared her body with him. The lapis was his mark and she wore it as a reminder to herself that she belonged to him. When he saw his stones draped on her, the Sultan knew that his slave belonged to him in all ways a woman can belong to a man."

Jane watched as he motioned to the young clerk that was busy dusting the shelves. When the man stood before him, Gavin reached into his waistcoat pocket and passed him his calling card. "Make an account for me and put this on it." He pointed at the bracelet and the clerk nodded, taking his leave. Then he returned his gaze to her. "The Sultan was extremely discriminating in who received his special gift, Jane. Not every woman was deserving."

"Really, it--"

"I have never given a woman a gift of lapis, Jane. In fact, I've never purchased a gift for a female who was not my mother or sister."

"Really, sir, I cannot accept such a gift."

His expression turned harder and his eyes raked coldly over her. "A simple thank you is all I require, Jane."

She looked down at the bracelet and then back up into his eyes. "Thank you does not seem like enough, my lord, for such an extravagant gift."

"It is enough, *shundori*."

She wanted to tell him how much she missed him, but she could not. To do so would be to make herself vulnerable, and Gavin was the last man she should let see her insecurities.

"When can I see you again?" he asked, stepping closer to her so that she was forced to tilt her face up to look at him.

"You are seeing me right now, my lord."

He cleared his throat and pretended to be civil, but she could see a muscle tensing and tightening in his jaw. "I meant, when will you be ready to continue your lessons?"

She looked nervously about the shop, trying to will herself not give in to temptation. "I'm not certain. I have quite a few obligations to see to."

"I see," he said, straightening away from her.

"Ah, there you are," Lord Winterbourne's voice called to her. "Still staring at those ugly stones, I see. You should be looking at diamonds and rubies, my dear. They would become you. Grayson," he started, stopping mid-sentence as if he couldn't quite believe the sight before him.

"Winterbourne."

"I didn't know you were acquainted with the viscount," he asked her, his blue eyes raking over her face, the wheels of his mind calculating and wondering just how intimately she knew Gavin.

"His lordship was telling me the fascinating tale behind the lapis."

"Was he?" Winterbourne said archly before reaching for her hand and placing it in the crook of his arm. "Well, I'm certain it was a rather fascinating tale. His people always put such a colorful bent to everything, but shall we, my dear? My sister is positively chomping at the bit--you know how impatient young girls can be."

"Indeed," she said, sweeping her gaze once more along Gavin's hard, unyielding face. "A very interesting lesson, my lord," she said, motioning to the bracelet. "I'm certain I won't forget it."

He looked at Winterbourne and then back to her, arching one black brow. "See that you don't."

* * * *

Raising his crystal goblet to his mouth, Gavin gulped at the port, watching with growing anger as the crowd of hot-blooded bucks surrounded Jane. Bloody hell, how had they discovered her so soon? A week ago she had blended into the background, barely garnering any notice--and now she had some of the most notorious men of the *ton* flocking about her. How had the caterpillar transformed so quickly into the sparkling butterfly?

Dammit could they see it also? Did they see that Jane's beauty was ethereal and fresh? Did their jaded eyes covet her refreshing innocence like he coveted it? Damn her, she shouldn't look at men that way. He slammed his glass down on the tray of a passing footman. Ignoring the servant's scowl, he helped himself to another glass of champagne and drank it in one long swallow, watching as Jane smiled sweetly. She might not flirt like the experienced women of the *ton*, but she damn well knew what she was about. She had her admirers eating from the palm of her hand with only a shy smile and the blush of pale skin.

How he wished he could stroll over to where she stood surrounded by these men and take her by the hand, showing everyone in the room that he was her lover and that she belonged to him. The pain of watching her amass admirers--that might one day become her lover--was akin to a drowning man watching the shore slip further and further away. He was drowning, he finally admitted. Drowning in the allure of Lady Jane Westbury.

Out of champagne, he searched the room for another footman, when he felt the coolness of crystal and the smoothness of silk glide along his hand.

"You look like you could use something."

Catriona Hamilton. Gavin stifled a groan. The last thing he needed or wanted was her.

"Such tedious company," she purred next to him. "I'm certain you can come up with ways to make the night more enjoyable."

She smiled behind her flickering fan and batted her eyelashes outrageously. Her flirting had no effect on him, and he unconsciously sought out Jane, noticing how his body reacted when she smiled shyly at Lord Winterbourne. No, Jane was a miserable failure in the art of flirting, but a veritable expert at wielding her innocence. How could any man resist her charm and openness? Indeed, no man could, not even him, a rake who was corrupt and jaded and immune to the charms of women.

Even now his cock was stirring to life in his breeches. She looked much too beautiful tonight in an ice blue gown that dipped far too low along her ample bosom. Every man was staring after her, intrigued by innocent smiles and blushes juxtaposed with a lush body that was made for sinning.

"Why don't we go out into the gardens?" Catriona whispered

behind her fan.

"I don't think so," Gavin mumbled before downing the entire glass of champagne. He really must control himself or else he'd be nothing but a stumbling drunkard. He had no desire for Jane to see in him such a state. To be drunk was weak, and he damn well would not let Lady Jane Westbury know that she could reduce to him to such lowness. Besides, he didn't want his senses dulled by imbibing too much. No, he could not have that. Tonight when he was fully sheathed in Jane's tight, welcoming body, he wanted to be fully aware of every tremor, every quake that rippled through her.

"Searching out other conquests?" Catriona's eyes narrowed and turned cold before she searched the room and found Jane. "Don't tell me you've fixed your roving eye on that one," she laughed. "The unbearably proper Lady Jane? Really, Grayson, she would run in fear from you. Why would she want a man who would ruin her the same way her husband did? Can you really imagine Jane Westbury enjoying lying beneath you? Good God," she chuckled, "the chit would swoon the minute she saw the size of you. And more importantly, she would never sully her reputation by having her name linked with yours. Everyone in the *ton* knows what sort of woman Lady Jane is. She's the maddening sort that wishes to be a wife and mother--she's certainly not about to become your whore."

Any thought Gavin had about giving Catriona the cut direct and heading for Jane vanished the second he heard her words. Any connection with him would surely ruin Jane's chances of making an advantageous match. No man would want her after discovering that she'd been with him.

Normally, he would have rejoiced in such an epiphany--but not in regards to Jane. With her he could not be the revenge-seeking viscount. She wasn't like the others--the ones who whispered behind his back and cut his mother and sister leaving them weeping and broken. Jane had never expressed anything more than curiosity and interest in his upbringing. She hadn't treated him like the India Rat; she hadn't looked at him like he was nothing better than a servant set to please her. Jane was good and kind, and he owed her some measure of decency. He owed it to her to stay away.

"She seems to be finally coming into her own after Westbury left her," Catriona muttered as her eyes contemptuously raked Jane. "I'm certain that discovering her insufferable husband's untimely demise in his mistress' bed no doubt vanquished any lingering regrets she might have felt about the man." She took a deep breath, making certain her large bosom brushed the arm of his jacket. "She's not very pretty, but that doesn't seem to detract Winterbourne and his friends from admiring her. Perhaps they like plump women." She shrugged. "Winterbourne has been by her side all week. I wonder if the two have become lovers?"

Gavin snapped his head from Catriona to Jane, who was being led out on to the floor by Winterbourne. His insides clenched when the music started and Jane curtseyed to Winterbourne, her cheeks pink. Her smile was almost intimate, and he swore that he'd kill him if he'd taken Jane as his lover. When he had seen them together that morning in the shop he had been irked, but thought it impossible that Jane would find the pompous Winterbourne worthy of her time or affections. That night in the maze, her retort about the pup had been said in the heat of anger, he was certain. Now, when he looked at them, as Winterbourne bowed slowly before her, he wondered if the bastard had already gotten between her thighs.

Was it possible Jane had found herself a suitor? Was that the reason she had rebuffed him all week, ignoring his presence in the ballrooms and his missives requesting that they continue their 'lessons'? Had she already learned all she could from him? Was Winterbourne tutoring her?

He saw Jane smile again as Winterbourne led her down the line, and Gavin realized he'd give his fortune to have her smile at him in such a way. Bloody hell, he'd give up what was left of his soul if only to have her in his life. But he was not like Winterbourne. He didn't come from impeccable bloodlines. He wasn't fair and blond and lithe. He was dark like the devil and tainted with the blood of a half-breed. He shouldn't covet Jane for himself, and he most certainly hadn't the right to be angry with her for attracting the attentions of such a man. After all, she had employed his skills for that purpose. He was to tutor her in the art of seduction, and it was obvious she was a master pupil.

"You've become rather dour," Catriona said, reminding him of her presence beside him. "I thought you were always game for sport in the bedroom."

"My tastes these days seem to settle on harder won quarry."

"I see," she said, fanning herself and looking away. "I suppose you're pining for Plain Jane. Well, let me tell you something, Grayson. After you've attempted to lure her into your bed, do not make the mistake of coming crawling back to me when she refuses you. For refuse you she will. You're not what she wants. You're the sort of gigolo that is exciting for a night, perhaps two, but nothing more."

"And you," he growled, "are not even the sort one remembers."

She snapped her fan shut and walked with swan-like grace through the crowd. Angry, Gavin stalked from the room, prepared to find something--anything that might take his mind off the way Jane looked in Winterbourne's company.

She looked right for the young lord and the thought that Winterbourne might have discovered the treasure he had already unearthed goaded him into a black fit of temper that he hadn't experienced since his youth.

Aye, he needed something to take his mind off Lady Jane Westbury.

Chapter Nine

Jane smiled up at Lord Winterbourne and over his lordship's shoulder watched Gavin's retreating form. Perhaps she had made a giant miscalculation when she set out to teach him his own lesson. Mayhap he would never yearn and burn, or be lured by her evasiveness. Obviously she was not the sort of woman to inspire such feeling in him. He had hardly looked at her since entering the ballroom, and Jane felt her heart constrict tightly in her chest when she thought of how Catriona had come sidling up beside him, her fan artfully swaying before her lovely face.

For some damnable reason their meeting that afternoon had filled her with hope that he might feel something for her. Obviously she had been a victim once more of her overly hopeful heart.

She watched as the countess stood by his side for some time, then left with Gavin following in her path not long after her departure. Was he going to her? Was he meeting her like he had the Duchess of Manchester and Lady Lennox that night a few short weeks ago?

Jealousy and fear consumed her and she lost concentration, stepping on Lord Winterbourne's foot. "I beg your pardon, my lord," she gasped, humiliated by her blunder.

"Don't be a goose, Lady Westbury, it was an accident I'm sure."

Jane tried to grin, but her lips froze in a grimace as she saw Lady Hamilton leave the room. Obviously she was meeting with the viscount.

"What is it?" Lord Winterbourne asked, pulling her by the arm to the fringes of the floor. "You've gone frighteningly pale, my dear. Are you ill? Can I bring you a refreshment?"

"Just some fresh air," she asked, as numerous eyes looked their way. "And perhaps some privacy."

"Of course," he said, placing her gloved hand on his arm and navigating them to one of the doors. "Let us find a quiet room in which to sit and refresh yourself. In truth you've gone quite white. Are you certain you're not ill?"

"Merely warm," she said as Lord Winterbourne guided her down the candlelit hall and opened a door. They were in a small salon, and Lord Winterbourne strolled over to a window and opened it, letting in a breeze that immediately cooled her heated skin.

"Why do you not sit and make yourself comfortable?"

Jane looked to the settee and then to Winterbourne. "I'm not certain that Lady Wessex would approve of us in her salon."

Winterbourne waved her comment aside and reached for her hand, pulling her to the settee. "We shan't dawdle here. Surely you could sit for a minute or two to revive your constitution."

Jane gulped uneasily as his lordship helped her to sit. He plopped himself beside her and grazed his finger along her cheek. "Might I kiss you, dearest Jane?" he began. "I've wondered all week what your rosebud lips would feel like against mine."

Her heart lurched, and Jane was powerless to move. She didn't want to be kissed by Winterbourne. She wanted Lord Grayson-- Gavin. Gavin would never have asked her if he could kiss her. No, he would have just done so, not allowing her an opportunity to refuse. Gavin never asked, he took and controlled, and Jane always felt herself breathless at his mastery. She didn't want a weak man. Archie had been weak. Winterbourne was only a boy given to romantic poetry. Gavin was a man. She would give anything to have Gavin desire her.

"Lady Jane," Winterbourne murmured as he pressed closer, taking her hand in his. "I have thought of no one but you. You have enchanted me, my lady and I will stop at nothing to possess you."

"Lord Winterbourne!" Jane gasped when she felt his weight atop her.

Gavin heard the startled shriek as he was helping himself to Lord Wessex's brandy. Replacing the decanter, he strolled to the door that separated the study from another room. Cracking it open he saw Lord Winterbourne atop Jane.

His first instinct was to hurtle himself into the room and tear Winterbourne to shreds, but something stopped him. The desire to find out just how Jane would respond to Winterbourne's cumbersome attempt at seduction froze him in his spot.

"Jane," Winterbourne grunted as he reached for her mouth and missed, hitting her chin. "My lovely Jane. How I want you."

"Lord Winterbourne," Jane panted, pinned beneath his weight.

"I'm certain that this is not the place for such behavior. We shall be discovered."

"Then tell me, dearest Jane, where is the place? Where can we indulge this desire that is growing steadily between us?"

Gavin's hand squeezed the latch until his fingers went numb and white. Damn Winterbourne, he was saying all the right things. It would only be a matter of minutes before the bastard had his hand up her skirt. And that, Gavin could not watch.

"I would do anything for you, Jane," Winterbourne pleaded, hugging Jane in his arms while he nuzzled his face between her décolletage. "I want to spend forever with you. If I've learned nothing else from our time spent together this past week, it's that I want to spend the rest of my life with you."

Gavin felt like he'd been punched, unsuspecting, in the gut. He fought through the pain and realized that Jane and Winterbourne had been spending time together. While *he* had been brooding and lonely, *she* had been lifting her skirts for the young pup, implementing every lesson she'd learned at his hands.

"I really must be going," she said, straightening her bodice before raising her hands to her hair. "Perhaps tomorrow we might continue this discussion."

"I shall be there, dearest Jane," Winterbourne vowed. "I will be there tonight if only you would allow me."

"Lord Winterbourne," Jane said, smiling that damnable smile that made him lose his train of thought. "I'm afraid I cannot. Not tonight."

"Then I shall lie awake all night praying for a quick end to the darkness and for the sunlight to carry me to your doorstep."

Bloody fool, Gavin thought as he watched the young pup go on bended knee and kiss Jane's hand. He was making an ass of himself. Gavin would have felt some measure of pity for the young man had he not set his sights on the woman that *he* wanted.

The door closed behind Jane, and Gavin let himself into the salon.

"Get up, Winterbourne."

The young man stood, shock registering in his face. "Grayson."

"A touching scene and one that will never be repeated, do you understand?"

"I'm afraid you have me at a disadvantage, for I have no idea of what you are speaking of."

"Jane Westbury," Gavin said through clenched teeth. "You're

not to see her again, do you understand me?"

The insolent pup at the audacity to laugh. "And who are you to issue orders to me? What is Jane Westbury to you? You are beneath her, sir."

"You've been warned, Winterbourne," he growled, thinking it prudent to leave the young lordling before he beat him to a bloody pulp.

"And what if I choose not to heed your warning?"

"Then you and I shall meet at dawn and I will take great delight in slicing you open from your throat to your ballocks."

Winterbourne blanched but refused to back down. "I'm not certain why you've chosen to interfere in my affairs, Grayson, but I will tell you now, that Jane is mine."

"You've been warned."

"I will not give her up to some half-breed son of a whore who thinks he can strong-arm me."

Blinding anger seized him, and Gavin found himself tossing Winterbourne against the wall, his forearm pressing against Winterbourne's lace covered throat. "Do not tempt me, Winterbourne. My half-breed blood is boiling and I'll have no compunction about killing you here without benefit of the niceties. Now," he said in his most threatening voice, "you will not throw yourself on Lady Westbury again. If I find that you've been bothering her, I'll see to emasculating you."

"What the bloody hell do you know, Grayson? We spent the afternoon together. She didn't even mention your name."

Fearing that he'd kill him right then and there, Gavin thrust Winterbourne against the wall and left the room. Bloody hell, he was out of control. He couldn't think, couldn't even see straight as he stalked down the hall and into the foyer where a footman opened the door for him.

Where the hell was Jane? Probably off with more of her suitors. Well, there was one sure way to meet up with the Lady.

Barking out orders to the coachman, Gavin waved away the assistance of a footman and let himself into the carriage. Slumping onto the leather squabs he flung his frock coat into the corner and loosened his waistcoat and cravat. His blood swam hot and angry in his veins and with a vicious jerk he pulled the cravat from his neck and tossed it atop the coat.

Voices came from the house and Gavin recognized Jane's melodic laughter followed by Winterbourne's baritone rumble. Bloody hell, he was going to have to do something about him.

THE ART OF PLEASURE

The carriage door opened and a woman climbed in and closed the door. "Good evening, Jane."

With a gasp, she covered her mouth, her dark eyes luminous and sparkling in the lantern light.

"Lord Grayson. Whatever are you doing in my carriage, sir?"

"Tutoring you, madam," he said, reaching for the straining buttons of his breeches. "Your education resumes with lesson number three, and that is--what a lady can expect when she plays games with a man. And you, Jane have been playing games with me."

Chapter Ten

"No ... I'm ... that is I'm not playing games...." Jane trailed off as the carriage lurched forward. Eyes wide, she moved the curtains aside to watch the enormous façade of the Wessex's townhouse disappear behind them.

A large hand reached out and captured her chin, forcing her to meet his hard gaze. "Think well before you lie to me, madam, for I am in no mood to indulge you."

Jane looked around the carriage and then to the window. Gray mist was rolling into the city and she felt as though she was being engulfed by a shroud as the carriage was lost in a thick patch of fog, blinding her. Gavin's fingers suddenly left her chin, only to land atop her hand. Uncurling her fingers from the velvet curtain, he grasped her hand in his and brought her wrist up to the lantern light. His fingers, dark against the ivory lace, pulled the cuff of her sleeve back, revealing the lapis bracelet he had purchased for her.

His gaze slid to hers and he arched a brow in smug satisfaction before he started to tug her toward him. "Now, Jane, you may arouse me with your hand."

"Surely you don't mean to do that sort of thing here?" He did not release his hold and instead increased the pressure of his hand on her fingers, pulling her from her seat until she was kneeling between his parted thighs.

"I can think of no better place to sit back and watch a lady pleasure me." He bent his leg, propping his boot on the bench, allowing her full access to the huge bulge in his breeches. His thighs were hard, the muscles pulling the delicate seams of his silk breeches taut, outlining the sheer strength in his legs. The negligent way he was sprawled on the bench contrasted with the commanding power Jane heard in his words, and the way his fingers, firm and assured, forced her with the barest touch to sink lower to the carriage floor.

"You've succeeded, Jane," he said as he reached once more for the gold buttons of his breeches, opening them one by one. "You've made me burn for you. Now is the time to wield your power, Jane. Seduce me." He reached for her hand and slid it up the length of his thigh to his groin, where she felt his erection lift and thicken beneath the silk. His eyes were riveted on her face. She could feel the heat of his stare, but her gaze was fixed firmly on her pale hand covered with his dark one as he slowly folded back the opening of his breeches and forced her fingers around the thick width of him.

"I am at your mercy, Jane," he sighed as she slid her hand up the silky length of him, the gold streaks in her lapis bracelet twinkling in the yellow lantern light. "But do not take too much comfort in that fact, Jane. I am quite certain our positions shall be reversed, for I shall have you at my mercy before the night is through."

"Would you like that?" she asked boldly as she watched the way her fingers traced the tip of his erection.

"The question is," he said, pushing the sleeves of her gown down over shoulders, "would you like it?" She gasped when the cool air met her skin, and her nipples tightened as her breasts swelled over the edge of her corset. Before she could react, he reached inside her corset and lifted her breasts, baring them to his burning eyes. Then he sat forward and grasped her about the waist, bringing her to the juncture of his thighs. Pulling her hand from his erection, he licked two of her fingers then brought them to the valley of her breasts, wetting her skin. Jane watched as he slowly stroked his erection, then brought its glistening tip to the firm mounds of her breasts before he circled her nipple with the wet tip.

"What shall I do with my cock, Jane?"

Her eyes flew to his face, searching for some sign of his intentions. Archie had never talked during their encounters and Jane was unaware that words between lovers could also arouse.

"You have beautiful breasts, Jane," he said as he brushed her nipple again with the wet tip of his erection. "I'd like to slide my cock between them. Part them for me, so that I may watch you with your hands on your breasts and my cock sliding between your flesh."

Her heart was beating maddeningly fast, and Jane was certain she had never been quite so wicked as she was when she was in the company of the viscount. He was so dark and commanding that Jane couldn't help but imagine him as a Sultan, and she, his dutiful slave, catering to his every whim and desire.

"That's it," he said, sliding the pink tip between her breasts. His hands covered hers on the sides, crushing her breasts together so that only the wet tip of his phallus could be seen. Jane watched in fascination as her breasts engulfed his erection, the deep breaths coming from him told her that he was watching too.

His fingers moved along her breasts until they reached her nipples. Taking each one between his fingers, he traced, pinched, then soothed them with the pad of his thumb. He thrust a few more times, watching as her breasts took his erection in.

"Have you ever had a cock in your mouth, Jane?"

Her eyes flew first to his shaft between her breasts then to his face. He was watching her carefully, and Jane thought she saw uncertainty flash in his eyes.

"I have not, my lord." Needing to please him, wanting to pleasure him, she lowered her head and touched the tip of her tongue to his penis. She heard him suck in a breath, and Jane, feeling emboldened, swirled her tongue around the tip.

"Take off your dress, Jane," he said, pulling his erection free. "I want you naked while you're on your knees. I want to see every inch of you before me. You've denied me, Jane, but not for much longer."

He wanted her. He had longed for her during the past week. The knowledge made her feel powerful, and maybe just a bit secure in the fact that the viscount sought her out this night, not because he was her tutor, but because he was thinking of himself as her lover.

Slowly she shed her gown, the silk puddled around her thighs like a blue cloud. Leaning forward, he placed his lips below her ear and kissed the sensitive flesh while his fingers stole around her back, loosening the ties of her corset.

"You're going to look stunning in nothing but ivory flesh and my cock in your mouth, do you know that, Jane?" She whimpered at the words and the feel of his tongue on her skin. "I have waited for more than a week to see you thus, and I will not wait an instant longer. This is what waiting does to a man, Jane." He tossed her corset to the floor and ripped her chemise down the center until her sex and thighs were bared to him. "It makes a man eager and rough. Does my crudeness offend you, Jane?" He removed the tattered chemise and smoothed his hand down her softly rounded belly. "Is your whimper out of fear or desire?"

She looked shyly away from him and attempted, almost unconsciously, to cover herself with her arms. Her bravado left her the instant she was naked. All of Archie's taunts came rushing back, and she squeezed her arms tightly around her middle as if to ward off Archie and Catriona's insults.

"Jane," he whispered, raking his hands through her hair and disturbing her coiffure. "This isn't what I desire. I do not want to see your arms shielding your beauty. I have not waited a week in order to have you hide from me." He raised her face to his mouth and kissed the corner of her lips. "Move your arms to your sides and let me look at you."

She shook her head, refusing to meet his gaze. She couldn't bear to see disappointment in his magnificent green eyes. She only wanted to see desire there. But he refused to listen to her pleas, and instead, took her hands and wrapped her arms around her waist. He secured her wrists against her bottom, holding her still with one of his hands. His other hand traced her skin from the hollow of her throat to the thatch of hair that shielded her sex. He let out a sigh and said something in Indian before resting his gaze on her face.

"Now then," he murmured. "Was your whimper out of fear or desire?"

"Desire," she said quietly.

"Then show me your desire, Jane." His fingers traced her face to her hair where he brushed her curls over shoulders until her hair trailed down her back. "Take me into your lovely mouth, my *shundori,* and show me your desire for me."

His fingers curled about her neck and slowly he lowered her head until her lips met the pink tip. His hand fisted around the shaft as he circled her mouth with his erection. Jane let her tongue come out in small, delicate flicks, first testing the feel and taste of him, then purposely drawing short, sucking breaths from him.

"Long licks, Jane. Trail your tongue along my cock. Let me see the pinkness of it against my skin."

Jane leaned forward and angled her head so that she slid her tongue from the base of his phallus to the very tip where a pearl-white drop rested. Unable to tear her gaze from his, she reached out and captured the drop with her tongue.

His lids lowered and Jane watched as he rested his head against the back of the squabs. He did not close his eyes, instead, he traced her cheeks, then her lips as she pleasured him with her tongue. When he began to squirm on the bench and his hand fisted tightly in her hair, she looked up and met his beautiful gaze, rendered turquoise in his desire. "Swallow my cock, Jane."

Then with his hand in her hair, he lowered her mouth to his swollen tip, forcing it past her lips, until the hard length of him was in her mouth.

"Bloody hell," he groaned as he flexed his hips, forcing his length further into her mouth. "You're going to make me come, Jane, and it's too bloody soon." Then he angled his hips again, and Jane sucked on his hard length, eliciting a long groan and a string of words she had never heard used. "Another time," he said, pulling his erection from her mouth. "Another time and I shall allow myself the sinful pleasure of coming in your hot mouth. But now," he said, reaching for her jewelled wrist and dragging her up from her knees. "I want to come inside your scalding heat. Are you hot and wet for me, Jane?"

He brought her atop him. Parting her thighs, she straddled his muscular legs. She felt shockingly exposed in this position, and she didn't know if she liked it or not.

"You're hot and wet, I can feel your honey seeping through the silk of my breeches. You're a *houri*, aren't you?" he whispered as he traced the contours of her body. "You're mine to command, aren't you, Jane?"

"Gavin...." his name was a breathless sigh as he captured her breasts in his hand. The rocking motion of the coach made her full breasts sway, and Jane saw that he watched them move with a look of longing and hunger.

"Raise your hands to the ceiling, Jane, and do not lower them until I say you may do so."

Lowering her bottom onto his lap, Jane reached above her head, her fingers entwined tightly together as the tips brushed the velvet covered ceiling.

"Up on your knees," he commanded, lifting her from his lap. "Now, arch your back and neck, Jane."

Closing her eyes, Jane did as he asked. Her long hair trailed down her back until the curling ends grazed against his breeches. Her hips were pushed forward, as were her breasts, and the rhythm of the coach made them sway provocatively until the peaks were hard buds, aching to be touched.

"Very nice," he purred, as his hands skimmed over her belly and hips. His fingers stole around to her buttocks then to the inner facing of her thighs, only to move up again and glide through the ends of her hair. His hands roamed her body, and Jane felt as though she were a slave he was examining before buying. His touch was soft and provocative, yet masterful, and

Jane responded to his words and his touch so easily. "You have a body made for a man to worship, Jane. Soft, welcoming, everything is there to indulge a man and his senses." Her breath left her lungs when he brushed her breasts with his hands, leaving them full and swaying--the nipples painfully hard. He repeated the motion, only this time firmer, leaving her breasts swaying more. She felt his erection stir beneath her and she saw that he stroked himself slowly while he watched her breasts bounce. "Tell me, Jane." His free hand kneaded a path from her belly to her mound. "How long has it been since you've had a cock imbedded in your sheath?"

Her lips trembled and she bit them, fighting the urge to whimper and writhe. When she squeezed her eyes shut, he reached for her bottom and spread her thighs further apart, then, sliding his finger along her wetness, he parted her sex and searched for the tight bud of flesh. Slowly he circled it, wetting it, sensitizing it until she lowered herself closer to the erect shaft that he began to rub along her wetness.

"How long, Jane?" he whispered against her throat, "since you've been with a man? A month?" He licked her neck as he swirled his erection around the bud, slowly building her desire. "A week?"

She moaned when he traced tiny circles beneath her ear, then matched the rhythm as he traced the outline of her opening. "How long, dearest Jane, since a man has slipped into your body and stretched you?"

"I-I ... don't know," she panted moving her hips in an attempt to have him slide his erection inside her. But he stilled her with a strong hand on her hip.

"Has it been a day, Jane?"

She looked down at him and felt his eyes, accusing and turbulent cut through her desire. When she tried to lower her hands, he shackled her wrists with his fingers and held her arms above her.

"Has Winterbourne been inside you, Jane?" His eyes swept over her body to where his phallus continued to outline the entrance of her clenching body. When he looked up at her, his eyes were daring and dark. "Have you let him fuck you, Jane?"

"No."

His fingers tightened around her wrists and his breathing became harsh in the quiet of the carriage. "How long, Jane? How long has it been since you've felt a man deep inside you, loving you, bringing you to completion?"

"Never," she whispered as he lowered her arms and brought her lips down against his.

"Then I shall be the first, Jane."

She felt his hands glide down her bottom and the tip of his shaft was nudging her entrance. "Let me inside, Jane," he whispered, "but only a little. I want to feel you stretch around me, inch by inch."

She did as he asked, sliding her body onto his erection and not resisting when he planted his hands around her waist and raised her, allowing the very tip of his erection to stay inside her.

"Again," he commanded.

Over and over, she sank her body on his length. Each time he allowed her to go further, and each time she moaned and tossed her head back, enjoying the feel of his hard length. When she went to slide down again, he stopped her and instead reached for her wrist, bringing it to his groin so that her fingers curled around his sex. It was hard and slick with her arousal and her stomach clenched as wetness seeped out of her body when she felt what would soon be claiming her. For that was his intention, she knew, as she raised her head and met his gaze. He wanted her to feel him, to know what and who would be deep inside her, loving her, completing her.

She stroked him, up and down, firming her grip on his shaft until his lids lowered and his fingers pinched and grasped her buttocks and then she leaned forward, and slowly impaled herself on his rampant length. He bucked up against her and reached for her hand, the one glistening with their arousal, and pressed it to her breast. When her nipple was wet and straining, he slipped it between his lips and sucked, his hips moving wildly beneath her as her breasts bounced in his mouth and his fingers tightened on her bottom.

"Gavin," she cried, matching his pace and forcing him to quicken his.

He said nothing, but placed his strong fingers on her buttocks, parting her and running his finger along her stretched rim. Knowing he was feeling himself penetrate her body made her eager and wet. With a small cry, she felt her body stiffen and allowed him to thrust deep inside her.

Her climax was quite literally blinding, and she fell against him, breathing harshly and tasting the saltiness of the sweat on his neck. But he would not let her rest. Instead, he palmed her again while he stroked her deeply. When his fingers were drenched with her arousal, he brought them to his lips and licked them. "I love your taste, my *shundori*," he murmured, and she felt his body tense beneath her. "I can't get enough of it. I can't get enough of you." He splashed his seed deep inside her and clutched her tight to his chest.

Jane clenched her body around his and he groaned, forcing her hips lower onto his erection. She toyed with the ends of his hair that had loosened from his queue and kissed his damp neck. The carriage continued to rock along the road, lulling her into sated sleep. "Should we not be at my house by now?"

"We're going to Richmond, my *shundori*," he said as he smoothed a hand down her back. "And there we will continue your lessons."

"Lessons in pleasuring men?"

"No," he said, clutching her face in his hands. "Lessons in pleasuring me."

Chapter Eleven

The carriage rumbled along the limestone drive of Gavin's Richmond house. As the coach swayed, his arms instinctively wrapped around Jane, bringing her to his chest. Closing his eyes, he rested his head against the squabs and forced himself to cease staring at Jane as she slept in his arms.

Any minute they would approach the house, and Prakash would be awaiting their arrival. Any minute, he would be free of Jane, and his body would no longer burn for her. It was only because her sweet curves were nestled tightly against his belly and chest that he could not seem to think straight. Distance between them would soon get rid of these ludicrous thoughts running rampant through his mind.

The coach rocked to a stop. Lifting Jane from his lap, he waited until the door opened and carried her down the stair and up the entrance of the house. Prakash was waiting for them. Gavin was thankful that he'd had the presence of mind to dress Jane.

"A hot bath awaits you, my lord. I have put the bath in the gardens, *bondhu*, as you requested."

"And the rest?" he asked over his shoulder.

"Everything is as you asked."

"Good night, Prakash."

"Good night, *bondhu*."

Gavin nodded, dismissing Prakash, then continued down the long hall to the bank of French doors that lay open. Stepping inside the conservatory he saw that every one of his orders had been followed.

"Jane," he whispered as he laid her down on a black divan, "awake."

Her honey colored lashes flickered then parted before slowly lifting to reveal her intoxicating eyes. "Have we arrived?"

Her smile was soft and womanly and Gavin felt his insides begin to melt. Distance, he told himself. He couldn't let Jane's shy smiles be his undoing.

Straightening away from her, he motioned to the tub. "A warm bath awaits you."

Her eyes widened as he stepped away from her and she reached for him. "Will you not stay?"

"No." He couldn't stay, not now, not when he was feeling his heart fill with a strange wistfulness he had never before experienced. Her lashes lowered, but not before she could conceal the look of confusion in them. "I will meet you here in a while. I have business to attend to."

He left her then, strolling to the path that led to his study door. He heard her rise from the divan, the rustle of silk sounding over the gentle cascade from the nearby waterfall. His blood ran hot and thick, slowing in his veins as he thought of the dress being shed from her body. He thought of how her ivory skin would look in the golden candlelight, and he imagined her hands soaping her body--her fingers gliding over her breasts, down her belly only to slide between her thighs.

The crinkling of silk once again drew his attention and he mindlessly stepped back and peered between the branches of a palm tree only to see the silk gown skim down along her back and over her waist till it fell onto the floor. Her arms came up over her head and he could see the sides of her breast, full and soft and begging for a touch of his hand. She wound her hair up into a bun and secured it with pins, before turning and stepping into the tub.

A voyeur, he watched as she sank into the water, the bubbles of the jasmine scented water covering her body, shielding her secrets from him. But his mind supplanted the image of full breasts with coral nipples, a softly rounded belly that he couldn't wait to kiss and feel beneath his mouth, and legs, soft and feminine that would fit perfectly around his waist.

The images in his mind, coupled with seeing her arms move beneath the water made his brain ignite with yearning. She was washing herself, he knew it although he couldn't see her hands touching her skin. He wanted to go to her, to stand beside the tub, yet the sight before him kept him entranced.

Her hands sank under the water and she leaned forward. Her little foot, covered with bubbles and arched like a ballet dancer's, rested on the edge of the copper tub. She moaned, a soft, husky sound, then rested her head back, closing her eyes as she did so.

Was she touching herself? Re-enacting what he had done to her? Did her breasts yearn for him? Was she wet and aching for his cock? Was she pleasuring herself while she thought of him? Good God, he was inflamed--consumed by the very thought of having her thinking of him.

A soft purring sound came from deep in her throat and her neck arched back. Water splashed over the sides and he was gifted with the sight of her breasts, wet and shining in the water. When he thought he'd give in to his desires and go to her, he saw her hand, the lapis bracelet sparkling beneath a froth of bubbles glide along her breast. Her neck arched once more, and her mouth parted on a breath that made his cock stiffen further. Bloody hell, he'd never seen a sight more enticing.

There was very little he hadn't done in his extensive sexual escapades, but watching a lady at her toilette had never been one of them. He shouldn't be intruding on her privacy, but he couldn't move, couldn't take his eyes off her hand and the bracelet he'd purchased for her. He knew she was rubbing her fingers along her nipples, hardening them but the bubbles concealed the most graphic vision of it. If one looked quickly one would think she was merely soaping her body and enjoying the water, but his gaze lingered, taking in how her dainty foot arched with each movement of her hand and how her lashes fluttered and her lips parted on silent moans and whimpers. He knew then that she was doing much more than bathing. She was thinking about him and what he'd done to her.

The water splashed over the sides of the tub once again, nudging him into walking toward her. He'd already shed his clothing and his cock was hard and soaring to the ceiling. He stood behind her and without a word, he lifted her from the tub, ignoring her gasp of surprise. He brought her body, bubbles and all, against him. His mouth came down hard on hers and his tongue pushed past her lips, into her mouth, savoring every inch of her. She did not resist him. Instead she loosened the silk tie holding his hair, letting the length tumble about his shoulders while she threaded her fingers through it.

She moaned when he reached for her thighs and parted them, lifting her so that she straddled his waist. Her soft belly rubbed against his hard one and his cock leapt, searching for the entrance to her body. He could take her like this, he knew. She was weak and willing and would allow him to surge up inside her, but he pushed the inclination out of his mind. He had never been granted the privilege of seeing a lady soak in a tub, much less given an opportunity to join her. It was a thought that made his fevered brain burn hotter. He stepped into the tub, sinking down with her still astride him without missing one stroke of his tongue.

"The floor," she murmured against his lips when his large frame sent half the water sloshing out of the sides of the tub.

"To hell with the floor, madam," he groaned, nipping her lips and cupping his hand around her neck to bring her closer to him. "I'm certain it'll be much wetter before the night is through."

He ran his hand up her back, soaping it with the sea sponge she had been using. She purred in appreciation, and he repeated the action while he kissed her. Over and over, his mouth ravished hers, with drugging kisses that dulled his thoughts and made him swell further against her belly.

Growing restless, Jane rubbed her slick mound against him and he felt his cock leap against her. It was so hard to resist what she flagrantly offered. Breaking the contact with her mouth, he turned her so that her back was against him and his searching member was far from her reach.

Picking up the sponge, he soaped her arms then breasts before slowly gliding down her silky middle. She purred and writhed, torturing him further with quick flashes of erect, coral nipples that bobbed up from the water. Gritting his teeth, he ignored them, focusing instead on the sponge that was slowly making its way to the brown curls shielding her secrets.

He wanted to do more than please her tonight. The thought shocked him into stillness and Jane glanced up at him, her eyes worried.

The feeling became deeper as he looked down at her. His heart raced and he felt altogether different than he ever had before.

"Gavin?" she asked uneasily.

"I want you, Jane," he said, hoping she understood how difficult it was for him to need anything from anyone. "I need to feel your heat. I want your smiles."

She smiled and rose out of the water like a mermaid arising from sea foam. She was standing naked before him, bubbles sliding down her skin and she was trying bravely to bear his bold perusal. Jane, he wanted say, haven't you figured out how much I adore you? Do you not understand how beautiful you are, how your body inflames me? But he couldn't. He had never been able to utter the flowery words that tripped easily off other men's tongues. He hadn't the knack for sweet seduction and as he looked up the length of Jane's body, he wondered if that was what she had meant when she said Winterbourne gave her what she needed.

"My lord?"

He saw her arms slowly leave her sides, and he knew then exactly what she needed. He caught her hands in his and rose very slowly from the water. "Wait here."

He left the tub and reached for one of the towels that Prakash had set on a nearby chair. He quickly dried himself, all the while feeling her dark eyes travelling the length of him. When he was finished, he discarded the towel onto the floor and reached for a dry one.

He towelled her off quickly, ignoring her gasps when he reached between her legs and dried her thighs. He bit back the urge to capture her mouth in his and replace the towel with his hand. He was determined to do something that he had never done before--he was going to give Jane a glimpse inside his soul. He was going to offer her a piece of himself.

Gavin picked her up as if she weighed nothing more than a feather and carried her inside the silk tent, where he put her down and told her to close her eyes. Her heart raced. She felt exceedingly vulnerable standing naked before him, not being able to see his expression. Was he looking at her? Scrutinizing her hips and thighs? Was he comparing her to Catriona Hamilton? Her eyes flew open and met Gavin's green gaze.

"Have you ever looked at yourself, Jane?" He traced the back of his hand along her cheek.

"Yes," she said with a grimace.

"Have you ever looked at your body through a man's eyes?"

Her eyes darted to the cushions that littered the floor. A silk coverlet awaited her, she only had to reach for it and hide behind it.

"Come," he murmured when he saw the direction of her gaze. "I want to awaken you to your considerable charms, Jane."

She allowed him to take her hand and pull her to the cushions. She sank to her knees as he came down behind her and trailed the tips of his fingers along her spine, making gooseflesh rise on her already sensitized body.

"Such beautiful skin," he whispered before his lips caressed the nape of her neck. "So soft, so responsive to my touch." His lips moved lower and he placed a kiss between her shoulders. She was on already on fire for him, and yet she somehow knew it would be a long while yet before she felt Gavin inside her.

His lips moved downward, and he pressed her forward so that she was leaning over her knees. His hands continued to skim the length of her back, up and down, studying her.

"I like this, Jane, where your waist indents to your hips. I like sliding my hands along your curves, feeling the flare of your hips. I like your bottom very much, Jane."

She felt her face turn hot and she was certain that every inch of her skin was flushed pink. His bold perusal was unsettling, and she gripped her knees tighter as if to protect herself from his far too seeing eyes.

"Have you any idea how good your bottom feels?" he asked, as he traced her derriere with his hands. "It's so wonderfully soft beneath my fingers. You have the type of bottom, Jane that drives me to distraction." One of his fingers traced the cleft and she gasped in surprise. She had never been touched there. "I'd like to take you from behind, Jane." She felt him sliding his erection along her buttocks. "I'd like to see my fingers grasp your hips and watch your spine curve gracefully as you take me into your tight sheath. I want to hear you gasp that way when I am inside stroking you, Jane."

He moved his phallus down her buttock then leaned closer and slid the tip along the petals of her sex. "I want to do it before a mirror, Jane. I want to see the look of pleasure on your lovely face. I want to see your lips part, your pink tongue dart out as you wet your lips as your passion escalates. I'd like to see your hands on your breasts as you play with them," she whimpered when she felt her nipples harden further and she squeezed her knees tighter. "I'd like to command you to do things, Jane. And I'd like to watch you do them. But not now, Jane. I am afraid that there is something more pressing I have to do. On your side," he commanded before helping her to assume the position he wanted. She was lying on her left side, her head propped in her hand and pillows scattered beneath her. He ran his hand down the length of her and she trembled. "You cannot hide your response to me, can you, my *shundori?*"

She shivered again as he leaned closer and brushed his lips against her shoulder. "Why would I want to hide it?"

"That is a game lovers play, Jane. But your passion runs much deeper than that, doesn't it?"

"I like feeling your hands on me."

"Where, Jane?" he asked, nuzzling her neck. "Where do you like to be touched? What do you want me to do? Tell me and I shall give it to you."

She didn't want to tell him what she desired, she wanted him to do what pleased him. She wanted just to experience his desire for her.

"I'd like to show you your beauty, Jane. Let me show it to you through my eyes."

She swallowed hard. A rush of trepidation coursed through her and she shoved it aside. She wanted this. This had been what she desired from him all along. It might be the only time he offered her such a thing. Indeed, it might be the last time that they were together.

"Close your eyes, Jane." She did, and he reached for her wrist. There was the tinkling of china, followed by something wet that dripped on her skin. "Now, Jane, you will not peek. You will let me study you for as long as I want. You will let me do whatever I want. Do you trust me, Jane?"

She bit her lips and nodded. She could do this. She wanted to do this.

"Very good, Jane, now rest your head on the pillow and lie very still...."

Chapter Twelve

Incense burned from the braziers, blanketing the tent in an exotic mix of sandalwood. Gavin waited until Jane was relaxed before he lowered his quill to the delicate skin of her inside wrist. She jumped when the red vegetable die met her skin. "Ssh," he whispered as he brushed the henna into familiar lines.

"What are you doing?" she asked, stiffening once again.

He looked up and saw that her eyes were tightly shut. "I am adorning you in my own way, Jane. I will show you what I have done when I am ready."

"Can't you tell me?" she asked, swallowing deeply.

He grinned. He felt her pulse quicken beneath his thumb, and he raised her hand to his mouth and kissed her fingertips. "I am choosing my favorite parts of your body, Jane. You may ponder that while you withstand my ministrations."

When she quieted, he returned to his task, the ancient art form of Henna. Instead of the traditional designs that women used to decorate their hands and feet, he created his own. A piece of him, written to her, on her, in Sanskrit.

She would never know what he said, she would think it was simply a design he placed on her most treasured body parts. He would be safe that way.

He glanced up and saw that her face was at last relaxed, and her breathing was heavy as his gaze followed the rise and fall of coral tipped breasts. Soon, he consoled his raging lust, soon he would be making love to her.

Ignoring his throbbing erection, he left her wrist and pondered where he would next write his words of desire. Her neck. The hollow behind her ear that his lips were drawn to, where he couldn't resist nuzzling.

He dipped his quill again and dragged it across her skin. She shivered and moaned and he purposely brushed the feathers of the quill along her shoulder. "I adore the space beneath your ear, Jane. It smells of you and it fits my mouth perfectly. I can feel your heartbeat pulse against my lips. I know the instant your heart beats faster for me, Jane."

Gooseflesh erupted on her skin and he felt arrogant satisfaction that he was responsible for it. She pleased him very much.

"Gavin. That feels very soothing."

"I'm glad," he said, before kissing her shoulder. "Now, roll onto your stomach, Jane, and I shall pacify you even more."

She hesitated only briefly before rolling over. His gaze skimmed along her back, to the indention that drew him above her buttocks. She was perfect there, he decided as he traced her bottom. He'd always been drawn to a good bottom and Jane Westbury had the most perfect heart-shaped derriere he'd ever seen. It seemed such a shame to cover it. So instead, he used the henna on the flat of her back and kissed her plump cheeks when he had finished. "I'm afraid I was unable to pay homage your bottom, Jane. It is simply far too perfect for words." With a final stroke of his hand on her cheek, he kissed her back then whispered into her ear. "Now, Jane, on your knees, facing me. Don't open your eyes, I will help you."

There was no awkwardness as she kneeled before him and when she tilted up her face, the candles bathed her skin in a golden glow. She took his breath. He started, feeling his chest burn and tighten. Something very strange happened, and he couldn't stop himself from clutching her face in his hands and lowering his mouth to hers. His kiss was slow and provocative. He slid his tongue between her lips and mimicked what his cock was straining to do to her. She moaned and he deepened it, but kept the pace slow and sensual. When her hands trailed down his belly, he pulled away, afraid he would not possess the self-control to stop before it was too late. Her whimper nearly undid his control, but he stayed his hands from reaching to cup her breasts, and instead he reached for the quill.

He circled her areole with the feathers and watched as the nipple hardened. His tongue burned to lave it, but he squelched the impulse, knowing that soon he would have her. He chose her left breast, the one with the charming freckle that never failed to capture his interest or imagination. "You have beautiful breasts, Jane, do you know that?" She shook her head and he smiled, watching the taut flesh tremble beneath the quill. "They're full and heavy and spill over my hand. I like that Jane, very much. When I am on top of you they rub against me and I'm reminded of your voluptuousness. When you're above me I can watch you and study the way you move. I like to watch you, Jane."

She sighed and tossed her head back and he set the quill to her.

He tickled the length of her midriff before reaching his most treasured spot. His finger replaced the quill and he circled her navel with it. He adored her soft belly. Loved touching it and putting his mouth to it. He couldn't wait to feel the soft and welcoming length of her beneath him. He looked up at her, her face lovely and serene. The emotion coursing inside him was so foreign, so strong that his hand shook when he dipped the quill in the henna and placed it on her navel.

His strokes were slow, thoughtful, and he wrote with all the emotion he had inside him. It didn't matter that she would never understand. He knew, and that was all that mattered. He couldn't tell her what her silky belly did to him, what thoughts wandered through his mind as he caressed her with his fingers and his mouth. But he did allow himself to kiss her softly and nuzzle her for the briefest of seconds. He was so close to her, he could smell her scent, and he knew she was aroused, and God help him he had never been more eager to part a woman's thighs and drive into her than he was now.

Letting the quill slip from his hands, he placed his fingertips on her mons and let his lips skim over the silky hair. Her fingers bit into his shoulders and the huskiness he heard deep in her throat made him thicken so painfully that he was forced to take his cock in his hand and soothe the ache that was now unbearable.

Willingly she parted her thighs for him and he flicked his tongue to taste her arousal. "So bloody beautiful," he groaned. "Lay back, *shundori*," he growled. "I have to have all of you. I need you in my mouth and on my tongue."

"Gavin," she sighed, raking her fingers through his hair. "Is there nothing you haven't done?"

He looked up at her then, and brought her down to meet him. "There is," he said, trailing his hands down her back to cup her lush bottom.

"Tell me."

"I have never made love, Jane."

Her eyes flew open and he kissed her, laying her back on the pillows, he came down on top of her, his breath coming in short pants. "Show me what it is like, Jane. I need to know, I need to know what it is like with you. Love me, Jane," he said before claiming her mouth in a kiss he knew would destroy him.

Chapter Thirteen

The early morning light filtered through the bed curtains. Jane stretched and yawned and thought about the wondrous night she had spent in Gavin's arms.

He had made love to her so thoroughly throughout the night and throughout nearly every room in the house that it was a wonder she was even awake at all. She smiled sheepishly, remembering the things he had done to her and the scandalous and most deliciously wicked things he had said to her as he carried her up to his room.

"Gavin," she whispered, reaching for him. But he was not beside her. She sat up and brought the sheet around her. She searched the room and called out his name. There was no answer.

In a rush of panic, she pulled the sheet from the bed, wrapped it tightly around her and stepped onto the cool floor. There, on the table before the window sat a folded paper with her name written boldly across the front.

She reached for it, her fingers shaking so fiercely that she could hardly open it. Already her eyes blurred with tears, her mind already knew what her heart refused to acknowledge.

Dearest Jane,

I have never been good with words, nor have I any experience with good-byes. I hope that you will forgive me for writing this, but you must know that I thought this the only way to keep from hurting you with my clumsy tongue.

Good-bye, Jane. You haven't any need for more lessons. You never really needed them. You always possessed the qualities to attract a man. You only needed the confidence to let them shine through. You never needed me or anyone else to show you the way, Jane. It was there all along, waiting to break free of your chrysalis.

I will never forget watching you emerge from your shell. I will always remember how you looked when you became aware of your beauty, the image of your smile and parted lips will forever be etched in my mind.

Take care, Jane, and remember me once in a while when you're entertaining your admirers. Spare me a smile or two in the ballrooms and I will know that you have not forgotten me.

Good-bye, Jane.

It was signed simply, *Gavin.*

Fat, scalding tears burned a trail down her cheeks. Why, she wanted to scream. Why couldn't he love her? Why had he lulled her last night into believing that she meant something to him?

Raising her hand to swipe away the tears, she remembered for the first time what he had done to her. Grasping the sheet in her hand, she stalked to the cheval looking glass and lowered the sheet, baring the red designs on her body.

She had never seen anything like it. His marks weren't recognizable, at least to her eyes. She twisted to her side and let the sheet drop lower revealing the large patch on her lower back. It was covered with the same sort of design.

What had he done to her, and why had he done it if he intended to leave her before she awoke?

The door cracked opened and Jane covered herself, but not before the maid peeked around the corner. Her dark eyes widened before she lowered them and kept her gaze averted from her while she put a bowl of steaming water on the commode.

She was Indian, Jane knew. Perhaps she would know what these strange markings were and where the artist was hiding.

"Maya," she said, remembering the girl's name. "Where is his lordship?"

Maya's hands were clenched tightly before her, and Jane could not help but notice how her gold bangles tinkled together as her hands shook.

"He is not at home, my lady."

"Where has he gone?" she asked, her voice breaking on a sob. She looked away and hoped that Maya would see fit to ignore her obvious distress.

"To London."

Jane nodded and tried blink back the tears that fell uncontrollably from her eyes. She felt utterly wretched, like her heart had been ripped from her chest. She had never felt so miserable. Not even Archie leaving her for Arabella had made her feel this hopeless.

"Do not cry, my lady," Maya whispered. The servant's hands raked through her hair and smoothed it against her back. "He wouldn't want you to cry."

"How do you know?" she said through trembling lips.

"I know him very well and I know that he wouldn't want to see tears from you."

"He doesn't care." Jane pressed her fingers to her eyes. "He wouldn't have left if he did."

"You spill these tears for you, or for him?" she asked, as she picked up a brush and began stroking it through Jane's riotous curls.

"Both," she whispered before her breath hitched and made a tiny hiccup. She sniffled against the sheet and forced back a sob. "I'm crying because my heart is breaking. And my heart is breaking because of him--because I can't make him love me."

Maya's eyes met hers in the mirror and Jane felt the tears begin well again. "You can't?" she asked, before taking her hair and pushing it over her shoulder so that her curls lay against her breast. "Did he tell you about these?" Fingers pressed into her skin on her neck, and Maya reached for her wrist to examine it.

"No, he did not." Jane huffed.

"It is henna. Women of my culture wear it to make our bodies more attractive to men. Our men--Indian men," she corrected, "have a special attraction for hands and feet. It is one of the only things that they are not forbidden to see, so we decorate them to entice them."

"What do the designs mean?"

"Nothing, really," Maya shrugged. "We create our own, whatever we want. But he has not done it in the traditional way. He has put his English touch to this ancient tradition."

"What has he done, Maya?"

"Show me and I will tell you."

Jane lowered the sheet, revealing her breasts and her navel, making sure the cotton dipped low enough on her back for Maya to see.

"He has written you a letter."

Her mouth parted in shock as she met Maya's smile in the looking glass. "Read it to me."

"Show me how. Tell me where to begin."

Jane presented Maya with her wrist and the servant turned it to examine it closer. "He has written it in Sanskrit," she said, looking up from her dark lashes.

"He didn't want me to know."

"Perhaps," Maya smiled secretly. "Now then," she murmured.

"This says, 'A moth seeking the flame.'" Jane frowned and looked at her wrist. "Where is the next one?" Maya asked.

Her neck. She remembered how he had kissed and tickled her shoulder. She recalled the feel of his face pressed into the hollow beneath her ear.

"Ah," Maya nodded, holding her hair away. "'A drop seeking the sea.'" Jane covered her breast with her hands and closed her eyes as Maya read the next one. "'My heart seeking yours.'"

She tried to say something, but Maya halted her. "Your back, my lady, that is next, I think." Jane swallowed hard and closed her eyes, waiting to hear what Gavin had written. "It is a poem that all Bengalis, perhaps all Indians treasure. It is by Rumi and it is the most beautiful of all his works."

"Tell me, Maya," she said unable to stand the suspense any longer.

Maya smiled and started to read. "From the moment you smiled at me I was yours. You captivated me so that I was constantly looking for you. How foolish of me to not know that lovers do not finally meet somewhere. They're in each other all along." Maya met her gaze and brushed a lock of hair behind her ear. "He has fixed it to suit his needs, I see. How very English of him." She grinned.

Her heart was beating much too fast. Gavin had written that? What did this mean? Was he attracted to her? Did he desire her? *Did he love her?*

"And this," she asked impulsively, showing Maya her middle, "what has he said here?" Maya glanced at her naval then picked up the brush and resumed running it through her hair.

"I cannot tell you that," she said very softly. "He must be the one to tell you."

"But he won't," Jane cried. "I don't even know where he is."

"Why do you want to find him?"

Jane stepped back and blinked. She couldn't believe that Maya didn't understand the depths of her feelings. "Because I love him," she said as if she were talking to a simpleton. "I don't want to lose him. I have to tell him, Maya."

The servant smiled brightly and reached for her hand. "Come with me, *bondhu*, and I will show you what to do."

"Where are you taking me?" she asked, grasping the sheet tightly against her breasts.

Maya turned and held her finger to her lips. "To the room of feminine secrets."

"I've never heard of such a room," Jane said suspiciously.

"That is because you are English. But we will fix that," Maya grinned. "And I shall tell you all the secrets there are to know about getting the man of your dreams."

Chapter Fourteen

Gavin glanced around his opulent surroundings and took a sip of port. He had been away from Jane less than a day and here he was, finding himself supporting the wall at Lord Manwarring's masquerade. What a joke, he thought as he took another drink. The costumes were nothing short of scandalous and the masquerade nothing less than a pretext to host an orgy.

His lips curled in disgust, but whether it was due to the couple who were fondling each other on the stairs beside him or himself for being there, he hadn't yet decided.

The groans from the amorous woman on the stairs made him turn away. Unconsciously he compared the husky, almost overdone sounds to that of Jane's breathless pleas and entreaties. What was she doing now? he wondered. Was she with Winterbourne? Did he have his mouth and hands all over her? Was her body clamouring for Winterbourne as it had for him the night before?

Bloody madness! He growled, finishing his drink. What the devil was he thinking? He was in a room full of writhing women waiting for a tup. He only had to glance at one of them and he would find his breeches undone and an eager mouth swallowing him. But when he looked down between his parted thighs it would not be Jane's face he saw. It would be some harpy who meant nothing to him.

He should never have admitted a blessed thing to himself. What had he been about spouting off nonsense about making love? *I've never made love, Jane. Show me....* What a fool he'd been.

"Where is your mask, darling?" a familiar voice cooed behind him. "Or was it your intention for me to find you this evening?"

He turned around and looked down into the masked face and the much displayed charms of Catriona Hamilton.

"Well," she said, pouting sulkily, "have you come to your senses? Have you realized that Plain Jane is not worth your time, or," she said huskily, pressing her breasts against him, "your precious energy?"

He tried to make himself reach for the sheer scrap of muslin that was supposed to be Catriona's toga. He tried to make himself bare her breasts and kiss her lips, but he couldn't.

"Now then," she purred, boldly stroking the front of his breeches. "Why don't you show me just how magnificent your stallion really is?"

She was so typical of the women he knew. She thought her boldness was making him hard and randy, but in fact it was only vulgar. Her beauty was gauche. There was nothing about her that was genuine.

A month ago he might not have even noticed, or cared for that matter, but tonight he did. Tonight he wouldn't be able to achieve an erection if had three women such as Catriona working on his member. There was only one woman who could satisfy his needs. And yet, he wasn't the right man for her needs.

"Come, Grayson, show me your sword and I'll give you something to sheathe it in." He looked away from her glittering eyes and pouting lips. "Perhaps you want to be someplace more private," she teased. "Perhaps you've got something very naughty in store for me. Is that it Grayson? You want me to be a naughty girl so that you may punish me?"

A ripple of murmurs suddenly erupted amongst the groans and moans that filled the ballroom. Looking away from Catriona, he searched the room for a sign of whatever had sparked the hushed excitement he heard.

A vision in jade green floated from the doorway into the room and his body reacted like it had not had release in months.

"Mmm, very nice," Catriona hummed. "You're certainly big enough, aren't you?"

He ignored her and her searching hand and studied the woman in the jade chiffon, dressed as though she had walked straight out of a Sultan's harem. He grinned. She certainly looked at home in a skirt that was slung low on her hips with a jewelled top that molded her breasts into perfect mounds. His mouth went dry as his gaze flickered up to hair that was left loose and flowing. The color of her hair was his favorite--honey brown.

"Come my lord," Catriona encouraged. "Let us not wait another minute."

His lady in jade scanned the room and he wished he were closer so that he could see her face clearer. Were her eyes outlined in kohl? Did she look as mysterious and forbidden behind her face veil as he had imagined she would?

His body tightened and he folded his arms across his chest to keep from running to her. He was not what she wanted. He was a half-breed, the son of a mother who had been a concubine. He had spent his life bent on revenge, not caring who he destroyed. He didn't deserve her. His mind knew that, but his heart, and his damnable cock had yet to register the fact.

Her eyes scanned the ballroom and his heart squeezed fiercely in his chest. Good God what was she doing here? Was she meeting Winterbourne? Was she meeting someone new? Would she even notice him? His heart hammered along and he felt prickles of perspiration trickle down his back.

"Grayson?" Catriona asked, as she followed his gaze. "Who is that?"

"She's beautiful, isn't she?" he said, scanning the jade lady's lovely and very scantily clad body.

"She looks like a Sultan's whore."

"Hmm." He grinned, not even bothering to look at Catriona. "I have a penchant for Sultan's whores. You will recall that my mother was one."

Catriona gasped and tugged on his lace sleeve. "I didn't mean it that way, my lord. I just meant...."

The odalisque finally saw him and their eyes locked from across the room. Without a moment's hesitation she stepped forward, her hips swaying most invitingly, calling to his straining body.

"Tell her to go away," the countess hissed. "I'm not sharing you tonight."

"You tell her to go away and see what she says."

He followed her with a hungry gaze as she came closer. His gut wrenched uncomfortably. What was she doing at a party such as this, dressed like that? For whom was she playing the vixen?

Catriona squished herself closer to him, but he kept his gaze focused on *her*. She hardly blinked and he was suddenly very intrigued by the confidence he saw shining in those beautiful, kohl-lined eyes.

"Go away," Catriona hissed, before draping herself on his chest. "Can't you see we're busy? You're not wanted here."

His lovely odalisque glanced at Catriona before returning her heated brown gaze to him. "Is that true, my lord?" she said, her voice laced with sensuality. "I am not wanted?"

Good God, he thought, swallowing hard as he hungrily raked his eyes over her voluptuous form. Not wanted? He wanted nothing more than to tear the chiffon from her body and bare her beautiful heart-shaped bottom to his gaze and his hands. Then, he thought feverishly, he'd free her breasts and suck them until she begged him to fill her with his cock--a cock that was growing bigger with each passing second.

"My lord?" she asked again, and he could see her red-painted mouth pout beneath the veil. "You do not want me?"

"Do you know what you're about?" he asked, freeing himself from Catriona's cloying embrace. "Do you know what you're letting yourself in for by choosing me out of all the men who are clamoring for your attention?"

"I do," she whispered.

"I am a half-breed, madam. My blood is tainted and I have lived a sordid life. I have not always acted with honor. Now are you certain you wish to choose me?"

"The only person I want is you, Gavin."

He picked her up then and swung her into his arms, ignoring the stamping of Catriona's silk slipper against the marble floor. Before he could think of what he was doing he was climbing the stairs in search of an empty bedroom. He had to have her. Now.

"You do realize that you've just given up your chance to find yourself a husband."

"I have?"

"You have."

"Do you know who I am?" she asked.

He heard the brief flicker of hesitation in her voice before she tried to mask it. His eyes darted to the lapis bracelet and inwardly he grinned. He didn't need to see his gift encircling her wrist to know whom he held in his arms. "I do."

"Who am I?"

He flung open the first door he found unlocked and placed her in the middle of the bed. He returned to the door and locked it, all the time ruthlessly untying his cravat and the buttons of his waistcoat. He flung his frock coat onto the floor and kicked off his shoes as she watched him with those unbelievably beautiful eyes.

Her gaze followed his shirt as it landed on the floor, followed by his breeches. He tossed his cravat on the bed and waited for her to look up at him. Their gazes locked and with a grin he put his knee on the bed and captured her chin in his hand.

"Good evening, Lady Jane Westbury."

"Gavin," she cried, flinging her arms around his neck.

"Jane," he groaned, pulling the veil from her face and ravishing her mouth with his. He was kissing her like a starving man. He couldn't keep his hands off her and more importantly--he didn't want to.

Pulling the ties that secured her beaded top, he freed her breasts and captured them in his palms. She moaned and arched forward, filling his hands with hardened nipples. The silky material of her skirt grazed his knee, reminding him of the barrier that was still between them.

Sliding his hand down her belly, his finger grazed something cool and sharp. He pulled away and glanced down between their heaving bodies. When he looked up he knew he was grinning like a first class rake.

"You did this for me?"

She nodded and ran her finger down the jade ring that pierced her belly. "It reminded me of your eyes."

"God, Jane," he groaned. "Your navel was a distraction to me before, but do you know what the sight of it does to me now?"

"Arouses you, I hope."

He glanced down at his throbbing erection and then back up at her. "There's no hiding my arousal."

She smiled a secret, womanly smile and stroked her finger along the length of him. "Lay back, my lord," she whispered, pushing him down and straddling his legs. She reached for his hands, letting her breasts graze his chest. He chuckled deep in his throat and nipped at her pert nipples when they were level with his mouth. "My, Lady Jane, what fabulous breasts you have."

He tried to move his hand and bring her breast to his mouth so he could tease her with his lips, but it was frozen, stuck to the bed. He glanced up and saw that one wrist was already shackled to the bed with his lace cravat. He looked to the other side to see her securing the other with his stocking.

"What is the meaning of this, Jane?" he asked, trying to twist himself free. "How do you expect me to get my hands on you, now?"

"Let me arouse you with my mouth, my lord." She smiled wickedly.

His cock leapt and she grasped it in her hand. Her tongue came out and stroked the length of him and he nearly went off right there. She looked utterly exotic and seductive peering up from his cock with her lined eyes and the jade and pearl headpiece that came down the middle of her hair and dangled provocatively on her brow. Their eyes met, and she held his gaze as she swirled her tongue along the head of his erection. Then she smiled and took the whole length of him into her mouth.

"Jesus, Jane," he swore as he fisted his hands. "You look so damn beautiful."

"Do I?" she purred between flicks of her tongue.

"God yes," he groaned, feeling his climax upon him.

"I'll be anything you want," she said huskily as he met his eyes again. "I'll do anything you ask of me, if you will make me one promise."

He groaned as she began to pump him with her hand. He jutted his hips forward, begging her to stroke him faster. "Promise me, Gavin."

He thrust his length into her mouth and groaned. "God yes, Jane, take me into your mouth. Suck me, Jane. Show me how much you want this--want me."

She played with him and brought him to the pinnacle of ecstasy, had him teetering just on the edge of coming most magnificently when she pulled away, letting him slide inch by excruciating inch out of her wet mouth.

"Jane," he begged, not caring how he sounded. "I have to come. I *need* to come."

"Soon," she said, kissing his belly.

"No, now, Jane," he cried, twisting his hands, trying to free himself from his lace bonds.

"Your promise," she murmured as she sat up and grasped her breasts between her hands. His mouth went dry has he watched her stroke her breasts before him. His eyes travelled down the length of her, to the intriguing jade stone that dangled in her navel and the Sanskrit words that circled her luscious belly.

Bringing her finger to her mouth, she wet it and brought it to her nipple, hardening it further. Damn her, he was going to make her pay for this. Good God, what was she about? Was this Jane, shy, little Jane? *His Jane?*

"Well?" she asked, resting back on her heels as she slid her hands down her breasts, past her belly to skim, every so slightly on her sex before gliding down her thighs where she raised the hem of her skirt and slowly parted her thighs.

He waited, the roaring of his blood in his ears the only thing he could hear. His heart was pounding, his mind racing as he waited with hungry eyes for her to reveal her pink silk.

"Gavin," she crooned, inching the fabric up until he could see a dark shadow between her legs. "Will you promise me one thing?"

He couldn't talk, could barely even move. Lord he just wanted a glimpse. A tiny look to steady his raging lust. A glimpse of her to sate his overwrought nerves. She was Siren, an *houri*. His body was on fire for her, for just a glimpse of the honey between her thighs.

She took her finger and circled her belly, making the jade stone dangle. He watched as she lovingly traced each word that he'd written around her navel. She met his eyes. "Will you promise to read this to me?"

Oh God, he couldn't promise her a damn thing. And yet he so desperately wanted to. He was on fire for her. He wanted to be the man she wanted, and yet he wasn't sure of himself.

"Let me free," he gritted out, testing the lace that bound his wrists to the headboard. "I want my hands on you. *You* want my hands on you."

"True." She smiled. "But perhaps you'd care to see *my* hands on *me*."

He choked then. Truly to God he thought he'd disgrace himself. What the hell had happened to her? Had she imbibed too much alcohol? Had he been poisoned to be this sexually frenzied? God, he was worked up.

"I missed you this morning," she said teasingly as her hands slid up her thighs and over to where her mound was hidden from him.

"Untie me and I will give you more pleasure than you ever knew was possible, Jane."

She closed her eyes and parted her mouth as her finger stroked through the fabric. God help him, he had to look. Had to glance down to see how she straddled his thighs, he could feel the wetness from her body seeping onto his skin. His cock was painfully hard and he was tied, God damn it, to the bed like a caged beast with a prime bit of beef out of its reach.

"I thought about you all afternoon," she whispered, then met his gaze while she stroked his throbbing erection.

"Jane," he gritted his teeth to stop himself from crying out. "I have to come. I need your hand, your mouth, your beautiful quim around me. *Something*," he pleaded, feeling like he was ready to explode.

And then he felt the softness of her skirt float about his thighs and he looked down, over his erect cock and straight at the sight he'd been dying for.

"Well?" she smiled seductively. "All for your pleasure, for the cost of a promise."

He tossed his head back on the mattress and forced what he had just seen from his mind. She'd shaved her quim--just for him. He'd always dreamed of having a woman who indulged in the eastern tradition. He'd always fantasized about watching his cock slide in and out of a shaven quim. Lord, he'd never been so hot for a woman in his life. He was burning for Jane, and if she didn't give him what he wanted, he'd end up nothing but ash.

"Maya says that all the Indian women do it. It's supposed to be for the man's pleasure, but do you know what I think," she purred, parting her swollen sex and letting him watch as she expertly pleasured herself. "I think it's so I can watch your beautiful mouth on me."

"And do you know what I think," he said, breaking free of his bonds and reaching for her. "I'm going to tease you as mercilessly as you've done to me."

Jane gasped as Gavin pushed her back and slid his body down atop hers. He nipped her belly, which was still tender from the piercing before he moved lower. She moaned when he settled his mouth on her.

"Look at you. God, you're beautiful," he whispered, nuzzling her sex and parting her with his fingers before flicking his tongue against the swollen bud. "Why, Jane?"

"Because I wanted to please you."

He looked up at her, eyes filled with emotion, and possibly fear. "Why have you come here tonight?"

She could no longer hold back. Her love and desire was spinning out of control. "Because I want you."

"For how long, Jane?"

"Forever."

"Jane," he whispered sliding up her belly and tracing the words he'd written on her flesh. "Will you be anything I want if I give you this promise you claim to want so badly?"

"Yes," she panted as he filled her slowly. It had been torture teasing him and waiting to feel his hardness inside her.

"Will you be my lover, Jane?"

Her heart raced and she nodded. "Yes."

"Will you let me look at you whenever I wish? Will you come to me naked and confident?"

"Y-y-yes," she stammered, feeling her passion begin to crest with each of his strokes.

"Will you be my wife?"

"Yes," she cried, clasping his face in her hands.

"The mother of my children?"

Tears streamed down her face and she nodded, arching her back allowing him to stroke her deeper.

"Will you be the person who loves me forever, Jane? Who keeps the coldness away and makes me forget the person I have been?"

"Yes."

"Will you never become ashamed that you have given yourself to someone like me, Jane? Will you never regret marrying me or bearing my children?"

"Gavin, I could never be ashamed of you or our children. I want this to happen. I want you."

He nuzzled the hollow beneath her ear. "Will you be the one person I want more than anything?"

She raised her head and peered into his eyes. He stilled inside her and traced her painted lips with fingers that trembled. "Who is it you want, Gavin?" she said more breathlessly than she had wanted.

He smiled and filled her once more. "The woman I love," he whispered. "Lady Jane Westbury."

"Oh, Gavin, I love you so," she cried bringing him closer to her.

Raising himself up, he cupped Jane's bottom in his hands and brought her legs around his waist, stroking her slowly, watching as her body took him in and loved him. Looking up from their joined bodies, he reached out and placed his finger on her belly, tracing each word as he read them aloud. "I never knew love till I met you, or pain until I knew I must leave you. I will love you for all time and I only wish I wasn't afraid to tell you." She clutched him tightly to her, her tears streaming down her cheeks and running on to his. "That is what is written on my most favorite part of you, Jane. Those words are the piece of me I hoped you'd carry forever."

"Oh, Gavin, I'll do anything to make you happy, I'll be anything--anyone."

"Jane, all I want is the woman who smiled at me and captured my heart. I only want you, Jane."

"Not the odalisque?" she teased.

"Perhaps from time to time." He grinned, rolling off of her and pulling her down on top of him. "But not tonight. Tonight I want Lady Jane Westbury, soon to be Lady Jane Grayson."

"Just Plain Jane?" she teased kissing his throat and then his neck.

"Never plain, Jane," he said, grasping her bottom in his hands. "You've always been beautiful to me, and now, if you will cease teasing me, I'd like to make love to my future wife."

"She would like that."

"Would she?" he laughed, playfully slapping her bottom. "Well then, let me get on with the duties of a husband."

"She would like that very much."

"As would he," he groaned, taking her lips in his and loving her with such fierceness she would never again question her ability to entice and enrapture. For he was firmly enticed and perfectly enraptured with the idea of spending the rest of his life tutoring Lady Jane.

The End

Printed in the United States
67131LVS00002B/1-30